THE WORLD OF PREMCHAND

The World of Premchand

SELECTED STORIES OF PREMCHAND
TRANSLATED BY DAVID RUBIN

INDIANA UNIVERSITY PRESS
Bloomington and London

For Ainslie and Sue Embree

ACKNOWLEDGEMENTS

I would like to express my appreciation to Mrs Bonnie
R. Crown, Director of the Asian Literature Program
of the Asia Society, for her encouragement and assistance
in the publication of this book; to Sripat Rai,
Premchand's son, for generously giving permission for
this publication; to S. P. Nirash of Delhi University
for his expert counsel in matters of idiom and dialect in
Premchand's stories; to Mrs Shaista Rahman of Aligarh
University, Robert Swan of Duke University, and
Gordon Roadarmel and Edith Irwin of the University
of California at Berkeley for many valuable suggestions;
and to the American Institute of Indian Studies for the
fellowship which made this undertaking possible.

Contents

Introduction

To Premchand belongs the distinction of creating the genre of the serious short story—and the serious novel as well—in both Hindi and Urdu. Virtually single-handed he lifted fiction in these languages from a quagmire of aimless romantic chronicles to a high level of realistic narrative comparable to European fiction of the time; and in both languages, he has, in addition, remained an unsurpassed master.

Dhanpat Rai, known from 1910 on by the pen-name of 'Premchand', was born in a village near Banaras in 1880, in humble circumstances but with access to a good education in Persian and Urdu letters, as was to be expected in a literate family of the Kayasth community. Many of the difficulties of his early years are described in the autobiographical sketches that conclude this volume.

From the time he began writing, near the beginning of this century, Premchand's life was extraordinarily active. When he died in 1936 Premchand left twelve published novels, about three hundred short stories, countless letters, editorials and essays, several plays and screen-plays and a number of translations and adaptations. He had also had a busy career as editor and publisher. His productivity is all the more astonishing when one realizes that he suffered poor health throughout much of his life.

From the early to the late fiction there is a steady and easily perceptible growth. The first stories, written often with a patriotic or nationalistic bias, tend towards romantic evocations of heroic exploits from Indian history or legend. In the early years Premchand also had a penchant for rather thin yarns about ghosts, lamias and the like. There is probably some influence of Maupassant in the occasional surprise or trick endings. These early stories, like most of his work into the 1920's, were written in Urdu—not so much a distinct language from Hindi as a distinct phase of the same language, with a different alphabet, but sharing with Hindi almost its entire grammatical system and a major proportion of the working vocabulary. Premchand supervised the

Hindi versions of most of this work and gradually switched over to Hindi as his chief writing language.

He very soon discovered the domain which was to remain the richest inspiration for his work—the life of the village. The villages of the eastern Uttar Pradesh, specifically the country districts around Allahabad and Banaras—apparently perfectly ordered according to mechanically exact social regulations that had functioned more or less unchanged for centuries—offered to Premchand an endlessly fascinating stage for the interplay of diverse personalities, at every stage of evolution, with a rigid, efficient, and often cruel social order. Caste snobbery—though it is more than snobbery, being a function of religion; the yearning for sons (a desire that overwhelms all others) to carry on the family and perform the rituals; the terror at the possibility of disgrace or loss of face; the shame of widowhood; the proverbial conservatism—and cunning—of the peasant: these are some of the recurring strands in the fabric of his portrayal of the village. In the early stories there is a tendency to editorialize, even sermonize, and to be redundant, which decreases gradually; the best stories of the late twenties and thirties are free of it entirely. But even in the early stories—'The Power of a Curse,' for example—Premchard's compassion, humour and psychological understanding of the villagers are apparent.

Influenced by Dickens, Tolstoy and Gandhi, among others, and strongly impressed by Marx, Premchand very early directed his fiction toward social reform. The inhumanity of caste hierarchies, the struggle for India's independence and the wretched plight of women are some of the problems that arouse his indignation most frequently. With his maturing as a writer his narration becomes increasingly dramatic and (at least, on the surface) objective, and the presentation of character immeasurably subtler than in the early works. The range of the later stories expands beyond the village to the world of those struck by what one of his characters calls 'the new light,' young intellectuals and emancipated women, people often further from happiness than uneducated villagers. Gandhian influence, perhaps, but more likely a matter of Premchand's own vision. Though the stories continue to be preoccupied with social problems their tone and technique become increasingly Chekhovian. Melodrama and moral thesis give way to tragi-comedy. In 'My Big Brother' a potentially ludicrous situation is developed with pathos, although the touch remains light and the story is genuinely comic; in 'The Shroud' the scarcely tolerable grimness of the characters' lives is developed in the mode of grotesque comedy.

Despite the changes in India since Independence, Premchand's world is still very much in evidence, particularly in the villages. Here and there the surface of daily life has changed but it would be premature to say that there has been any radical transformation. What may strike a Western reader as false, perhaps, or melodramatic in some of these stories is merely commonplace in India, as a perusal of today's Indian newspapers serves to confirm. No matter how much they are officially discouraged, in the countryside caste restrictions have weakened little; the mother-in-law still rules her sons' wives in the joint family; and above all, the swiftness, the unexpectedness of death—and the resignation with which it is accepted—can still be said to constitute a fundamental element of Indian life in both village and town.

Premchand's indignation and his very choice of subject matter tend somewhat to set him apart from contemporary Hindi fiction. Although he has had considerable influence, and there are still writers who deal with social problems and village life, the dominant trend at present seems to be more toward a psychological literature, more refined (and alas, more chic) in nuance and language and consequently less vigorous. The new Hindi writing is often heavily larded with Sanskrit, much of it gleaned from thesauri and lacking in any rich connotative power—indeed, denotative as well in some instances—and of course cleansed of Premchand's inexhaustible fund of humble metaphors and proverbs; similarly, the subject matter tends to be the restricted world and psyche of the writer himself, turned inward, away from the epic horizons of Premchand's multifarious world. Premchand makes many of the present generation of writers—to apply Katherine Mansfield's remark about the novelists who followed Dickens—look very small, 'and such pencil sharpeners!'

In presenting these stories here my division into three groups is, in part, arbitrary. Stories like 'A Day in the Life of a Debt-Collector' and 'A Car-Splashing' might well be assigned to the village world, though it seemed to me that there is a certain urbanity in both and in one the very presence of the automobile, suggesting the larger sphere of the town. The stories in the third division are more involved in problems of individuality and growth in awareness, while 'The Shroud' and 'Deliverance', though they are clearly village stories, transcend the limitations of earlier village tales and attain to a decided universality of utterance.

There are certain special problems in translating Premchand, both because of the nature of Hindi and Premchand's style. Translation from Hindi cannot be quite so precise as—ideally, at least—it may be from French or German. Certain elements of the structure of the language are fairly distinct—in the whole matter of subordination and coordination, for example, and the tendency of Hindi to elliptical and abbreviated statement. Idioms and proverbs, naturally, unlike those in European language, are apt to lack any corresponding equivalent in English. There is, furthermore, the special problem of allusion to subjects which are immediately clear to an Indian reader but which require special explanation to anyone from another culture. In regard to this, I have occasionally interpolated a phrase of explanation to avoid resorting to footnotes. Then, particularly in the village stories, Premchand's characters speak in a highly metaphorical language, full of allusions, proverbs and elaborate images. Many of these would be unintelligible if simply 'translated'; obviously, a suitable equivalent has to be found—or invented—and this I have tried to do. At the same time, whenever possible I have maintained the original idiom. When the Hindi has, 'Neyur went home as happy as if God's hand had touched his head', it seemed to me a falsification to replace it with 'Neyur went home extremely happy', and so I have retained the original simile. And of course many of the proverbial expressions are plain enough and need no interpretation—'to try to stop a hurricane with a broom' comes to mind as a good example. In the matter of the dialect spoken by some characters I have preferred not to represent it by any English dialect, as some have done, but attempted instead to simplify the language and retain whatever of the original idioms I could.

It should be borne in mind that the few stories selected here were culled from eleven volumes. The following from among these stories have previously been translated into English: 'January Night', 'The Shroud', and 'The Thakur's Well'. Abridged English

16

versions of 'Deliverance', 'My Big Brother', 'Neyur', and 'The Road to Salvation' have also been published. Of these, so far as I know only 'The Shroud' has been available in the United States and Great Britain before.

Here, then, is a mere sampling of the vast treasure of Premchand's writings, but one which I hope may serve to introduce this greatest of Hindi writers to the English-speaking public.

1 The Village

The Road to Salvation

The pride the peasant takes in seeing his fields flourishing is like the soldier's in his red turban, the coquette's in her jewels or the doctor's in the patients seated before him. Whenever Jhingur looked at his cane fields a sort of intoxication came over him. He had three *bighas* of land which would earn him an easy 600 rupees. And if God saw to it that the rates went up, then who could complain? Both his bullocks were old so he'd buy a new pair at the Batesar fair. If he could hook on to another two *bighas,* so much the better. Why should he worry about money? The merchants were already beginning to fawn on him. He was convinced that nobody was as good as himself—and so there was scarcely anyone in the village he hadn't quarrelled with.

One evening when he was sitting with his son in his lap, shelling peas, he saw a flock of sheep coming towards him. He said to himself, 'The sheep path doesn't come that way. Can't those sheep go along the bank? What's the idea, coming over here? They'll trample and gobble up the crop and who'll make good for it? I bet it's Buddhu the shepherd—just look at his nerve! He can see me here but he won't drive his sheep back. What good will it do me to put up with *this*? If I try to buy a ram from him he actually asks for five rupees, and everybody sells blankets for four rupees but he won't settle for less than five.'

By now the sheep were close to the cane-field. Jhingur yelled, '*Arrey,* where do you think you're taking those sheep, you?'

Buddhu said meekly, 'Chief, they're coming by way of the boundary embankment. If I take them back around it will mean a couple of miles extra.'

'And I'm supposed to let you trample my field to save you a detour? Why didn't you take them by way of some other boundary path? Do you think I'm some bull-skinning nobody or has your money turned your head? Turn 'em back!'

'Chief, just let them through today. If I ever come back this way again you can punish me any way you want.'

21

'I told you to get them out. If just one of them crosses the line you're going to be in a pack of trouble.'

'Chief,' Buddhu said, 'if even one blade of grass gets under my sheeps' feet you can call me anything you want.'

Although Buddhu was still speaking meekly he had decided that it would be a loss of face to turn back. 'If I drive the flock back for a few little threats,' he thought, 'how will I graze my sheep? Turn back today and tomorrow I won't find anybody willing to let me through, they'll all start bullying me.'

And Buddhu was a tough man too. He owned 240 sheep and he was able to get eight annas per night to leave them in people's fields to manure them, and he sold their milk as well and made blankets from their wool. He thought, 'Why's he getting so angry? What can he do to me? I'm not his servant.'

When the sheep got a whiff of the green leaves they became restless and they broke into the field. Beating them with his stick Buddhu tried to push them back across the boundary line but they just broke in somewhere else. In a fury Jhingur said, 'You're trying to force your way through here but I'll teach you a lesson!'

Buddhu said, 'It's seeing you that's scared them. If you just get out of the way I'll clear them all out of the field.'

But Jhingur put down his son and grabbing up his cudgel he began to whack into the sheep. Not even a washerman would have beat his donkey so cruelly. He smashed legs and backs and while they bleated Buddhu stood silent watching the destruction of his army. He didn't yell at the sheep and he didn't say anything to Jhingur, no, he just watched the show. In just about two minutes, with the prowess of an epic hero, Jhingur had routed the enemy forces. After this carnage among the host of sheep Jhingur said with the pride of victory, 'Now move on straight! And don't ever think about coming this way again.'

Looking at his wounded sheep, Buddhu said, 'Jhingur, you've done a dirty job. You're going to regret it.'

2

To take vengeance on a farmer is easier than slicing a banana. Whatever wealth he has is in his fields or barns. The produce gets into the house only after innumerable afflictions of nature and the gods. And if it happens that a human enemy joins in alliance with those afflictions the poor farmer is apt to be left nowhere. When Jhingur came home and told his family about the battle, they started to give him advice.

'Jhingur, you've got yourself into real trouble! You knew what to do but you acted as though you didn't. Don't you realize what a tough customer Buddhu is? Even now it's not too late—go to him and make peace, otherwise the whole village will come to grief along with you.'

Jhingur thought it over. He began to regret that he'd stopped Buddhu at all. If the sheep had eaten up a little of his crop it wouldn't have ruined him. The fact is, a farmer's prosperity comes precisely from being humble—God doesn't like it when a peasant walks with his head high. Jhingur didn't enjoy the idea of going to Buddhu's house but urged on by the others he set out. It was the dead of winter, foggy, with the darkness settling in everywhere. He had just come out of the village when suddenly he was astonished to see a fire blazing over in the direction of his cane field. His heart started to hammer. A field had caught fire! He ran wildly, hoping it wasn't his own field, but as he got closer this deluded hope died. He'd been struck by the very misfortune he'd set out to avert. The bastard had started the fire and was ruining the whole village because of him. As he ran it seemed to him that today his field was a lot nearer than it used to be, as though the fallow land between had ceased to exist.

When he finally reached his field the fire had assumed dreadful proportions. Jhingur began to wail. The villagers were running and ripping up stalks of millet to beat the fire. A terrible battle between man and nature went on for several hours, each side winning in turn. The flames would subside and almost vanish only to strike back again with redoubled vigour like battle-crazed warriors. Among the men Buddhu was the most valiant fighter; with his dhoti tucked up around his waist he leapt into the fiery gulfs as though ready to subdue the enemy or die, and he'd emerge after many a narrow escape. In the end it was the men who triumphed, but the triumph amounted to defeat. The whole village's sugarcane crop was burned to ashes and with the cane all their hopes as well.

3

It was no secret who had started the fire. But no one dared say anything about it. There was no proof and what was the point of a case without any evidence? As for Jhingur, it had become difficult for him to show himself out of his house. Wherever he went he had to listen to abuse. People said right to his face, 'You were the cause of the fire! You ruined us. You were so stuck up your feet didn't touch the dirt. You yourself were ruined and you dragged the whole village down with you. If you hadn't fought with Buddhu would all this have happened?'

Jhingur was even more grieved by these taunts than by the destruction of his crop, and he would stay in his house the whole day.

Winter drew on. Where before the cane-press had turned all night and the fragrance of the crushed sugar filled the air and fires were lit with people sitting around them smoking their hookas, all was desolation now. Because of the cold people cursed Jhingur and, drawing their doors shut, went to bed as soon as it was dark. Sugarcane isn't only the farmers' wealth; their whole way of life depends on it. With the help of the cane they get through the winter. They drink the cane juice, warm themselves from fires made of its leaves and feed their livestock on the cuttings. All the village dogs that used to sleep in the warm ash of the fires died from the cold and many of the livestock too from lack of fodder. The cold was excessive and everybody in the village was seized with coughs and fevers. And it was Jhingur who'd brought about the whole catastrophe, that cursed, murdering Jhingur.

Jhingur thought and thought and decided that Buddhu had to be put in a situation exactly like his own. Buddhu had ruined him and he was wallowing in comfort, so Jhingur would ruin Buddhu too.

Since the day of their terrible quarrel Buddhu had ceased to come by Jhingur's. Jhingur decided to cultivate an intimacy with him; he wanted to show him he had no suspicion at all that Buddhu started the fire. One day, on the pretext of getting a blanket, he went to Buddhu, who greeted him with every courtesy and honour—for a man offers the hooka even to an enemy and won't let him depart without making him drink milk and syrup.

These days Jhingur was earning a living by working in a jute-wrapping mill. Usually he got several days' wages at once. Only by means of Buddhu's help could he meet his daily expenses between times. So it was that Jhingur re-established a friendly footing between them.

One day Buddhu asked, 'Say Jhingur, what would you do if you caught the man who burned your cane field? Tell me the truth.'

Solemnly Jhingur said, 'I'd tell him, "Brother, what you did was good. You put an end to my pride, you made me into a decent man."'

'If I were in your place,' Buddhu said, 'I wouldn't settle for anything less than burning down his house.'

'But what's the good of stirring up hatred in a life that lasts such a little while in all? I've been ruined already, what could I get out of ruining him?'

'Right, that's the way of a decent religious man,' Buddhu said, 'but when a fellow's in the grip of anger all his sense gets jumbled up.'

4

Spring came and the peasants were getting the fields ready for planting cane. Buddhu was doing a fine business. Everybody wanted his sheep. There were always a half dozen men at his door fawning on him, and he lorded it over everybody. He doubled the price of hiring out his sheep to manure the fields; if anybody objected he'd say bluntly, 'Look, brother, I'm not shoving my sheep on you. If you don't want them, don't take them. But I can't let you have them for a pice less than I said.' The result was that everybody swarmed around him, despite his rudeness, just like priests after some pilgrim.

Lakshmi, goddess of wealth, is of no great size; she can, according to the occasion, shrink or expand, to such a degree that sometimes she can contract her most magnificent manifestation into the form of a few small figures printed on paper. There are times

25

when she makes some man's tongue her throne and her size is reduced to nothing. But just the same she needs a lot of elbow-room for her permanent living quarters. If she comes into somebody's house, the house should grow accordingly, she can't put up with a small one. Buddhu's house also began to grow. A veranda was built in front of the door, six rooms replaced the former two. In short the house was done over from top to bottom. Buddhu got the wood from a peasant, from another the cowdung cakes for the kiln fuel to make the tiles; somebody else gave him the bamboo and reeds for the mats. He had to pay for having the walls put up but he didn't give any cash even for this, he gave some lambs. Such is the power of Lakshmi: the whole job—and it was quite a good house, all in all—was put up for nothing. They began to prepare for a house-warming.

Jhingur was still labouring all day without getting enough to half fill his belly, while gold was raining on Buddhu's house. If Jhingur was angry, who could blame him? Nobody could put up with such injustice.

One day Jhingur went out walking in the direction of the untouchable tanners' settlement. He called for Harihar, who came out, greeting him with '*Ram Ram!*' and filled the hooka. They began to smoke. Harihar, the leader of the tanners, was a mean fellow and there wasn't a peasant who didn't tremble at the sight of him.

After smoking a bit, Jhingur said, 'No singing for the spring festival these days? We haven't heard you.'

'What festival? The belly can't take a holiday. Tell me, how are you getting on lately?'

'Getting by,' Jhingur said. 'Hard times mean a hard life. If I work all day in the mill there's a fire in my stove. But these days only Buddhu's making money. He doesn't have room to store it! He's built a new house, bought more sheep. Now there's a big fuss about his house-warming. He's sent *pan* to the headmen of all the seven villages around to invite everybody to it.'

'When Mother Lakshmi comes men don't see so clearly,' Harihar said. 'And if you see him, he's not walking on the same ground as you or I. If he talks, it's only to brag.'

'Why shouldn't he brag? Who in the village can equal him? But friend, I'm not going to put up with injustice. When God gives

I bow my head and accept it. It's not that I think nobody's equal to me but when I hear *him* bragging it's as though my body started to burn. "A cheat yesterday, a banker today." He's stepped on us to get ahead. Only yesterday he was hiring himself out in the fields with just a loincloth on to chase crows and today his lamp's burning in the skies.'

'Speak,' Harihar said, 'Is there something I can do?'

'What can you do? He doesn't keep any cows or buffaloes just because he's afraid somebody will do something to them to get at him.'

'But he keeps sheep, doesn't he?'

'You mean, "hunt a heron and get a grouse"?'

'Think about it again.'

'It's got to be a plan that will keep him from ever getting rich again.'

Then they began to whisper. It's a mystery why there's just as much love among the wicked as malice among the good. Scholars, holy men and poets sizzle with jealousy when they see other scholars, holy men and poets. But a gambler sympathizes with another gambler and helps him, and it's the same with drunkards and thieves. Now, if a Brahman Pandit stumbles in the dark and falls then another Pandit, instead of giving him a hand, will give him a couple of kicks so he won't be able to get up. But when a thief finds another thief in distress he helps him. Everybody's united in hating evil so the wicked have to love one another; while everybody praises virtue so the virtuous are jealous of each other. What does a thief get by killing another thief? Contempt. A scholar who slanders another scholar attains to glory.

Jhingur and Harihar consulted, plotting their course of action —the method, the time and all the steps. When Jhingur left he was strutting—he'd already overcome his enemy, there was no way for Buddhu to escape now.

On his way to work the next day he stopped by Buddhu's house. Buddhu asked him, 'Aren't you working today?'

'I'm on my way, but I came by to ask you if you wouldn't let my calf graze with your sheep. The poor thing's dying tied up to the post while I'm away all day, she doesn't get enough grass and fodder to eat.'

'Brother, I don't keep cows and buffaloes. You know the tan-

27

ners, they're all killers.That Harihar killed my two cows, I don't
know what he fed them. Since then I've vowed never again to keep
cattle. But yours is just a calf, there'd be no profit to anyone in
harming that. Bring her over whenever you want.'

Then he began to show Jhingur the arrangements for the house-
warming. Ghee, sugar, flour and vegetables were all on hand. All
they were waiting for was the Satyanarayan ceremony. Jhingur's
eyes were popping.

When he came home after work the first thing he did was bring
his calf to Buddhu's house. That night the ceremony was performed and a feast offered to the Brahmans. The whole night
passed in lavishing hospitality on the priests. Buddhu had no
opportunity to go to look after his flock of sheep.

The feasting went on until morning. Buddhu had just got up
and had his breakfast when a man came and said, 'Buddhu, while
you've been sitting around here, out there in your flock the calf
has died. You're a fine one! The rope was still around its neck.'

When Buddhu heard this it was as though he'd been punched.
Jhingur, who was there having some breakfast too, said, 'Oh God,
my calf! Come on, I want to see her! But listen, I never tied her
with a rope. I brought her to the flock of sheep and went back
home. When did you have her tied with a rope, Buddhu?'

'God's my witness, I never touched any rope! I haven't been
back to my sheep since then.'

'If you didn't, then who put the rope on her?' Jhingur said. 'You
must have done it and forgotten it.'

'And it was in your flock,' one of the Brahmans said. 'People
are going to say that whoever tied the rope, that heifer died because
of Buddhu's negligence.'

Harihar came along just then and said, 'I saw him tying the
rope around the calf's neck last night.'

'Me?' Buddhu said.

'Wasn't that you with your stick over your shoulder tying up
the heifer?'

'And you're an honest fellow, I suppose!' Buddhu said. 'You
saw me tying her up?'

'Why get angry with me, brother? Let's just say you didn't tie
her up, if that's what you want.'

'We will have to decide about it,' one of the Brahmans said.

28

'A cow slaughterer should be stoned—it's no laughing matter.'

'Maharaj,' Jhingur said, 'the killing was accidental.'

'What's that got to do with it?' the Brahman said. 'It's set down that no cow is ever to be done to death in any way.'

'That's right,' Jhingur said. 'Just to tie a cow up is a fiendish act.'

'In the Scriptures it's called the greatest sin,' the Brahman said. 'Killing a cow is no less than killing a Brahman.'

'That's right,' Jhingur said. 'The cow's got a high place, that's why we respect her, isn't it? The cow is like a mother. But Maharaj, it was an accident—figure out something to get the poor fellow off.'

Buddhu stood listening while the charge of murder was brought against him like the simplest thing in the world. He had no doubt it was Jhingur's plotting, but if he said a thousand times that he hadn't put the rope on the calf nobody would pay any attention to it. They'd say he was trying to escape the penance.

The Brahman, that divinity, also stood to profit from the imposition of a penance. Naturally, he was not one to neglect an opportunity like this. The outcome was that Buddhu was charged with the death of a cow; the Brahman had got very incensed about it too and he determined the manner of compensation. The punishment consisted of three months of begging in the streets, then a pilgrimage to the seven holy places, and in addition the price for five cows and feeding 500 Brahmans. Stunned, Buddhu listened to it. He began to weep, and after that the period of begging was reduced by one month. Apart from this he received no favour. There was no one to appeal to, no one to complain to. He had to accept the punishment.

He gave up his sheep to God's care. His children were young and all by herself what could his wife do? The poor fellow would stand in one door after another hiding his face and saying, 'Even the gods are banished for cow-slaughter!' He received alms but along with them he had to listen to bitter insults. Whatever he picked up during the day he'd cook in the evening under some tree and then go to sleep right there. He did not mind the hardship, for he was used to wandering all day with his sheep and sleeping beneath trees, and his food at home hadn't been much better than this, but he was ashamed of having to beg, especially when some harridan

29

would taunt him with, 'You've found a fine way to earn your bread!' That sort of thing hurt him profoundly, but what could he do?

He came home after two months. His hair was long, and he was as weak as though he were sixty years old. He had to arrange for the money for his pilgrimage, and where's the moneylender who loans to shepherds? You couldn't depend on sheep. Sometimes there are epidemics and you're cleaned out of the whole flock in one night. Furthermore, it was the middle of the hot weather when there was no hope of profit from the sheep. There was an oil-dealer who was willing to loan him money at an interest of two annas per rupee—in eight months the interest would equal the principal. Buddhu did not dare borrow on such terms. During the two months many of his sheep had been stolen. When the children took them to graze the other villagers would hide one or two sheep away in a field or hut and afterwards slaughter them and eat them. The boys, poor lads, couldn't catch a single one of them, and even when they saw, how could they fight? The whole village was banded together. It was an awful dilemma. Helpless, Buddhu sent for a butcher and sold the whole flock to him for 500 rupees. He took 200 and started out on his pilgrimage. The rest of the money he set aside for feeding the Brahmans.

When Buddhu left, his house was burgled twice, but by good fortune the family woke up and the money was saved.

5

It was Savan, month of rains, with everything lush green. Jhingur, who had no bullocks now, had rented out his field to share-croppers. Buddhu had been freed from his penitential obligations and along with them his delusions about wealth. Neither one of them had anything left; neither could be angry with the other—there was nothing left to be angry about.

Because the jute mill had closed down Jhingur went to work with pick and shovel in town where a very large rest-house for pilgrims was being built. There were a thousand labourers on the job. Every seventh day Jhingur would take his pay home and after spending the night there go back the next morning.

The Road to Salvation

Buddhu came to the same place looking for work. The foreman saw that he was a skinny little fellow who wouldn't be able to do any heavy work so he had him take mortar to the labourers. Once when Buddhu was going with a shallow pan on his head to get mortar Jhingur saw him. '*Ram Ram*' they said to one another and Jhingur filled the pan. Buddhu picked it up. For the rest of the day they went about their work in silence.

At the end of the day Jhingur asked, 'Are you going to cook something?'

'How can I eat if I don't?' Buddhu said.

'I eat solid food only once a day,' Jhingur said. 'I get by just drinking water with ground meal in it in the evenings. Why fuss?'

'Pick up some of those sticks lying around,' Buddhu said. 'I brought some flour from home. I had it ground there—it costs a lot here in town. I'll knead it on the flat side of this rock. Since you won't eat food I cook I'll get it ready and you cook it.'

'But there's no frying pan.'

'There are lots of frying pans,' Buddhu said. 'I'll scour out one of these mortar trays.'

The fire was lit, the flour kneaded. Jhingur cooked the chapatties, Buddhu brought the water. They both ate the bread with salt and red pepper. Then they filled the bowl of the hooka. They both lay down on the stony ground and smoked.

Buddhu said, 'I was the one who set fire to your cane field.'

Jhingur said light-heartedly, 'I know.'

After a little while he said, 'I tied up the heifer and Harihar fed it something.'

In the same light-hearted tone Buddhu said, 'I know.'

Then the two of them went to sleep.

NOTE

Original title, '*Mukti-Mārg*', 'Salvation Road'. First published in 1924. One of Premchand's finest stories of village life for its sympathy and objectivity and the mock epic humour of its battle scenes and satire.

The 'Satyanarayan' ceremony, held to honour auspicious occasions like housewarmings, consists of special prayers, the recitation of the exploits of Lord Vishnu, specially consecrated foods and banquets for the Brahmans.

The conclusion of the story makes it clear that Buddhu is of a lower social community than Jhingur. The higher caste may not eat food prepared by the lower unless, as in this case, the actual cooking is done by the higher-ranking man, since fire purifies everything it touches.

A Feast for the Holy Man

A wandering holy man appeared in the doorway of Ramdhan the farmer and said:

'May you prosper, son, if you put your faith in the holy man.'

Ramdhan went to his wife and said, 'A sadhu's at the door, we have to give him something.'

His wife had been scouring pots, all the while worried about what they were going to eat that day, for there was not a speck of grain in the house. During the last spring season even at noon the skies were dark. The barn had been emptied of its stocks—the money-lenders had taken half, the landowner's agents had gobbled up the other half, the straw had been sold to get the ox-trader off their necks—that was all. For themselves they had saved one small sack. By threshing it over and over again they managed to get scarcely a maund of grain out of it. Somehow or other they had reached the end of spring, but God knew how they would go on or what the oxen would eat or even the people in the house. But a holy man had come to their door—how could they send him away disappointed, what would he think in his heart? She said:

'What am I going to give him when there's nothing at all left?'

Ramdhan said, 'Go look in the clay jug, if there's any flour bring it.'

'Yesterday I used whatever I could scrape out of it—what kind of miracle do you expect from it?'

'I'm not going to be heard telling the baba that there's nothing in the house. Borrow something from one of the neighbours.'

'Look what I've already borrowed without ever paying anything back! What kind of face can I show them now?'

'Isn't there something set aside for an offering to the gods?' Ramdhan said. 'Get it and I'll give it to him.'

'And where are we going to get something to offer the gods?'

'The gods don't come a-begging. If you've got something to give, you give it, if you haven't then you don't.'

'And I suppose you think we've got ten or twenty pounds of meal set aside for them! With luck there's about a pound. After

that's gone what if another sadhu comes? You'll have to send him
about his business.'

'We'll face that problem when it comes.'

Grumbling, she got up and picked up a small clay pot in which
there was scarcely a pound of flour. With the greatest difficulty it
had been kept aside as an offering to the gods. Ramdhan stood
reflecting a moment. Then he put the flour in a bowl, went outside and poured it into the sadhu's sack.

2

When he'd taken the flour the mahatma said, 'My child, for today we intend to linger here. Give me a little *dal* and then the
sadhu's meal will be complete.'

Ramdhan went in again and told his wife. By chance there was
some *dal* left in the house. Ramdhan took it with some salt and
some cowdung cakes for fuel. Then he fetched water from the well.
Ceremoniously the holy man shaped the flour into cakes, cooked
the *dal* and took some potatoes from his sack and set them on
the fire. When the food was ready he said to Ramdhan, 'Child,
for a proper offering to the Lord we need just a spoonful of ghee.
If the food is not prepared according to the ritual, then what
kind of an offering will it be?'

'Babaji,' Ramdhan said, 'there isn't any ghee in the house.'

'Child, don't say such things—God has given you much.'

'Maharaj, I have no cows or bulls, so how should I have ghee?'

'Child, in God's storerooms there's a little of everything—so go
and ask the mistress of the house.'

Ramdhan went back in and said to his wife, 'He's asking for
ghee—he's a beggar who begs his way but he can't get his food
down without ghee!'

'Then take some of this *dal* and bring it to the banya. After
everything else, why be angry with the Baba just for this?'

They got the ghee. The holy man took out a handful of food
as an offering to the Lord, rang a little bell and sat down to enjoy
his meal.

He ate his fill, then folding his hands on his belly lay down on the threshold. Ramdhan brought the sadhu's plate, pot and ladle into the house to scour them.

That night nothing was cooked in Ramdhan's house. They just warmed up plain *dal* and drank it.

When he lay down to sleep, Ramdhan said to himself, 'Well, he's a better man than I am!'

NOTE

Original title: '*Bābāji kā Bhog*', 'The Sadhu's Repast'. Ramdhan is described as an *ahir*, a community associated with cow-herding; in this case Ramdhan is a farmer and, ironically, has no cattle but only plough oxen. The handful of food which the sadhu sets aside for the gods may be disposed of in various ways—fed to a cow, thrown into a river, etc., but is not to be consumed by humans. Although in his catalogue Amrit Rai gives no date for this story, it is a fine example of the compression and absence of editorial comment which characterize Premchand's last stories.

The Power of a Curse

Munshi Ramsevak came out of his house frowning and said, 'Death would be better than living like this.' Death gets quite a few invitations of this sort; if she accepted them all the whole world would be depopulated by now.

In the village of Chandpur Munshi Ramsevak was a very rich man and he was full of all the special qualities of very rich men. The foibles of human nature provided the foundation of his living. He could be seen every day seated on a broken bench under a neem tree within the precincts of the open-air small-pleas court, his satchel crammed with papers opened up in front of him. Nobody had ever seen him presenting a brief before the tribunal or arguing a case; but everyone called him 'attorney'. It might blow up a storm, rain or hail, but the attorney could not be budged from his bench. Whenever he made his way to the open court the villagers crowded after him. He was regarded by everyone with respect and trust, and he was renowned for possessing the eloquence of the divine Saraswati herself. Call it an attorneyship or a legal practice, but it was only maintaining a family tradition. He had no very great income; people might talk about silver coins but even copper coins rarely came his way. Though there was no doubt about Ramsevak's legal knowlege, he was compelled by complications to forego a real lawyer's job. Anyway, whatever it was, his profession was kept up only for the sake of continuing the family tradition. In actual fact his real means of livelihood was provided by widows without family but rich in the good things of life and by old men with lots of money and little sense. The widows handed over their money to him for safe-keeping and old men who feared their wastrel sons entrusted their wealth to him. But once any money went into his fist it forgot the way to come out again. When the need arose he himself would borrow—after all, without borrowing whose work would make any headway? He borrowed in the morning to give back by evening, but the evening never came. In brief, Munshi Ramsevak knew how to borrow but not to give. This too was the family tradition.

All these matters frequently presented obstacles to Ramsevak's peace and quiet, but he had not the least fear of law and justice. To oppose him in this sort of business was like tackling a crocodile in the water. And still whenever any wretch did tangle with him, cast aspersions on his honesty or insulted him, Ramsevak was deeply hurt. And this sort of unfortunate incident kept on happening; there were shallow creatures everywhere who took delight in demeaning others. Egged on by such people, petty fellows would sometimes slander him. Otherwise, to take one example, how would an insignificant green-grocer's widow have the audacity to march right into his courtyard and curse him? He'd been an old customer of hers, for years he'd got vegetables from her. If he didn't pay, the woman ought to have been content—sooner or later she would have received it. But the foul-mouthed bean-monger went to pieces about it after only a couple of years and for a matter of a few pice tried to disgrace an established gentleman. Munshi Ramsevak got so irritated he was ready to do away with himself—he was not to blame for any of it.

2

In the same village lived a Brahman widow named Munga. Her husband had been a sergeant in the native Indian battalion in Burma and had died in battle there. In view of his fine service, the government had bestowed a sum of 500 rupees on her. Being a widow and times being hard, the poor creature entrusted all her money to Ramsevak, and begging back tiny sums every month she managed to eke out a living.

Munshiji had carried out his duty for several years now with full honesty. But when Munga had grown old without any sign of dying and he realized that perhaps from the whole amount she did not intend to leave even half to pay for her funeral expenses, he said to her one day, 'Munga, are you going to die or aren't you? Or just say straight out that you'll look after your own funeral fees.' That day Munga's eyes were opened, her dream dispelled, and she said, 'Give me back the full amount!' The account book was ready: not a pice of it remained according to the book. She violently grabbed his hand and said, 'You've made off with 250 rupees of mine but I won't let you keep a pice of it!'

But a poor widow's anger is just the sound of a blank bullet that may scare a child but has no real effect at all. She didn't have any influence in the courts, she couldn't read or write or keep accounts. To be sure, there was some hope in the panchayat, the village council. The panchayat met, people gathered from several villages. Munshi Ramsevak was ready and agreeable; he stood up in the council and addressed the members: 'Friends! You are all noble and devoted to the truth. I bow to you all. I am grateful to the core to you for your generosity and mercy, your charity and love. Do you people think I really made off with the money of this unfortunate widow?'

With one voice the councillors said, 'No, no! You couldn't do such a thing!'

Munshiji said, 'If you all agree that I've stolen her money, then there'll be nothing left for me except to drown myself. I'm not a rich man, nor can I take pride in being munificent. But thanks to my pen and to your kindness I cannot call myself needy. Am I so petty as to embezzle a widow's money?'

The councillors were unanimous. 'No, no, you couldn't do such a thing!'

They had had a taste of his money and that was that. The council acquitted him and adjourned.

Munga heaved a sigh and, making the most of it, said to herself, 'If I'm not to get it here, then all right, I won't, but I'll get it back in heaven.'

3

There was nobody now to help Munga or listen to her grieving. Whatever woes poverty bestowed she had to bear them all. She was strong of body and if she had wanted she could have worked hard. But from the day the panchayat gave its judgment she swore she wouldn't work. Now she was obsessed with the thought of her money. All day and all night, walking or sitting, she had only one idea: to inveigh against Munshi Ramsevak. Seated day and night at the door of her hut she fervently cursed him. For the most

part in her pronouncements she employed poetic speech and
metaphors so that people who heard her were astonished.

Gradually her mind gave way. Bare-headed, bare-bodied, with
a little hatchet in her hand, she would sit in desolate places.
She abandoned her hut and was seen wondering around the ruins
in a cremation ghat along the river—dishevelled, red-eyed, grim-
acing crazily, her arms and legs emaciated. When they saw her
like this people were frightened. Now no one teased her even for
fun. Whenever she came out in the village, women shut the doors of
their houses, men slinked away and children ran off screeching. But
there was one child who didn't run away and that was Munshiji's
son Ramgulam. Whatever defect had been omitted in the father
was to be found in the son, and he was always getting the other
boys into trouble too. The village one-eyes and lame men hated
the sight of him.* And he enjoyed insults as much as though they
were compliments. He would keep after Munga, clapping his
hands and taking the village dogs with him, until the poor woman,
utterly bewildered, would flee the hamlet. Having lost her mind
along with her money she had earned the title of the local madwoman. She would sit alone, talking to herself for hours, express-
ing her intense desire to eat, smash, pinch and tear Ramsevak's
flesh, bones, eyes, liver and the like, and when her hatred reached
its climax she would turn her face toward Ramsevak's house and
shriek the terrible words, 'I'll drink your blood!'

Women were frightened when they heard her howling voice in
the stillness of the night. But more terrible than her words was her
wild laughter. In the imagined pleasure of drinking Munshiji's
blood she would burst into laughter that resounded with such
demoniacal violence, such bestial ferocity that when people heard
it in the night their blood was chilled. It seemed as though hundreds of owls were hooting together. Munshiji was a man of great
courage and tenacity, not one to be afraid of a madwoman any
more than of the courts, but when he heard Munga's awful words
he was scared. We may not be afraid of human justice but the
fear of God's justice resides by nature in every man's heart—
Munga's dreadul night-wanderings sometimes inspired such
reflections in Ramsevak's mind, and even more in his wife's. Nagin,

*This suggests both that he tormented them and that he was even uglier
than they.

who was pregnant now, was a very shrewd woman. She advised her husband about all his business dealings. The people who said Munshiji possessed the eloquence of Goddess Saraswati were mistaken: this virtue really belonged to his wife. She was as brilliant in speech as he in writing. And these two, husband and wife, would now consult together on what to do about this situation in which they found themselves powerless.

One midnight when Munshiji, according to his regular custom, had banished his troubles with a few swallows of liquor and gone to sleep, suddenly Munga let out a shriek right on his doorstep and howled, 'I'll drink your blood!'

Munshiji was electrified by her horrible peals of laughter. His legs shook with fear, his heart thumped. Gathering up his courage with a great effort he opened the door and woke Nagin. Peevishly she said, 'What's the matter?' Munshiji whispered, 'She's standing on the door step.'

Nagin sat up. 'What's she saying?'

'Don't be stupid, what do you think she's saying?'

'You mean she's right at the door?'

'Yes, can't you hear her?'

Nagin was not afraid of Munga but she was very much afraid of the misdeed she symbolized; still, she believed she could get the best of her by talking. 'Just let me talk to her,' she said but Munshiji forbade her.

The two of them tiptoed to the threshold and peeking from the door they saw Munga's dim figure lying on the ground, they heard her panting. In her hungering for Munshiji's flesh and blood she had completely used up her own: even a child could have knocked her down—and yet she could make the whole town tremble.

The night passed. The door was shut but Ramsevak and Nagin spent the hours sitting up. Munga could not get inside but who could stop her voice? Her voice was the most terrible thing about her.

At dawn Munshiji went outside and said to her, 'Why are you lying there?'

'I'll drink your blood,' Munga said.

Rearing up, Nagin said, 'I'll knock your head right off!'

But Nagin's venomous tone had no effect on Munga, who

40

shrieked with laughter. Disconcerted, Nagin fell silent before that laughter. Then Munshiji spoke again:

'Get up!'

'I won't!'

'Just how long do you think you're going to lie here?'

'I'll go when I've drunk your blood!'

In these straits Munshiji's pungent pen was of no use and Nagin's fiery eloquence grew cold. They went inside to consult on how to put an end to this calamitous situation.

When the Goddess comes she has a drink of goat's blood and goes on her way, but this witch came to drink human blood, the very blood which, if even a drop of it was spilled while Munshiji was sharpening a pen nib, was lamented throughout the household for weeks and months while the event was related from house to house in the village. Would Munga's shrivelled body become young again from drinking that blood?

The news got around the village that Munga was squatting on Munshiji's doorstep. The villagers took great delight in his embarrassment and loss of face. Whole flocks of people gathered around at once. Little Ramgulam didn't like this crowd and he got so angry with Munga that if he had had the power he would have flung her into a well. As soon as an idea like this struck him he would be so tickled that he could hardly control his laughter. Oh, what fun it would be to dump her into a well! But the bitch wouldn't get away from the door, what could you do? Munshiji, as it happened, kept a cow; Ramgulam collected the dung of this cow in a pot and flung it at the poor woman. Some of it splashed on the on-lookers too. Munga was completely covered and the people hastily retreated, saying, 'This is Munshi Ramgulam's door where you can expect such fine manners! Get away quickly or there'll be some even greater show of courtesy.' While the crowd dispersed Ramgulam went into the house and had a good laugh and clapped his hands. Munshiji congratulated his amiable son on this ingenious and appealing way of getting rid of that good-for-nothing crowd. The whole mob finally disappeared, but Munga went on lying there exactly as before.

Noontime came. Munga ate nothing. Then it was evening. Even after a barrage of threats and abuse she refused to eat. The village headman came and coaxed her, and Munshiji even begged her

41

with folded hands, but she would not agree. Finally he got up and went inside. He said that hunger alone could overcome so fierce a hatred.

That night Munga neither ate nor drank anything and once again Munshiji and Nagin lay awake until morning. By now Munga's howling and laughing were heard much less frequently. The people of the household assumed that the worst was over. As soon as it was daylight Munshiji opened the door and saw Munga lying motionless. Flies were already buzzing around her mouth; her breathing had stopped. She had come just to die at his door. To the man who'd taken her life savings she had entrusted her corpse as well, she was making him a gift of the very clay of her body.

Is is impossible to describe the sensation this event produced in the village and the extent of Ramsevak's disgrace. As much of a commotion as there can be in such a tiny village over such an extraordinary event, well, it was even greater than that, and Munshiji's dishonour was not a whit less than it ought to have been. Whatever prestige he'd been able to maintain vanished. Now not even the leather-tanners would have accepted water from him or touched him. If a cow in somebody's household dies while tied to a peg, then that man goes around for months begging from door to door; no barber will shave him, no water-carrier bring him water, nor anyone touch him: such is the penance for cowslaughter. The punishment for the murder of a Brahman is even stiffer and the disgrace immeasurable. Knowing this, Munga had come to die on his doorstep. She knew she could not accomplish much alive but dead she could do a great deal.

5

Munshi Ramsevak was versed in law: according to the law he was innocent. Munga had not died according to any legal instance, no example of it could be found in the Indian Penal Code. Therefore those people who wished to impose a penance on him were entirely mistaken. There was no great harm so far as he was concerned: if the water-carrier did not want to draw his water, Munshiji would draw it himself—anyway, what was wrong with doing such little chores for yourself? And what if the barber wouldn't shave him?—what's the use of getting shaved? The beard's a lovely thing, the very glory and embellishment of man. And then if later you get fed up with the beard, you can always buy a razor for a paltry sum. He wasn't worried when the dhobi refused to wash his clothes. In any street in town there was nothing cheaper than soap. With just one cake a whole pile of clothes could be made clean as a duck's feathers. How could the dhobi make clothes that clean? He whips them on the stones until they're in tatters. He wears your clothes, rents them out to others, throws them into his boiling cauldron and steeps them in fuller's earth. And of course they're ruined. That's why shirts don't last more than two or three years. If that hadn't been the case grandfather would have got along with having only two jackets and two shirts made every fifth year. Throughout the day Munshiji and his wife consoled themselves with such reasoning. But as soon as it was evening their rationalizing petered out.

Fear took hold of them when darkness fell. As the hour turned late this fear grew all the stronger. They'd left the front door open by mistake and not one of them was daring enough to get up and shut it. Finally Nagin took a lamp, Munshiji his axe and Ramgulam the sickle, and the three of them, quaking and shrinking, went to the door. There Munshiji boldly tackled the problem: he made a valiant attempt to go outside. Trembling but with a loud voice he said to Nagin, 'You're frightened for nothing. Do you think she's sitting out there?' But his loving Nagin pulled him back inside and said angrily, 'You're wicked to joke about it.' Having won this tilt the three of them went into the kitchen and began to cook something.

But Munga had gotten under their skins. Seeing their own shadow they'd jump, sure it was Munga. It seemed to them that she was sitting in every dark corner. That emaciated body and scattered hair, the mad look, the horrible eyes—it was Munga to a tee!

In the kitchen they had set several large clay pots for flour and pulse and there were some old rags lying around too. Driven by hunger a mouse came out looking for the grain which those pots in fact had never had a taste of—but it was well-known in the village that in this house the mice had to be resourceful thieves.

The mouse crept under the rags with a rustling sound. The way those rags were spread out they looked exactly like Munga's skinny legs. When she saw them Nagin jumped and let out a shriek. Losing his head completely Munshiji sprang for the door and Ramgulam started running and got entangled in his father's legs. Just then the mouse emeged and when they saw it they recovered their wits. Ramsevak walked boldly toward the pot. 'Leave it alone,' Nagin said. 'We've seen how brave you are.'

Her contempt made Munshiji very angry. 'Do you think I was afraid?' he said. 'What was there to be afraid of? Munga's dead, so how could she be there? Didn't I go outside yesterday? You tried to stop me but I didn't pay any attention.'

This argument silenced Nagin. Yesterday it had been no ordinary deed to go outside the door or even to try to. Whoever had shown such evidence of bravery could not be called a coward by anybody. Nagin was just being perverse.

After they'd eaten the three of them came into the bedroom. But even there Munga did not leave them alone. They were talking, enjoying themselves. Nagin told the tale of Raja Hardaul and Rani Sarandha, Munshiji recounted the circumstances of several criminal cases. But even in these diversions Munga's image refused to leave their minds. The very slightest tap would startle them. If there was a rustling of leaves the hair would stand up on all three of them. Several times a low voice reached them from within the earth: 'I'll drink your blood . . .'

At midnight Nagin was startled from her sleep. It seemed to her that Munga, with her red eyes and sharp pointed teeth, was sitting on her chest. Nagin screamed. She started running toward the courtyard like a madwoman, and suddenly she fell senseless to the ground, sweating all over. Munshiji had been awakened by her yell but he was so frightened he didn't open his eyes. Like a blind man he felt his way to the door. After a long while he found it and came into the courtyard. Nagin was lying on the ground writhing. He lifted her up and brought her inside, but she didn't open her eyes the whole night. Toward dawn she began to rave incoherently. In a little while her fever rose, her body turned hot as a griddle. By evening she was in a delirium and at midnight when all the world was plunged in silence she took her leave of it forever. Fear of Munga had killed her. While Munga lived she had always feared Nagin's hissing. But sacrificing her own life, she could now take Nagin's.

The night passed, day drew on, but not one person in the village showed up to bear Nagin's corpse away, Munshiji went from house to house, but no one answered the door. After all, who will go to a murderer's house? who will do honour to the corpse of an assassin? This time Munshiji's prestige, his genius at law and the fear of his mighty pen were of no use to him at all. Rejected everywhere, he turned back to his house. Here everything appeared to him as gloomy as possible. He came as far as his door but he didn't set foot inside. Outside was Munga, inside Nagin. Mustering his courage, he finally entered the house reciting passages from the 'Holy Acts of God Hanuman'. Only he knew what was passing in his mind. There was the corpse: no one of the earlier generation was left, no one from the coming except his son. To be sure, he might marry again. This last spring he'd only reached fifty. But where could he find a worthy and sweet-tongued wife? What a loss! Who was there now to cope with dunning creditors, who could silence them? Who could keep the accounts of all his transactions so well? Whose sharp voice could shoot out like an arrow to pierce the hearts of his creditors? There was no compensation for such a loss. The next day Munshiji loaded the body on to a wheel-barrow and went toward holy Ganges.

6

The number of people attending the cremation was not large. There was Munshiji himself and one other, his dear son Ramgulam. Even Munga's corpse had not had to suffer such humiliation.

Having done away with Nagin, Munga was not going to leave Munshiji alone. At every moment her image remained before his eyes. Wherever he might be his mind always harked back to her. If he could have devised any little diversion perhaps he might not have been so nervous, but not even the village scarecrows would give him a nod. The poor man had to draw his own water and even wash the pots. No mind can remain stable with only worry, anger, anxiety and fear before it, especially this mind that had been preoccupied every day with the disputes of law.

Like a prisoner in solitary confinement, somehow or other he managed to get through the next ten or twelve days. At the end of two weeks, his mourning over, Munshiji changed his clothes and with his mat and satchel went to the open court. Today his expression was a little brighter. Today, he thought, his clients would flock around him, they'd condole with him and he'd shed a few tears. Then there would be an abundance of foreclosures, settlements and mortgages and he'd be rolling in money. In the evening he would celebrate a little with some liquor—giving *that* up had increased his depression. Full of these thoughts he reached the court.

But there, instead of the abundance of mortgages and the flood of foreclosures and the merry greetings of clients, he encountered the sandy wastes of disappointment. He sat for hours with his satchel open but nobody came near him, or even inquired about how he was. Not only were there no new clients but very old ones, whose business Munshiji's family had handled for generations, today hid their faces from him. That incompetent and loutish Ramzan, whom Munshiji used to laugh at and who could not even write properly, today he was as mobbed as Krishna among the milkmaids. It was all a matter of fate. The clients walked around with their faces averted as though they didn't know him. After wasting his whole day at the court Munshiji went home, sunk in worry and disappointment. As soon as he came close to the house Munga's image rose before him. He was so nervous that when on opening the door two dogs, shut in by Ramgulam, came rushing out he completely lost his wits, let out a shriek and fell senseless to the ground.

What happened to Munshiji after this is not known. For several days people saw him go to the court and come back drooping. It was his duty to go to the court and although there was a dearth of clients there this was now the only trick left to keep the creditors off his back and inspire confidence in them. After that he went off to the shrine of Badrinath and was not seen for several months.

One day a sadhu came to the village—on his forehead ashes, locks long and matted, a clay waterpot in his hand. His countenance closely resembled Ramsevak's and his speech also was not much different. He sat in meditation beneath a tree. That night smoke rose from Ramsevak's house, then the glow of a fire was visible and then a burst of flame. All the villagers came running— not to put the fire out but to see the fun.

As for Ramgulam, when Munshiji disappeared he went off to live with an uncle and stayed there a while, but no one there could put up with his ways.

One day he was digging up radishes in somebody's field. The owner gave him a few slaps. This made him so angry that he went into the man's granary and set it on fire. It burned down completely and thousands of rupees went up in smoke. The police investigated and Ramgulam was arrested. For this offence he is at present in the reformatory at Chunar.

NOTE

Original title, '*Garib ki Hāy*', 'The Lament of the Poor'. First published in 1911. In this quite early story there is a good deal of the moralizing that so often characterizes the earlier work and considerable redundancy as well. I have cut this where it seemed in the interests of the story.

It is worth noting that in this tale Munshi Ramsevak is ostracized not because he is a wicked man—which everyone has accepted throughout his career—but because he is technically the cause of a Brahman's death. Premchand's attitude toward the villagers is no less critical than it is toward Munshiji.

The name 'Nagin' suggests '*nag*', a cobra, hence the reference to her hissing, rearing up, etc.

A Catastrophe

In Banaras district there is a village called Bira in which an old,
childless widow used to live. She was a Gond woman named
Bhungi and she didn't own either a scrap of land or a house to
live in. The only source of her livelihood was a parching oven. The
village folk customarily have one meal a day of parched grains,
so there was always a crowd around Bhungi's oven. Whatever
grain she was paid for parching she would grind or fry and eat
it. She slept in a corner of the same little shack that sheltered the
oven. As soon as it was light she'd get up and go out to gather
dry leaves from all around to make her fire. She would stack the
leaves right next to the oven and, after twelve o'clock, light the
fire. But when, according to custom, she did not start her fire on
such fast days as the eleventh of the month and the day of the
full moon, or on the days when she had to parch grain for Pandit
Udaybhan Pandey, the owner of the village, on those days she
went to bed hungry. She was not only obliged to work without pay
for Pandit Udaybhan but she also had to fetch the water for his
house. And, for this reason, from time to time the oven was not
lit. She lived in the Pandit's village, therefore he had full authority to make her do any sort of odd job. It couldn't be called an
injustice; it would have been an injustice only if he'd paid her for
it. In his opinion if she received food for working for him, how
could it be considered as work done without pay? The peasant
has a full right to tether his bulls without feeding them
after they've worked a full day in the fields. If he doesn't do this,
it's not from any kindness of his but only concern for his profit.
Panditji did not have this worry because Bhungi wasn't going
to drop dead after staying hungry for a couple of days. And if by
chance she should die, then some other Gond could very easily be
found to fill her place. He was doing her a favour, as a matter of
fact, by letting her live in the village at all.

It was spring, the sun was moving into a new sign of the
zodiac, a day on which the fresh grain was fried and eaten and
given as a gift. No fire was lit in the houses. Bhungi's oven was

48

being put to good use today. There was a crowd worthy of a village fair around her. She had scarcely opportunity to draw a breath. Because of the customers' impatience squabbles kept breaking out. Then two servants arrived, each carrying a heaped basket of grain from Pandit Udaybhan with the order to parch it right away. When Bhungi saw the two baskets she was very alarmed. It was already after twelve and even by sunset she would not have time to parch so much grain. With one or two hours more she could have earned enough food for a whole week. But God had not seen fit to allow it, instead he had sent these two fatal messengers. Now she would have to stay at the oven parching until after dark for no payment. In despair she took the two baskets.

One of the flunkeys said menacingly, 'Don't waste any time or you'll be sorry.'

'Sit here and wait,' she said, 'and when it's parched take it and go. Cut off my hand if I touch anybody else's grain.'

'Who's got time to sit around and wait? Just have it done by sundown.'

With this command the servants went away and Bhungi began to parch the grain. It's no laughing matter to parch a whole maund of grain. She had to keep stopping from the parching in order to keep the oven fire going. So by sundown not even half the work was done. She was afraid Panditji's men would be coming and as soon as they'd arrived insult and beat her. She began to move her hands all the more frantically. She would look toward the road and go on throwing sand into the trough until the sand got cold and the grain began to come out only half-roasted. She couldn't figure out what to do—she couldn't parch and she couldn't stop, and she began to realize what a catastrophe it was. What sort of bread did Panditji give her for her work? He wasn't one to wipe her tears! If she worked herself to the bone it was to earn some kind of food, but as soon as Panditji caught sight of her he'd threaten her, and just because she occupied four inches of his land. So high a price for so little land? And so many plots in the village lying fallow, so many cottages deserted. Saffron didn't grow in those empty fields, why should he be after her every hour of the day? When anything happened he'd threaten to dig up her oven and ruin it. If only she had a man to protect her she wouldn't have to put up with this.

While she was caught up in these gloomy thoughts the servants returned and said, 'Well, is the grain parched?'

Feeling bold, Bhungi said, 'Can't you see? I'm parching it now.'

'The whole day's gone and you haven't finished any more grain than this? Have you been roasting it or spoiling it? This is completely uncooked! How's it going to be used for food? It's the ruin of us! You'll see what Panditji does to you for this.'

The result was that that night the oven was dug up and Bhungi was left without a means of livelihood.

To punish her for not finishing,

Pan

3

Bhungi now had no means of support. The villagers suffered a good deal too from the destruction of the oven. In many houses even at noon cooked cereal was no longer available. People went to Panditji and asked him to give the order for the old woman's oven to be rebuilt and the fire once more lighted, but he paid no attention to them. He could not suffer a loss of face. A few people who wished her well urged her to move to another village. But her heart would not accept this suggestion. She had spent her fifty miserable years in this village and she loved every leaf on every tree. Here she had known the sorrows and pleasures of life; she could not give it up now in the last days. The very idea of moving distressed her. Sorrow in this village was preferable to happiness in another.

A month went by. Very early one morning Pandit Udaybhan, taking his little band of servants with him, went out to collect his rents—he didn't have any confidence in estate agents. He wouldn't allow any other person to share in his dues, his fines and his fees for religious services. Now when he looked toward the old woman's oven he fell into a violent rage: it was being resurrected. *REBUILT RE* Bhungi was energetically rebuilding it with balls of clay. Most likely she'd spent the night at this work and wanted to finish it before the sun was high. She did not in the least doubt that she was going against the Pandit's wishes, but she had no conception of how long-lasting anger can be, she could not realize that such a great person could have so much hatred for a pathetic old woman. She naturally assumed that human character had somehow to be loftier than that. But alas, the poor creature had grown old without growing wise.

Suddenly Panditji shouted, 'By whose order?'

Bewildered, Bhungi saw that he was standing before her.

He demanded once again, 'By whose order are you building it?'

In a fright she said, 'Everybody [ALL THE VILLAGERS] said I should build it and so I'm building it.'

'I'll have it smashed again.' With this he kicked the oven. The wet clay collapsed in a heap. He kicked at the trough again but she ran in front of it and took the kick in her side. Rubbing her ribs she said, 'Maharaj, you're not afraid of anybody but you ought to fear God. What good does it do you to ruin me like this? Do you think gold is going to grow out of this foot of ground? For your own good, I'm telling you, don't torment poor people, don't be the death of me.'

'You're not going to build any oven here again.'

'If I don't how am I going to be able to eat?'

'I'm not responsible for your belly.'

'But if I do nothing except chores for you where will I go for food?'

'If you're going to stay in the village you'll have to do my chores.'

'I'll do them when I've built my oven. I can't do your work just for the sake of staying in the village.'

'Then don't, just get out of the village.'

'How can I? After twelve [FIFTY] years of working a field the tenant earns a share in it. I've grown old in this hut. My in-laws and their grandparents lived in this same hut. Except for Yama, king of death, nobody's going to force me out of it now.' ·

'Excellent, now you're quoting Scripture!' Pandit Udaybhan said. 'If you'd worked hard I might have let you stay, but after this I won't rest until I've had you thrown out.' To his attendants he said, 'Go get a pile of leaves right away and set fire to the whole thing; we'll show her how to make an oven.'

4

In a moment there was a tremendous racket. The flames leapt toward the sky, the blaze spread wildly in all directions. The people of the whole village came clustering around this mountain of fire. Hopelessly, Bhungi stood by her oven watching the conflagration. Suddenly, with a violent dash, she hurled herself into the flames. They came running from everywhere but no one had the courage to go into the mouth of the blaze. In a matter of seconds her withered body was completely consumed.

At that moment the wind rose with a gust. The liberated flames began to race toward the east. There were some peasants' huts near the oven which were engulfed by the fierce flames. Fed in this way, the blaze spread even further. Panditji's barn was in its path and it pounced upon it. By now the whole village was in a panic. They began to band together to put out the fire but the sprinkle of water acted like oil on it and the flames kept mounting higher. Pandit Udaybhan's splendid mansion was swallowed up; while he watched, it tossed like a ship amid wild waves and disappeared in the sea of fire. The sound of lamentation that broke out amidst the ashes was even more pitiful than Bhungi's grievous cries.

NOTE

Original title, '*Vidhvans*', 'Destruction'. Written in the early twenties. Though usually designating a tribal community, in the eastern Uttar Pradesh 'Gond' indicates a person of a very low-ranking social group who are privileged, according to the complicated rules regulating the preparation of food, to handle food for high-caste groups. Cf. 'Deliverance'.

January Night

Halku came in and said to his wife, 'The landlord's come! Get the rupees you set aside, I'll give him the money and somehow or other we'll get along without it.'

Munni had been sweeping. She turned around and said, 'But there are only three rupees. If you give them to him where's the blanket going to come from? How are you going to get through these January nights in the fields? Tell him we'll pay him after the harvest, not right now.'

For a moment Halku stood hesitating. January was on top of them. Without a blanket he couldn't possibly sleep in the fields at night. But the landlord wouldn't be put off, he'd threaten and insult him. So what did it matter if they died in the cold weather as long as they could just take care of this calamity right now? As he thought this he moved his heavy body (that gave the lie to his name)* and came close to his wife. Trying to coax her he said, 'Come on, give it to me. We'll manage. I'll figure out some other plan to get the blanket.'

Munni drew away from him. Her eyes angry, she said, 'You've already tried "some other plan". You just tell me what other plan can be found. Is somebody going to give you a blanket? God knows how many debts are always left over that we can't pay off. What I say is, give up this tenant farming! The work's killing you, whatever you harvest goes to pay up the arrears, so why not finish with it? Were we born just to keep paying off debts? Earn some money for your own belly, give up that kind of farming. I won't give you the money, I won't!'

Sadly Halku said, 'Then I'll have to put up with his abuse.'

Losing her temper, Munni said, 'Why should he abuse you— is this his kingdom?'

But as she said it her brows relaxed from the frown. The bitter truth in Halku's words came charging at her like a wild beast.

She went to the niche in the wall, took out the rupees and handed them over to Halku. Then she said, 'Give up farming

*_Halku_ is derived from _halka_, meaning 'light'.

this time. If you work as a hired labourer you'll at least get enough food to eat from it. No one will be yelling insults at you. Fine work, farming someone else's land! Whatever you earn you throw back into it and get insulted in the bargain.'

Halku took the money and went outside looking as though he were tearing his heart out and giving it away. He'd saved the rupees from his work, pice by pice, for his blanket. Today he was going to throw it away. With every step his head sank lower under the burden of his poverty.

2

A dark January night. In the sky even the stars seemed to be shivering. At the edge of his field, underneath a shelter of cane leaves, Halku lay on a bamboo cot wrapped up in his old burlap shawl, shivering. Underneath the cot his friend, Jabra the dog, was whimpering with his muzzle pressed into his belly. Neither one of them was able to sleep.

Halku curled up drawing his knees close against his chin and said, 'Cold, Jabra? Didn't I tell you, in the house you could lie in the paddy straw? So why did you come out here? Now you'll have to bear the cold, there's nothing I can do. You thought I was coming out here to eat *puris* and sweets and you came running on ahead of me. Now you can moan all you want.'

Jabra wagged his tail without getting up, protracted his whimpering into a long yawn, and was silent. Perhaps in his canine wisdom he guessed that his whimpering was keeping his master awake.

Halku reached out his hand and patted Jabra's cold back. 'From tomorrow on stop coming with me or the cold will get you. This bitch of a west wind comes from nobody knows where bringing the icy cold with it. Let me get up and fill my pipe. I've smoked eight pipefuls already but we'll get through the night somehow. This is the reward you get for farming. Some lucky fellows are lying in houses where if the cold comes after them the heat just drives it away. A good thick quilt, warm covers, a blanket! Just let the winter cold try to get them! Fortune's arranged everything very well. While we do the hard work somebody else gets the joy of it.'

He got up, took some embers from the pit and filled his pipe. Jabra got up too.

Smoking, Halku said, 'If you smoke the cold's just as bad but at least you feel a little better.'

Jabra looked at him with eyes overflowing with love.

'You have to put up with just one more cold night. Tomorrow I'll spread some straw. When you bed down in that you won't feel the cold.'

Jabra put his paws on Halku's knees and brought his muzzle close. Halku felt his warm breath.

After he finished smoking Halku lay down and made up his mind that however things were he would sleep now. But in only one minute his heart began to pound. He turned from side to side, but like some kind of witch the cold weather continued to torment him.

When he could no longer bear it he gently picked Jabra up and, patting his head, got him to fall asleep in his lap. The dog's body gave off some kind of stink but Halku, hugging him tight, experienced a happiness he hadn't felt for months. Jabra probably thought he was in heaven, and in Halku's innocent heart there was no resentment of his smell. He embraced him with the very same affection he would have felt for a brother or a friend. He was not crippled by the poverty which had reduced him to these straits at present. Rather it was as though this singular friendship had opened all the doors to his heart and brilliantly illuminated every atom of it.

Suddenly Jabra picked up the noise of some animal. This special intimacy had produced a new alertness in him that disdained the onslaught of the wind. Springing up, he ran out of the shelter and began to bark. Halku whistled and called him several times. But Jabra would not come back to him. He went on barking while he ran around through the furrows of the field. He would come back for a moment, then dash off again at once. The sense of duty had taken possession of him as though it were desire.

3

Another hour passed. The night fanned up the cold with the

wind. Halku sat up and bringing both knees tight against his chest hid his face between them, but the cold was just as biting. It seemed as though all his blood had frozen, that ice rather than blood filled his veins. He leaned back to look at the skies. How much of the night was still left! The Dipper had not yet climbed half the sky. By the time it was overhead it would probably be morning. Night would last another three hours or so.

Only a stone's throw from Halku's field there was a mango grove. The leaves had begun to fall and they were heaped in the grove. Halku thought, 'If I go and get a pile of leaves I can make a fire of them and keep warm. If anybody sees me gathering the leaves in the dead of night they'll think it is a ghost. Of course there's a chance some animal's hidden in my field waiting, but I can't stand sitting here any longer.'

He ripped up some stalks from a near-by field, made a broom out of them and picking up a lighted cowdung cake went toward the grove. Jabra watched him coming and ran to him wagging his tail.

Halku said, 'I couldn't stand it any more, Jabra. Come along, let's go into the orchard and gather leaves to warm up with. When we're toasted we'll come back and sleep. The night's still far from over.'

Jabra barked his agreement and trotted on toward the orchard.

Under the trees it was pitch dark and in the darkness the bitter wind blew, buffeting the leaves, and drops of dew dripped from the branches.

Suddenly a gust carried the scent of henna blossoms to him. 'Where's that sweet smell coming from, Jabra? Or can't your nose make out anything as fragrant as this?'

Jabra had found a bone lying somewhere and he was chewing on it. Halku set his fire down on the ground and began to gather the leaves. In a little while he had a great heap. His hands were frozen, his bare feet numb. But he'd piled up a regular mountain of the leaves and by making a fire out of them he'd burn away the cold.

In a little while the fire was burning merrily. The flames leapt upward licking at the overhanging branches. In the flickering light the immense trees of the grove looked as though they were carrying the vast darkness on their heads. In the blissful sea of darkness the firelight seemed to pitch and toss alike a boat.

Halku sat before the fire and let it warm him. After a while he took off his shawl and tucked it behind him, then he spread out both feet as though challenging the cold to do its worst. Victorious over the immense power of the winter, he could not repress his pride in his triumph.

He said to Jabra, 'Well, Jabra, you're not cold now, are you?'

Jabra barked as though to say, 'How could I feel cold now?'

'We should have thought of this plan before, then we'd never have become so chilled.' Jabra wagged his tail. 'Fine, now what do you say we jump over the fire? Let's see how we manage it. But if you get scorched I've got no medicine for you.'

Jabra looked fearfully at the fire.

'We mustn't tell Munti tomorrow or there'll be a row.'

With that he jumped up and cleared the fire in one leap. He got his legs singed but he didn't care. Jabra ran around the fire and came up to him. Halku said, 'Go on, no more of this, jump over the fire!' He leaped again and came back to the other side.

4

The leaves were all burned up. Darkness covered the orchard again. Under the ashes a few embers smouldered and when a gust of wind blew over them they stirred up briefly, then flickered out again.

Halku wrapped himself up in his shawl again and sat by the warm ashes humming a tune. The fire had warmed him through but as the cold began to spread he felt drowsy.

Jabra gave a loud bark and ran toward the field. Halku realized that this meant a pack of wild animals had probably broken into the field. They might be bluebuck. He distinctly heard the noise of their moving around. Then it seemed to him they must be grazing; he began to hear the sound of nibbling.

He thought, 'No, with Jabra around no animal can get into the field, he'd rip it to shreds. I must have been mistaken. Now there's no sound at all. How could I have been mistaken?'

He shouted, 'Jabra! Jabra!'

Jabra went on barking and did not come to him.

Then again there was the sound of munching and crunching in the field. He could not have been mistaken this time. It really hurt to think about getting up from where he was. It was so comfortable there that it seemed intolerable to go to the field in this cold and chase after animals. He didn't stir.

He shouted at the top of his lungs, 'Hillo! Hillo! Hillo!'

Jabra started barking again. There were animals eating his field just when the crop was ready. What a fine crop it was! And these cursed animals were destroying it. With a firm resolve he got up and took a few steps. But suddenly a gust of wind pierced him with a sting like a scorpion's so that he went back and sat again by the extinguished fire and stirred up the ashes to warm his chilled body.

Jabra was barking his lungs out, the bluebuck were devastating his field and Halku went on sitting peacefully near the warm ashes. His drowsiness held him motionless as though with ropes. Wrapped in his shawl he fell asleep on the warmed ground near the ashes.

When he woke in the morning the sun was high and Munni was saying, 'Do you think you're going to sleep all day? You came out here and had a fine time while the whole field was being flattened!'

Halku got up and said, 'Then you've just come from the field?'

'Yes, the whole field's ruined. And you could sleep like that! Why did you bother to put up the shelter anyway?'

Halku sought an excuse. 'I nearly died and just managed to get through the night and you worry about your crop. I had such a pain in my belly that I can't describe it.'

Then the two of them walked to the edge of their land. He looked: the whole field had been trampled and Jabra was stretched out underneath the shelter as though he were dead.

They continued to stare at the ruined field. Munni's face was shadowed with grief but Halku was content.

Munni said, 'Now you'll have to hire yourself out to earn some money to pay off the rent and taxes.'

With a contented smile Halku said, 'But I won't have to sleep nights out here in the cold.'

January Night

NOTE

Original title, '*Pús ki Rāt*', 'A Night in the Month of Pus'. (*Pús*, a month in the Hindu solar calendar corresponding to December-January.) First published in 1930.

Observe, at the beginning of the story, the powerful motivation provided by fear of being insulted or spoken harshly to.

Neyur

In the sky silver mountains raced along and bumped together. As though the sun and clouds were battling sometimes it was overcast, then again there was the glitter of dazzling sunshine. These were monsoon days that had turned sultry, the wind had died.

Outside the village several workmen were setting up a dike between two fields. Bare-bodied, drenched in sweat, dhotis tucked up tight around their hips, they were all busy shovelling the rain-softened earth into line.

Gobar rolled his blind eye and said, 'Brother, my hands won't move. But now they must have fired the signal gun. Let's have something to eat.'

'Finish the dike,' Neyur said, laughing, 'and then have your food. I started work even before you.'

Deena said, putting the basket on his head, 'The amount of ghee you ate up in your youth, Brother Neyur, why you don't even get that much water these days.'

Neyur was a short, husky, dark, nimble fellow of about fifty. But the strongest young fellows could not match him in working. Two or three years ago he was still wrestling; he'd given it up when his cow died.

'How can you go on without smoking a pipe, Brother Neyur?' Gobar asked. 'I can manage if I don't get any bread but I can't stand to be without tobacco.'

'And when you go home,' Deena said, 'will you have to cook your own supper? Doesn't your old woman do anything? I wouldn't put up for a day with a little wife like that.'

Neyur's wrinkled face with its tangled moustaches flashed a smiling line of laughter that lent a certain beauty to his ugliness. He said, 'Her young days have gone, son, she can't do any work these days—what can I do?'

'You've spoiled her,' Gobar said, 'otherwise why wouldn't she work? She has a fine time lying on her cot smoking her pipe and fighting with the whole village. You've grown old but she's stayed young right up to now.'

60

Deena said, 'She tries to give the young women a run for their money. All she thinks about is cinnabar, make-up and jasmine for her hair. You never see her without a fancy coloured sari and what's more she can't live without jewels. You're a donkey and go on taking care of her. Otherwise why would you put up with her scolding and slaps all this time?'

Gobar said, 'It makes me mad the way she fusses about dressing up. She won't do any work. But she has to dress up and eat the best.'

'What do you know about it, son?' said Neyur. 'When she came I had enough land under cultivation for seven plows. She would lie around like a queen. The times have changed now but what's happened to her? Her heart is still the same. If she sits for half an hour in front of the hearth her eyes get red and her head starts to pound. I can't stand looking at that. A man gets married for times just like these, otherwise why would he get involved at all in the worries of running a household? When I go home I make some bread, bring the water and she'll eat a couple of bites—if it weren't for that, well, I'd do the way you do and gobble down some scraps and a jug of water. Ever since the daughter died she's been a lot sadder, it was a very great blow to her. What do you and I know about the way a mother feels, son? Before, I used to scold her once in a while but how could I scold her now?'

Deena said, 'Why did you climb up the tree yesterday—are the figs ripe already?'

Neyur said, 'I was breaking off some leaves for the goat—we got her to have milk for our daughter. She's old now but she gives a little milk. My old woman lives just on bread and that goat's milk.'

After he got home Neyur had just taken a pot and the well cord to go and wash when his wife, lying on her cot, said, 'Why do you always come home so late? A man shouldn't sacrifice all his life for work. When everybody gets the same pay what's the use of killing yourself working?'

Neyur's heart melted with tenderness—in his wife's devotion to him, he told himself, there wasn't even a hint of selfishness. How much love there was! Who else cared about his comfort, about whether he lived or died? And that was why he would have given his life for her. He said, 'You must have been a goddess in another life, Budhiya, it's true!'

'All right, stop the flattering. Who's sitting here listening to us now that you should talk so fine?'

His heart bursting with pleasure, he went off to bathe. When he came back she was making thick chapatties and she'd put potatoes to roast in the fire. He mashed them, then they sat down to eat.

Budhiya said, 'You haven't had any happiness from marrying me. I lie around and eat and I worry and upset you. It would be much better if God took me off your hands.'

'If God comes, I'll tell him, "Take me first!" If he didn't I'd be left alone in this empty hut.'

'If you're not here what will it be like for me? Just to think about it makes my sight go dim. I must have done something very good to get you. Who else would put up with me?'

For such just sweet satisfaction Neyur was ready to do anything. Lazy, greedy, selfish Budhiya, just by sweetening her tongue the way a sportsman baits the hook, kept on making Neyur dance.

This was not their first conversation on the subject of who would die first. Many times before this had the question come up and been dropped in just the same way. But for some reason or another Neyur had come to the conclusion that he would be the first to go. For so long as Budhiya might survive him she was to live in comfort and not have to hold out her hand to anyone. It was precisely for this that he worked like a dog trying to scrape a few pice together. The hardest work, the work nobody else would do, Neyur would do it. After working the whole day with spade and hoe, during the sugar cane season he would press cane or guard the fields at night. But the days were slipping by and whatever he earned, that too was slipping away. Life for him without Budhiya would—but he couldn't even imagine that.

But this talk with her terrified Neyur today. Like one drop of dye in water the fear began to spread through his mind.

2

In the village there was no shortage of work for Neyur. He got the same wages he'd always got, but in this time of depression those wages didn't go very far.

Unexpectedly a sadhu came wandering into the village from somewhere and lit his ceremonial fire in the shade of the peepul tree right in front of Neyur's hut. The villagers took it as a stroke of good luck and they all gathered together to do reverence and honour to Babaji. They brought wood, spread out blankets, gave him flour and *dal*. Having nothing at home to give him, Neyur took on the job of making his meals. Intoxicating *charas* weed was brought and the holy man began to smoke.

In just two or three days the sadhu's fame had spread around. What an enlightened soul he was, he could tell the past and future and everything! And he was entirely without attachment to the world—he would not touch money with his hands, he scarcely ate anything. Throughout a whole day he would eat only a couple of pieces of bread. But his face shone like a lamp and how sweetly he spoke! Simple-hearted Neyur became the holy man's greatest devotee. If by some chance Babaji should take pity on him then he would find enlightenment, all his troubles would disappear.

The devotees had all gone home. The night was bitingly cold. Only Neyur was there, rubbing Babaji's feet.

Babaji said, 'Child, the world is illusion—why are you caught in its snares?'

'I'm an ignorant man, Maharaj,' Neyur said, bowing his head. 'What shall I do? There's my wife—how could I leave her?'

'You think *you*'re taking care of her?'

'Who else is there to help her, Babaji?'

'So God is nothing and you're everything?'

It was like a revelation to Neyur. How puffed up you've been, he told himself, how proud! You spend your life labouring and you think you're everything for Budhiya. You think you can meddle in the work of the Lord, who holds the whole world in his keeping. With the full sense of faith springing up in his simple villager's heart he reproached himself. He said, 'I'm an ignorant man, Maharaj.'

He could say no more than this. Tears of remorse fell from his eyes.

The holy man said majestically, 'You are about to learn the wonders of the Lord. If he wanted he could make you a millionaire in a second. In one second he could take away all your worries. I am merely a lowly servant of his, like the humble crow of the Puranas, but in me too there's enough power to make you rich. You're a pure-hearted, true and honest man, and I feel compassion for you. I've observed everybody in this village most carefully. There's no strength or faith in any of them. But in you I've found a devoted heart. Do you possess any silver?'

It seemed to Neyur that he stood before the gate of heaven.

'I must have about a half dozen rupees, Maharaj.'

'Haven't you got any old broken silver jewellery?'

'My wife has a little jewellery.'

'Tomorrow night bring me as much silver as you can find and see the greatness of God. Right in front of you I'll put the silver in a pot and set it in the fire. Come early in the morning and take the pot out of the fire, but be sure to remember that if you spend any of the gold sovereigns you get in drinking or gambling or any wicked deeds you'll become a leper. Go home to bed now, but just one word more: don't talk about this to anyone, not even your wife.'

Neyur went home as happy as if God's hand had touched his head and he could not sleep all night. In the morning he borrowed two or three rupees from each of various people and got fifty rupees together. People trusted him—he'd never done anybody out of a pice, he was a man of his word, a man of good will. It was not hard for him to get the fifty rupees. But how could he take Budhiya's jewellery? He played a trick. 'Your jewellery's become very dirty,' he told her. 'It ought to be cleaned with lemon juice. If it's left in the lemon juice overnight it'll be just like new.' So Budhiya put the ornaments in a pot and left them to soak. When she had gone to sleep that night Neyur put the money in the same pot and went to Babaji. Babaji recited a few spells. He set the pot in the ashes of his fire and after blessing Neyur sent him home.

The whole night Neyur tossed and turned and at the crack of dawn he went to pay a visit to the holy man. But there was no sign of Babaji. Alarmed, Neyur searched with his fingers through the burned-out ashes: the pot had disappeared. He beat his chest and desperately started out to look for the saint. Making his way toward the market he reached the edge of the pond. Ten minutes he waited, twenty, a half hour, but not a sign of the saint.

The devotees began to arrive, asking where Babaji had gone. Not even his blanket, not even his pots were there.

One man said, 'These wandering saints never stay for long—here today, there tomorrow. If they stayed in one place would they be saints? They might make friends with people and get trapped by worldly attachments.'

'He was enlightened,' another said.

'He had no lust for worldly things.'

'Where's Neyur? The saint was very kind to him—he must have told Neyur.'

They began to look for Neyur, but there wasn't a trace of him. Meantime Budhiya came out of the house calling for him. Then what a commotion!—Budhiya weeping and reviling Neyur.

Neyur was running along the boundary dikes between the fields as though he wanted to get clean out of this sinful world.

Somebody said, 'Yesterday Neyur borrowed five rupees from me. He said He'd give them back tonight.'

'He took two from me and promised to bring them back.'

Budhiya wept. 'The good-for-nothing took my jewellery. We'd saved twenty-five ruppes and he took them too.'

People understood that the saint was some kind of fraud and that he'd deceived Neyur. Lord, the cheats there are in the world! Nobody suspected Neyur of anything like that. The poor fellow was honest and he'd been tricked. He was probably hiding somewhere right now because of shame.

3

Three months passed.

In Jhansi district on the banks of the Dhasan there's a quite small village called Kashipur. The river banks are high ridges, and on one of them, for some time now, a sadhu had taken up his abode. A short, dark, well-knit fellow—Neyur, dressed up as a sadhu to deceive people, the same simple ingenuous Neyur who never looked at what belonged to somebody else, who was happy to earn his bread by his own hard labouring. He hadn't for a second ever forgotten his house, his village and Budhiya. After a few more days of this life he intended to go back and then he'd live happily with his little worries and his little hopes, laughing and playing in the village world. When he came home after the day's work bringing a bit of grain or a few pice, then with what tender affection Budhiya would welcome him. It was as though all his toil and fatigue were sweetened in that sweetness of hers. Alas, when would those days come again? He had no idea of how Budhiya was getting along. Who would treat her kindly? Who would cook for her and feed her? He'd left no money in the house, he'd lost even her jewellery. Then his rage rekindled and he wished he could get his hands on that saint. Alas, greed, greed!

Among Neyur's unquestioning devotees there was a beautiful young woman whose husband had abandoned her. Her father, who lived from an army pension, had married her to an educated man, but the fellow was under his mother's thumb and the girl could not get along with her mother-in-law. The girl wanted to live with her husband apart from his mother, but he would not agree to this. In a huff she'd walked out of the house. In the three years since this had happened the father-in-law's house had not once sent for her, nor had the husband even come to see her. The girl wanted to win control over her husband by any means— surely it could not be difficult for holy men to work a change in someone's heart if only they were compassionate!

One day she was alone with the saint describing her misfortune. It seemed to Neyur that he had found the prey he'd been stalking. He said solemnly, 'Daughter, I am not an enlightened man nor a mahatma, nor do I get involved in worldly problems, but when I see your faith and love I feel compassion for you. If God wishes, then your wish will be fulfilled.'

'You can bring it about, I have faith in you.'

'Whatever God wishes will come to pass.'

'Only you can bring the little boat of an unhappy woman like me safe across to the other shore.'

'Trust in the Lord.'

'You alone are my Lord.'

As though moved by religious scruple Neyur said, 'But daughter, to accomplish what you want a big ritual must be per- formed and the ceremony costs hundreds, thousands. I can't say if it will succeed in fulfilling your wish. I'll do what I can.

But everything's in the Lord's keeping. I don't touch money with my hands, but I can't bear to watch your suffering.'

That night she brought her gold jewellery in a basket and set it down at the saint's feet. With trembling hands he opened the basket and looked at the jewellery gleaming in the moonlight. He blinked. All this wealth was his! The girl was standing in front of him with folded hands. 'Accept it,' she said. There was nothing else for him to do, just take the basket and put it on the ground where he slept and send the girl off with a blessing. She would come early in the morning and he would be as far away as his legs could carry him. This was the luck he'd longed for! to go back to his village with bags full of rupees and to set them down before Budhiya. Oh! He couldn't have imagined a greater happiness than this.

But for some reason or other he could not bring himself to do the little he had to. He couldn't pick up the basket to stow it beneath his blanket. It was a trifle but he couldn't see how to do it, he could not even stretch out his hand toward the basket, he had no control over his hands. But if his hands were useless he still had a tongue, there would have been nothing world-shaking in saying, 'Daughter, pick it up and put it under my blanket,' his tongue would not be cut off for that. But it seemed to him now that he had no control even over his tongue. He could get what he wanted done with just a look, but now even his eyes refused to obey him. The master of his spirit, despite all its allies and ministers, was without power and without will. A hundred thousand rupees might be set before him, the naked sword might be in his hand and the cow tied with a strong rope but he could never bring that sword down on her neck. Even if someone were to kill him for it he could never do it. This abandoned woman was like such a cow to him. Finding the opportunity he'd been seeking for three months his soul was shaken. Greed, like some jungle beast eager for its prey, was chained, its claws drooped, its teeth lost their power.

With tears in his eyes he said, 'Daughter, pick up the basket and go. I was only testing you. Your wish will be fulfilled.'

On the far side of the river the moon had set in the bosom of the trees. Neyur got up slowly and after bathing in the Dhasan started on his way. He had come to loathe the cowdung ashes and sandalwood smeared on his forehead for his masquerade. He was astonished that he had ever gone out of his village. Just the fear of a little derision! He began to experience a strange elation, as though he had freed himself from his chains and won a great victory.

4

Neyur reached his village on the eighth day. Children came running, springing and jumping, to welcome him and took the stick out of his hand.

One boy said, 'Auntie's died, uncle.'

It was as though Neyur had been paralysed. The corners of his mouth fell, his eyes were stricken. He couldn't ask anything, he couldn't even speak. He stood for a second spellbound, then he ran furiously toward his hut. The swarm of children ran after him, but their meanness and mischief had left them. The hut lay open. Budhiya's cot was right where it had always been. Her pipe was set where it always was. In one corner were a few clay and brass pots. The children stood outside, not daring to go in, for Budhiya's ghost was there.

There was a great commotion in the village. Uncle Neyur had come back! A crowd collected at the door of the hut, everyone was asking questions. 'Where have you been all these days? She died on the third day after you went away. Night and day she cursed you. Even while she was dying she kept up abusing you. When we came on the third day, she was lying dead. Where have you been all this time?'

Neyur did not answer. He just looked at them with pitiable, desperate eyes, as though he had lost the power of speech. From that day on no one ever knew him to speak or cry or laugh.

A half mile from town there is a surfaced road, and a lot of people travel along it. Very early mornings Neyur goes and sits beneath a tree at the edge of the road. He asks for nothing from anybody. But travellers give him a little something—parched grain or wheat or small change. At evening he comes back to the hut, lights a lamp, makes supper, eats, and lies down on the same cot. The moving force of his life has vanished, he merely exists.

How profound humanity is! The plague came to the village;

Neyur

people abandoned their homes and fled. No one bothered about Neyur now; nobody feared him and nobody loved him. When the whole town ran away, Neyur did not leave his hut. Then Holi came, everyone made merry, but Neyur did not come out of his hut. And even today he can still be seen sitting silent, unmoving, lifeless, beneath the tree at the edge of the road.

NOTE

Original title, '*Neyur*'. First published in 1933. The name Neyur is a peasant name, a dialect derivation from 'neola', mongoose.

In the Urdu version of the story Premchand omitted the last two paragraphs, replacing them simply with this sentence: 'But he does his work exactly the way he used to and takes only a few crusts of bread for wages'.

The Thakur's Well

Jokhu brought the lota to his mouth but the water smelled foul. He said to Gangi, 'What kind of water is this? It stinks so much I can't drink it! My throat's burning and you give me water that's turned bad.'

Every evening Gangi filled the water jugs. The well was a long way off and it was hard for her to make several trips. She'd brought this water yesterday and there'd been no bad smell at all to it then. How could it be there now? She lifted the lota to her nostrils and it certainly stank. Surely some animal must have fallen into the well and died. But she didn't know where else she could get any water.

No one would let her walk up to the Thakur's well. Even while she was far off people would start yelling at her. At the other end of the village the shopkeeper had a well but even there they wouldn't let her draw any water. For people like herself there wasn't any well in the village.

Jokhu, who'd been sick for several days, held back his thirst for a little while. Then he said, 'I'm so thirsty I can't stand it. Bring me the water, I'll hold my nose and drink a little.'

Gangi gave it to him. His sickness would get worse from drinking bad water—that much she knew. But she didn't know that by boiling the water it would be made safe. She said, 'How can you drink it? Who knows what kind of beast has died in it? I'll go and get you some water from the well.'

Surprised, Jokhu stared at her. 'Where can you get more water?'

'The Thakur and the shopkeeper both have wells. Won't they let me fill just one lota?'

'You'll come back with your arms and legs broken, that's all. You'd better just sit down and keep quiet. The Brahman will give a curse, the Thakur'll beat you with a stick and that moneylending shopkeeper takes five for every one he gives. Who cares what people like us go through? Whatever they say about giving some help, we can just die and nobody will even come to this door to have a look. Do you think people like that are going to let you draw water from their well?'

The harsh truth was in these words and Gangi could not deny it. But she wouldn't let him drink that stinking water.

By nine o'clock at night the dead-tired field hands were fast asleep but a half dozen or so idlers were gathered at the Thakur's door. These were not the times—nor were there any occasions—for valour in the field; valour in the courtroom was the topic of the day. How cleverly the Thakur had bribed the local police chief in a certain case and come off scot-free! With what skill he'd managed to get his hands on a copy of the dossier in an important lawsuit. The clerks and magistrates had all said it was impossible to get a copy. One had demanded fifty for it, another a hundred, but for no money at all a copy had come flying. You had to know the right way to operate in these matters.

At this moment Gangi reached the Thakur's property to get water from his well.

The dim glow of a small oil lamp lit up the well. Gangi sat hidden behind the wall and began to wait for the right moment. Everybody in the village drank the water from this well. It was closed to nobody, only those unlucky ones like herself could not fill their buckets here.

Gangi's resentful heart cried out against the restraints and bars of the custom. Why was she so low and those others so high? Because they wore a thread around their necks? There wasn't one of them in the village who wasn't rotten. They stole, they cheated, they lied in court. That very day the Thakur had stolen a sheep from the poor shepherd, then killed and eaten it. They gambled in the priest's house all twelve months of the year. The shopkeeper mixed oil with the ghee before he sold it. They'd get you to do their work but they wouldn't pay wages for it to save their lives. Just how were they so high and mighty? It was only a matter of words. No, Gangi, thought, *we* don't go around shouting that we're better. Whenever she came into the village they looked at her with eyes full of lust, they were on fire with lust, every one of them, but they bragged that they were better than people like her.

71

She heard people coming to the well and her heart began to pound. If anybody saw her there'd be the devil to pay and she'd get an awful kicking out of it. She grabbed her bucket and rope and crept away to hide in the dark shadows of a tree. When had these people ever had pity on anybody? They beat poor Mahngu so hard that he spat blood for months, and the only reason was that he refused to work in the forced labour gang. Was this what made such people consider themselves better than everybody else?

Two women had come to draw water and they were talking. One said:

'There they were eating and they order *us* to get more water. There's no money for a jug.'

'The men folk get jealous if they think they see us sitting around taking it easy.'

'That's right, and you'll never see them pick up the pitcher and fetch it themselves. They just order us to get it as though we were slaves.'

'If you're not a slave what are you? You work for food and clothes and even to get nothing more than five or six rupees you have to snatch it on the sly. What's that if it isn't being a slave?'

'Don't shame me, sister! All I do is long for just a second's rest. If I did this much work for somebody else's family I'd have an easier time, and they might even be grateful. But here you could drop dead from overwork and they'd all just frown.'

When the two of them had filled their buckets and gone away Gangi came out from the shadow of the tree and drew close to the well platform. The idlers had left, the Thakur had shut his door and gone inside to the courtyard to sleep. Gangi took a moment to sigh with relief. On every side the field was clear. Probably even the prince who set out to steal nectar from the gods did not move more warily. Gangi tiptoed up on to the well platform. Never before had she felt such a sense of triumph.

She looped the rope around the bucket. Like some soldier stealing into the enemy's fortress at night she peered cautiously on every side. If she were caught now there was not the slightest hope of mercy or leniency. Finally, with a prayer to the gods, she mustered her courage and cast the bucket into the well.

Slowly, slowly it sank in the water. There was not the slightest sound. Gangi yanked it back up with all her might to the rim of the well. No strong-armed athlete could have dragged it up more swiftly.

She had just stooped to catch it and set it on the wall when suddenly the Thakur's door opened. The jaws of a tiger could not have terrified her more.

The rope escaped from her hand. With a crash the bucket fell into the water, the rope after it, and for a few seconds there were sounds of splashing.

Yelling 'Who's there? Who's there?' the Thakur came toward the well and Gangi jumped from the platform and ran away as fast as she could.

When she reached home Jokhu, with the lota at his mouth, was drinking that dirty, stinking water.

NOTE

Original title: '*Thākur ka Kuān*', 'The Thakur's Well', 'Thakur' is a title of Rajputs, members of the second highest caste and thus 'twice-born', entitled to wear the sacred thread Gangi refers to contemptuously. Almost precisely like the English title 'lord', 'Thakur' is also used to refer to the supreme deity. Whether Premchand meant it ironically is not certain, but the idea is reinforced by the irony of the protagonist's name, Gangi, with its inevitable suggestion of Ganga, the Ganges, whose water is the holiest in the world.

This is a late story (1932) and a fine example of Premchand's later simplicity and his rejection of the editorial comment that sometimes mars earlier stories. Despite the Indian constitution's outlawing of the sort of caste privilege that provoked Premchand's indignation, the story is by no means without contemporary significance. In rural areas such exclusion of the so-called scheduled communities is still encountered.

A Desperate Case

Some men are angry with their wives for giving birth to one daughter after another but never a son. They know it's not the wives' fault, or if it is, then no more than their own, but just the same whenever you see them they're vexed with their wives, call them unlucky and continue to torment them. Nirupma was one of these unlucky women and Ghamandi Lal Tripathi one of those cruel husbands. Nirupma had had three daughters in a row and everyone in the household gave her unkind looks. Her mother-in-law's and father-in-law's displeasure did not concern her particularly—they were old-fashioned people who considered daughters an unpleasant responsibility, the result of sins in earlier incarnations. But it was her husband's disaffection that grieved her, especially since even the fact that he was an educated man did not restrain him from speaking nastily to her. Far from loving her, he never spoke to her without getting angry; for days at a time he would not even come into the house and when he did he was so on edge that she trembled with fear lest there be a row. Although there was no lack of money in the family Nirupma never dared express a wish for even the most trivial object. She thought, 'I really am ill-omened—otherwise would God have created only girls in my womb?' She longed for a gentle smile from her husband, a tender word, to the point where she hesitated to show affection to her daughters lest people say, 'She's certainly making a lot of fuss over trifles!' When it was time for her husband to come home she would on one pretext or another keep the girls out of his sight. The greatest calamity was that Tripathi had threatened, if she had another girl next time, to leave the house forever rather than tolerate such hell for another second. Nirupma worried constantly about this too.

She fasted on Tuesdays, on Sundays, on the eleventh of the month of Jait and at countless other times. She was always performing rituals, but no ritual had fulfilled her wish. Continually putting up with disdain, insults, scolding and contempt, she had become disgusted with the world. It was in-

evitable that she should be disheartened in a house where, longing
for a tender word, a friendly glance, a loving embrace, no one
so much as bothered with her.

One day, feeling absolutely desperate, she wrote a letter to
her elder brother's wife; every word of it cost her an intolerable
pain. Her sister-in-law replied:

> Your brother is coming to fetch you right away. Recently a
> genuine saint has come to the village and his blessing has never
> been known to fail. Several childless women have had sons after
> his blessing. We have every hope that with you as well it will
> have the desired effect.

Nirupma showed this letter to her husband. Sadly he said,
'Saints have nothing to do with procreation and conception, it's
God's business.'

'Yes, but saints can attain to special powers.'

'Maybe so, but visiting them won't do any good.'

'Still, I'll go and visit this one.'

'Go if you want to.'

'If barren women have had sons, am I any less worthy than
they?'

'Didn't I tell you to go? When you do you'll find out. But it
seems to me that it's not in our fate to see a son's face.'

2

A few days later Nirupma went with her brother to her father's
house. She took the three girls with her. Sukeshi, her sister-in-law,
embraced her affectionately and said, 'The people of your house
are very cruel—to curse fate for having three such darlings! They
must be heavy for you, give them to me.'

When, after dinner, with Sukeshi and the younger brother's
wife, they were going to bed Nirupma asked, 'Where does this
saint live?'

'Why such haste?' Sukeshi said. 'I'll tell you in good time.'

'It's close by, isn't it?'

'Very close. When you want, I'll send for him.'

'He's very fond of you people, is he?'

'He's had dinner here twice. He lives right here.'

'Then why suffer when the doctor's already in the house?—I want to see him right away.'

'What will you give me?'

'What is there I could give you?' Nirupma said.

'Give me your youngest girl.'

'Go on, you're making fun of me.'

'All right, but you'll have to let him hug you just once.'

'Sister, if you laugh at me I'll go away!'

'This saint's very fond of pretty women.'

'Then he can go to the devil,' Nirupma said. 'He must be a scoundrel.'

'But that's the payment he demands for his blessing. He doesn't accept any other award.'

'The way you talk anybody'd think you were working for him.'

'Well, he arranges everything through me. I take the offerings, I also give the blessings, I also make the food for him,' Sukeshi said.

'So you made all this up, admit it, just to get me here!'

'No, not at all, I'm going to tell you of a plan that will allow you to live in peace in your own home.'

Then the two of them began to whisper. When Sukeshi had finished talking, Nirupma said, 'And what if it should be a girl again, after all?'

'So what? You'll have spent a little while in peace and quiet anyway. No one will be able to take those days away from you. If you have a son, then all will be fine; if it's a daughter then some new plan will have to be worked out. With the idiots you've got in your house what else can we do except resort to tricks like this?'

'I feel a little nervous about it.'

'In a couple of days write Tripathi and tell him you've seen the saint and that he's told you he'll grant your wish. God willing, from that day on you'll be treated with a lot more respect. Tripathi'll come on the run ready to sacrifice his life for you. For at least a year you'll have a pleasant time of it. After that, we'll see.'

'But won't it be a sin to lie to my husband?'

'To pull the wool over the eyes of a selfish fellow like him is a virtue!'

3

After three or four months Nirupma went home. Ghamandi Lal came to get her. Sukeshi was very detailed in her description of the saint. She said, 'It's never been known that a holy man gave a blessing like that without producing results. But of course, some people are so unlucky there's nothing to be done for them.'

Ghamandi Lal openly expressed his contempt for blessings and promises; he seemed ashamed to give credence to such things in this day and age, but there was no doubt that he was impressed.

Nirupma was welcomed back. When she became pregnant everyone's hearts thrilled with new hopes. The mother-in-law, who before had never done anything but revile her, treated her like a guest. 'Daughter, let it be, I'll make the supper, you'll get a head-ache.' Whenever Nirupma began to take out the water jug to fill it or to move a cot, then the mother-in-law would run to her. 'Daughter, leave it, I'm here, you mustn't lift anything heavy.' If she had been going to have a girl none of this would have had any effect on the child, but boys, even while they're still in the womb, begin to sit up and be proud. Now Nirupma was made to eat quantities of milk pudding so the boy would be robust and fair. Ghamandi Lal made a habit of getting clothes and jewellery for her, every month he would bring something new. Even when she'd been a new bride Nirupma had not led so pleasant an existence.

The months began to slip by. According to signs and omens she recognized Nirupma began to be convinced that it would be a girl this time too. But she kept this heretical opinion to herself. She would think, 'It's like a monsoon sunshine—how can you trust it? Enjoy it while you can, the rainclouds are going to cover it all.' She was jumpy about every little thing. She had never been particularly temperamental, but no one in the house would make the slightest noise lest she be upset and thus produce an ill effect upon the boy. Sometimes just to torment the family Nirupma would carry out a religious fast, and she found pleasure in tormenting them. She would think, 'The more I torment you selfish ones the better. You honour me, don't you, only because I'm going to give birth to a child who'll carry on your name. I'm nothing, the child alone is everything; I have no importance, everything hinges on your child. And this is my husband: at first how much he loved me, he wasn't worldly and greedy then. Now his love is a little trick to satisfy his selfishness. I'm an animal to be stuffed with fodder and water for the sake of my milk. If that's the way it is, fine, but now I can control you all. I'll make you give me as many jewels as I can, you won't be able to take them back.'

And so the nine months came to an end. Nirupma's two sisters-in-law were sent for from her father's house. Golden ornaments had already been made for the child; a fine milch-cow was purchased for his milk and Ghamandi Lal brought a little pram to take him on walks. On the day the labour pains started the astrologer was summoned to the door to cast the horoscope. A huntsman had been called to fire off the shotgun and women were gathered together to strike up a hymn. Everyone wanted details of what was happening inside the house. The English woman doctor had been sent for. The musicians sat waiting for the word; the village singer with his fiddle was ready to sound the strains of 'Let the mother be proud with Lord Krishna.' All the preparations, all the hopes, all the jubilation was hanging on one word only. With every moment of delay the impatience grew. To hide his excitement Ghamandi Lal was reading a newspaper, just as though it were all one whether it was a boy or a girl. But his old father was not so controlled. He could not restrain his exuberance, he talked to everybody and laughed and kept rattling a bag full of coins.

The huntsman said, 'I'll take a turban and scarf from the Master.'

Delighted, the old man said, 'Go on, how many turbans will you take? I'll give you such an expensive one every hair on your head will fall out.'

The singer said, 'And I'll accept something to live on from the master.'

'And how much will you eat? We'll feed you till your belly bursts.'

Suddenly a housemaid came out looking flustered. Before she

had managed to say anything the huntsman fired off the shotgun and immediately afterwards the pipes struck up a tune and the singer, hitching up his dhoti, sprang up to dance.

The maid shouted, 'Are you all drunk on *bhang,* you people?'

'What's happened?' the huntsman said.

'What's happened? It's a girl again, that's what's happened.'

'A girl?' the old man said, and with that he threw up his arms and sat down as though hit by a thunderbolt. Ghamandi Lal came out of his room and said, 'Go and ask the lady doctor—you just came running out here without really seeing anything.'

'Babuji,' the maid said, 'I saw with my own eyes.'

'And it's really a girl?'

'Such is our fate,' his father said. 'Go, everybody, get along. If it's written in your fate that you're not going to have something, then how can you ever get it? Go, run! Hundreds of rupees thrown away, all our preparations ruined!'

Ghamandi Lal said, 'We'll have to talk to this saint. I'll go today to make inquiries about the bastard.'

'He's a fraud, a fraud!' his father said.

'I'll expose all his cheating', Ghamandi Lal went on. 'If I don't crack his skull then I'll eat my words. He's some kind of swindler. Because of him I've thrown away hundreds of rupees. The pram, the cow, the swing, the golden ornaments—whose head can I throw them at? Think how many he must have cheated like this! If the score is paid off for once, then it will be some satisfaction.'

'Son, it's not his fault, it's the fault of fate.'

'Why did he claim this wouldn't happen? How much money women must have squandered on the cheat! He's got to be made to cough it all up, otherwise I'll report him to the police. The law has punishments for swindling too. From the very first I was afraid it might be a fraud. But my brother-in-law's wife fooled me—if she hadn't I'd never have been caught in such a swindler's trap. He's just a pig.'

'Be patient,' his father said. 'What God has wished he has wrought. Both girls and boys are gifts of God. And where there's three you can be sure there'll be another.'

Father and son went on talking. The singer, the huntsman and the others picked up their staffs and set out on their way. The house seemed to have gone into mourning. The lady doctor had also taken leave, and apart from the mother and the midwife there was no one in the lying-in room. The old mother was so disconsolate that she'd taken to her bed.

When the child's twelfth-day ceremony had been performed Ghamandi Lal went to his wife for the first time and said angrily, 'So it's a girl again!'

'What could I do,' Nirupma said, 'it's not in my control.'

'That wretched swindler really cheated us.'

'What can I say now? If he were a swindler, why would all those women keep going to the saint day and night? It's not in my fate. If he'd taken anything from anybody then I'd say he was a fraud, but I take an oath that I never gave a pice to him.'

'Whether he took anything or not I've spent a fortune. We've learned that it's our destiny not have a son. If the family line is coming to an end, then what does it matter if it happens now or in ten years? I'll go away somewhere, there's no joy left in this household.'

For a long time he stayed on bemoaning his fate; but Nirupma did not even lift her head.

The calamity had fallen on her once again, and again the same reproaches, the same insults and snubs, and no one cared whether she ate or not, whether she was sick, whether she was happy. Ghamandi Lal did not go away but the threat was almost always in Nirupma's mind. In this way several months passed and then once again Nirupma wrote Sukeshi to tell her she had put her in a more wretched situation than before, and now nobody even cared whether she lived or died. If this state of affairs went on, then whether her husband renounced the world and became an ascetic or not, she herself would certainly leave the world in a different way.

When she read this letter Sukeshi understood how things were. This time she did not invite Nirupma, knowing that they would not let her come, so she herself went, taking her husband along. She was a very lively, clever and fun-loving woman. As soon as she arrived she saw the baby girl in Nirupma's lap and said, '*Arrey!*, what's that?'

'It's fate—what else?' said Nirupma's mother-in-law.

'What do you mean fate? You must have made some mistake

in following the saint's instructions. It's not possible that whatever he's promised should fail to come about. Now tell me, did you fast on Tuesdays?'

'Without fail, I didn't skip one fast,' Nirupma said.

'And did you feed five Brahmans on Tuesdays also?'

'But he didn't tell me to do that.'

'Don't you tell me, I remember perfectly, he said it right in front of me and with a lot of emphasis too. You must have thought, "What's the point of feeding the Brahmans?" You didn't understand that unless you fulfilled every part of the ritual it wouldn't come out the way he said.'

'She never said anything about it,' the mother-in-law said. 'And why five? We would have fed ten Brahmans—we're not lacking in religion, after all.'

'Of course not, she just forgot, that's obvious. There's no possibility of getting a son this way. Great devotedness and piety are necessary and you were confused by just one Tuesday fast?'

'She's unlucky, what else?' said the mother-in-law.

Ghamandi Lal said, 'How could anybody not remember what he made such a fuss about saying? She's just trying to upset us all.'

'And I ask you,' his mother said, 'how the saint's words could fail to be fulfilled? For seven years I've lit the lamp and made offerings to the Goddess of the tulsi plant to get a grandson.'

'And she thought it was going to be easy as eating rice,' Ghamandi Lal said.

'Well,' Sukeshi said, 'what's happened has happened. Tomorrow's Tuesday, fast again and give a dinner to seven Brahmans. We'll see whether or not the saint's promise will be fulfilled.'

'It's useless,' Ghamandi Lal said, 'nothing will come of doing it.'

'Babuji,' Sukeshi said, 'you're educated, but with your learning how much your heart has shrunk! How old are you right now? How many sons would you like to have? If you don't have so many you're fed up with them I'll eat my words.'

The mother-in-law said, 'Daughter, how can anyone have that many sons?'

81

'If God wills,' Sukeshi said, 'then you'll get your wish. I got mine.'

'Are you listening, my dear?' Ghamandi Lal said. 'Don't make any mistakes this time. Make sure you understand everything sister-in-law tells you.'

'You can be sure,' Sukeshi said, 'I'll remind you. How to prepare the feast, how to go about everything, how to perform the ablutions, I'll write it all down for you and mother, and no more than eighteen months from today I'll claim a fat reward from you.'

Sukeshi stayed a week and after giving careful instructions to Nirupma she went back home.

5

Nirupma's star shone again; Ghamandi Lal was consoled with the thought that the future would redeem the past. Again Nirupma went from slave to queen, the mother-in-law treated her with the highest consideration, and everybody paid her the greatest attention.

The days passed. Nirupma would sometimes say, 'Mother, last night I dreamed that an old woman came to me and called out and gave me a coconut. She said, "This is what I've given you." ' And sometimes she would say, 'Mother, I don't know why but a great joy has sprung up in my heart, I long to hear beautiful singing, to bathe in the river. It's almost like being intoxicated.' When the mother-in-law heard these things she would smile and say, 'Daughter, these are good omens.'

Nirupma had bhang brought to her on the sly and ate it, because red and drunk-looking eyes meant a son, and then looking at Ghamandi Lal with her drowsy eyes she would say, 'Are my eyes red?'

'It seems as though you were actually drunk,' he would observe contentedly. 'This is a good omen.'

Nirupma had never been especially fond of perfume but now she was ready to give her life for a fragrant garland.

Before going to bed Ghamandi Lal now made a habit of reading heroic stories to her out of the Mahbharata; sometimes he would describe the glorious deeds of Guru Govind Singh. Nirupma was very fond of the story of Abhimanyu. Ghamandi Lal wanted to ensure that his unborn son would be a hero.

One day Nirupma said to him, 'What name will you give him?'

'I'm sure you've already picked one out. I haven't thought about it at all. It has to be a name associated with valour and glory. You think of a name.'

The two of them began to discuss names. They went through every name from Harischandra to Zoravar Lal but they couldn't pick one out for this extraordinary boy. Finally Ghamandi Lal said, 'What do you think of Teg Bahadur?'

'That's fine, I like it.'

'It's a splendid name. You've heard about the great deeds of Teg Bahadur. The name has a tremendous influence on the person.'

'The name is really everything,' Nirupma said. 'Whether it's Damri, Chhakauri, Ghurhu, or Katvaru, whenever you look at somebody's name you find, "As the name, so the man." Our child's name will be Teg Bahadur—the warrior's sword.'

6

The time for the delivery came. Nirupma knew what was about to happen. But outside everything was ready for the celebration. This time nobody had the slightest doubt. Everything had been made ready for the singing and dancing. A canopy had been put up and a throng of friends sat under it chatting. The sweets-maker took puris and sweets out of his boiling pan. Several sacks had been filled with grain so that as soon as the good tidings had been received it could be distributed among the beggars. To avoid all delay the sacks had already been opened.

But with every second Nirupma's heart sank. What would happen now? She had got through three years by some sort of deceit, and they'd been happy years, but now disaster was hovering over her head. Alas, she thought what a victim she was. To be punished this way without guilt. If it was God's wish that no sons should ever be born from her womb, what fault was it of hers? But who listened? She was really an unlucky woman, she ought to be abandoned, she was ill-omened, and that was why she was a victim. What was going to happen? In a second all the joy and jubilation would collapse in lamentation. They would begin to revile her, curse her inside and out. She was not afraid of her mother- and father-in-law, but her husband might once again cease to look at her, in his disappointment he might renounce his house and home. There was nothing but evil fortune on every side. 'Why should I live to see the misery of my family?' she said to herself. 'The trick is done with, there's no hope to be had from it any more. Ther used to be such longings in my heart; to bring up my darling girls, to get them married and see their children would have been happiness. But it's all finished now. Lord, be their father, look after them, but I'm going now.'

The woman doctor said, 'Well, it's a girl again.'

Inside and outside there were sounds of lamentation. Ghamandi Lal said, 'A curse on such a life, I'm ready for death!'

His father said, 'She's ill-omened, damned ill-omened.'

The beggars said, 'Weep your destiny, we're going to look for some other door!'

The noise had not died down when the doctor said, 'There's no hope for the mother, we can't save her—her heart has stopped.'

NOTE

Original title, '*Nairāshya*', 'Despair' or 'Disappointment'. First published 1924.

2 The Town

A Day in the Life of a Debt-Collector

Seth Chetaram bathed, poured water in sacrifice to Shiva, chewed two peppercorns, drank two pots of water and taking his stick went out to dun the people who owned him money.

Sethji was some fifty years old. The hair had fallen from his head and his skull was as clean as a sandy field. His eyes were small but absolutely round. Right under his head was his belly and beneath his belly his legs looking like two pegs stuck in a barrel. This barrel, by the way, wasn't empty. It was chock full of energy and vitality. The way it jiggled and danced when Sethji was putting the pressure on some defaulting debtor would have shamed an acrobat. He would glare so fiercely and roar so loudly that a regular mob would gather to watch him. But you couldn't call him a miser because, when he was in his shop, he threw down a pice to every beggar. Of course, at those times his frown was so severe and his eyes so terrible and his nose so wrinkled that the beggar would never go by his shop again.

He was absolutely dedicated to the theory that persistent dunning was the way to prosper. From right after breakfast until evening he was constantly occupied in dunning. In the course of his visits he would find a lunch set aside in one house, in another he would partake—at his debtor's expense—of milk, puris, sweets and other dishes. A free meal is nothing to be sneezed at. Save just one anna per meal and then for this one item in his thirty years of money-lending he would have saved some 800 rupees. Then when he came back a second time he would get milk, curds, oil, vegetables, and cowdung cakes or other fuel. Generally he didn't have to get his own dinner in the evening either. So he never failed to go out on his dunning expeditions. The heavens could burst asunder, fire rain down, a tornado strike, but Sethji, as though obeying an immutable law of nature, was sure to go out to collect his debts.

This morning his wife asked, 'Lunch?' 'No!' Sethji thundered. 'Supper?' 'We'll see when I get back.'

There was a farmer who owed Sethji five rupees. For six months the rogue had paid neither principal nor interest, he hadn't even come around with some little offering. His house was at least three miles away and therefore Sethji had put off going. He decided that he would go today and not leave without getting his money from the rascal no matter how much he might squirm and moan. But it was most unpleasant to make such a long journey on foot. People might say, 'A big name but a poor show! He wants to be called a Seth but he hops it on foot.' So he ambled along at a leisurely gait looking here and there and chatting with people he met so it would be understood that he was just out for a stroll.

Suddenly he met an ekka coming his way. The ekka driver, who was a Muslim, asked, 'Where do you have to go, Lala?'

'I don't have to go anywhere,' Sethji said. 'It's just two steps more. However, I suppose I might as well have a seat.'

The ekka driver gave Sethji a piercing look, and Sethji stared back with his fierce red eyes. Both of them understood that the other was going to prove a slippery proposition.

The ekka started to roll. Sethji made the first move. 'Where is your house, my good man?'

'Excellency, my house is wherever I lie down. When I had a house—well, then I had it. But now I'm houseless, homeless and, worst of all, wingless. Fate has clipped my wings, cut off my tail and abandoned me. My grandfather was a revenue collector for the Navab, excellency, the master of seven districts. Anybody he wanted shot was shot and if he wanted somebody hanged, he had him hanged. Even before the sun came up thousands and thousands of purses appeared before him. The Navab treated him like a brother. That was how it was then but now we're forced to work for people like you. Times change.'

Sethji realized that he was up against a tough opponent, a regular champion. It wasn't going to be easy to get the better of him, but since the challenge had been offered he'd have to take it up. He said, 'But surely you belong to the Imperial household? Your very appearance bears witness to that. Times change, brother, not every day turns out the same. At home we say that Lakshmi is fickle, she doesn't always act the same: today she comes to my house, tomorrow to yours. Your father must have left you a regular pile of rupees?'

'*Arrey,* Sethji, there was no counting that wealth. I don't know how many cellars it filled. The gold and silver were piled up by the boxful and there were baskets jammed full of jewels. Every single gem was worth half a million. The glitter was so great it put lamps to shame. But fate was still around to be reckoned with. One day Grand-daddy passed away and then we lost our connection with the Navab. The whole treasure was looted. People loaded trucks with the jewels and carted them off. Even then, enough was left in the house for Daddy to live out his days in luxury—the luxury a fool would live in. He used to go out in a palanquin carried by sixteen attendants. There were mace-bearers scurrying both in front and behind. And still he left enough for me to live on. If I'd lived sensibly I'd be well off today. But a rich man's son has got to live like a rich man. I used to get out of bed clutching a bottle of booze. All night long there'd be wild parties with whores dancing. How'd I know I'd have to suffer for it one day?'

Sethji said, 'Brother, thank Almighty God that you can look after your family honestly. Just think of how many of our brothers, on the other hand, tread the paths of wickedness day and night—nevertheless they stay as poor as churchmice. You've got to keep to religion, without religion you just live out your days—and what's the difference if you spend them eating fine things or chewing a dry crust? Religion's the big thing. As soon as I saw your face I knew you were a man of principle and integrity. When people are dishonest it's written all over their faces.'

'Sethji, what you say is true. You've got to keep up religion, it's everything. When I get four pice from you people I use it in feeding my children. Huzoor, just look at other ekka drivers—why, everyone of them is given up to bad habits, every one of them is. But I've taken the pledge. Why should you do something that just brings on misfortune? I have a big family, huzoor, my mother, my children, several dependent widows, and all my earnings come from this ekka. Still, somehow or other the good Lord looks after us.'

'He's the author of all things, Khan Sahib. May there always be abundance in your earnings.'

'That depends on the generosity of people like you.'

'It depends on the generosity of God. And you've turned out fine. I've had a lot of trouble from ekka drivers but now it seems that everywhere there are good and bad alike. I've never before met a man as honest and decent as you. What a fine nature you've got, I congratulate you!'

When the ekka man heard this fulsome praise he understood that the gentleman was a champion talker. He wouldn't have praised him, he thought, unless he intended to cheat him. So the ekka man decided he'd have to use some other angle to get what he wanted. It was going to be hard to get anything on the basis of generosity, so maybe he'd give if he was scared. The ekka driver said, 'But don't assume, Lalaji, that I'm as nice and honest as I look. I'm honest with the honest but with the bad ones I'm a regular son of a bitch. So just tell me, if you want me to shine your shoes I will. But when it comes to the fee I don't do any favours for anybody. If I did, how would I eat?'

Sethji had been convinced that once he did battle with the ekka man he'd finish his journey without so much as a pice in payment. But after this speech his ears pricked up. 'Brother,' he said, 'I don't do anybody any favours either when it's a matter of money. But there are times when it's a matter of friendship and then one's more or less obliged to give in. You too will have to make sacrifices from time to time. There should be no sharp dealings and harsh treatment from friends.'

The ekka man observed dourly, 'I'm not kind to anybody. No teacher taught *me* lessons in kindness. I'm about as kind as a rat. Who'd dare hold back a penny from me? I don't let even my wife get away with a penny, so how should I act with others? Other ekka drivers flatter their moneylenders, they hang around their doors. But I kick the moneylenders out. Everybody wails when they hear my name. When I get my hands on some money, I gobble it up plain and simple. Just see, friend, what you can get out of me, you can cart off anything I've got in my house—if you can.'

Sethji felt he was coming down with fever. He thought, 'This devil won't let me off without getting his money. If I'd known this calamity was in the offing I wouldn't have got into his ekka for anything. Who ever wore his feet out from such a little walk?

If I had to fork over money like this every day business would be ruined.'

Sethji was a pious soul. He had sacrificed to Shiva from the time he'd reached the age of reason and never once neglected the ceremony. Surely Shiva the Benevolent Lord would not fail to come to his aid on this occasion. Concentrating on the Lord, he said, 'Khan Sahib, extort from somebody else, but you'll have to cope with the police too, they don't show favouritism to anybody.'

The ekka driver burst out laughing. 'On the contrary,' he said, '*they* pay *me*. Whenever I find a victim I invite him in at once for a low rate and set out for the police station. I get my fare and I get a reward too. Who dares protest? I don't even have a license but I drive my ekka merrily right through the market. No bastard can touch me. I do best where there's the biggest crowd. I pick up the finest people and take them to the police station. Who comes out on top at the police station? There are twenty excuses to hold people. If it's a man they say it's suspected that he went chasing after a certain woman or if it's a woman they say that she's run away in a huff from her father-in-law's house. Then who can say anything? The police inspector may want to get out of it but even he can't leave. Don't think I'm honest. I'm a son of a bitch. When passengers don't agree on the fare I take them to the police station and get two for one. If they even make a squeak, I roll up my sleeves and get ready to take care of them —then there's nobody who can stand up to me.'

Sethji was aghast. True, he held his staff in his hand but he felt too weak to use it. He'd really got himself into a mess—there was no telling what evil omens had marked his leaving the house. If he fell foul of this wretch he might be laid up for a week or more. From now on he'd have to use his wits and get down and away as well as he could. Humble as a cat he said, 'Very well, Khan Sahib, stop now, we've reached my village. Tell me, how much do I owe you?'

The ekka man whipped the horse all the more and said roughly, 'Consider how much I've earned, brother. If you hadn't got on I could have taken three passengers. I would have been paid four annas from each one of them, which makes twelve. I'll just ask you for eight.'

Sethji was thunderstruck. In his whole life he'd never paid so

much for a ride. Under no circumstances could he pay such
a fare for a distance like this. In every man's life there are occasions
when he takes no heed of the consequences; for Sethji this was
such an occasion. If it had been a matter of one or two annas
then (though they would have been like drops of his own blood)
he would have given them. But for eight annas—why, it was
half a rupee—he was ready not only for an argument but even a
scuffle. Fully resolved, he sat firmly in his place.

At this moment they reached a hut at the edge of the road. The
ekka stopped, Sethji stepped down, took a two-anna coin from
the knot in his dhoti and reached to give it to the ekka driver, who
scowled back at him, accepting the fact that he'd lost this round.
The savour of the struggle had gone sour, it set his teeth on
edge. Souring it for Sethji as well was the only consolation. Gently
he said, 'Take it as a gift from me to buy your kids some candy.
Allah keep you in safety.'

Sethji took out another anna and said, 'Enough, now wag your
tongue all you like, I won't give a pice more.'

'No, master, as you yourself would say, how are we poor people
going to feed our children? We people are human too, huzoor.'

In the meantime a woman had come from inside the hut. She
wore a pink sari and was chewing on *pan*. She said, 'You took a
long time this morning.' Then she looked at Sethji. 'Fine, today
you got a high-class passenger, so I suppose you're in a mood for
some mischief. You must have hooked on to a coin—hand it over
this minute.'

With this she came up to Sethji and said, 'Sit down on our
charpoy and rest, Lala. It's great luck that we've got a glimpse
of you so early in the morning.'

A langorous fragrance came from her clothes. Sethji was all
attention and he leered at her. The woman was graceful, saucy,
mettlesome and tempting. The image of his wife rose before his
eyes: lumpish, flabby, clumsy, her clothes musty. Sethji was not
in the least of an amorous disposition but this time his eyes were
overwhelmed. Trying not to stare at her he took a seat on the
charpoy. He was still a mile off from his destination but he didn't
so much as think of that.

The woman picked up a small fan and began to wave it over
Sethji. With every motion of her hand a whiff of fragrance hit

him and intoxicated him. He'd never experienced such bliss. He was used to looking at everything with disgust, but now his very body was drunk. He tried to take the fan out of her hand.

'It's too much trouble for you, let me do the fanning.'

'Nonsense, Lalaji, you're in our home. Won't you let me take even this little trouble over you? What else would be fitting for us to do? Do you have far to go? It's late now—where are you headed for?'

Sethji turned his old sinner's eyes away and restrained his wicked thoughts. He said, 'There's a village I have to go to, not far from here. I'll be coming back right past here this evening.'

Delighted she said, 'So you'll be here again today! And where would you be going in the evening? For once you ought to have a little fun away from your house. Who knows when we'll meet again!'

The ekka man came in and said in Sethji's ear, 'Get your money out and I'll buy some snacks.'

Silently Sethji took out an eight anna coin and gave it to him.

Then the driver asked, 'Shall I fetch some sweets for you? We can find some sweets here worthy of you, they'll sweeten your mouth.'

Sethji said, 'No need to get me anything. Now this four-anna piece is for getting something nice for the children.'

Taking out the four-anna coin, Sethji threw it down with as much bold assurance as if he attached no value to it, but he wanted to see the expression on the woman's face, yet he was afraid lest she think that he was giving the coin as though he were paying somebody.

The ekka driver picked up the coin and was already leaving when his wife said, 'Give that four-anna bit back to Sethji! Aren't you ashamed of snatching it up like that? Take this rupee from me and go get eight annas worth of sweets.'

She took out a rupee and flung it down. Sethji was embarrassed —that a poor wife of an ekka driver who wasn't worth a brass farthing should show so much hospitality that she would dig out a whole rupee, well, how could he stand for that? 'No, no,' he said, 'I won't permit it. Take back your rupee.' His delighted eyes gobbled her up. 'I'll give a rupee, take this and get eight annas worth.'

The ekka man went off then to see to the sweets and snacks, and his wife said to Sethji, 'It's going to take him some time—while he's gone have some *pan*.'

Sethji looked around him, for he could not take *pan* made by these people. 'But there's no *pan* shop around here,' he said.

'What,' she said, giving him a teasing glance, 'won't the *pan* I make be as good as what you get from a shop?'

Embarrassed, Sethji said, 'No, no, I didn't mean that. But aren't you Muslim?'

Playfully insistent she said, 'God's oath, for saying that I'll feed you *pan* and then leave you.'

Then she took a betel leaf from a *pan* box and walked towards Sethji. For a moment he hemmed and hawed, then stretched out with both hands trying to push her away and shut his lips tight, but when she would in no wise accept his refusal Sethji made a mad dash to escape. He left his staff on the charpoy. After he'd run about twenty steps he stopped, panting, and said, 'Look, you shouldn't go against somebody's religion like that. If we people take food you've touched we're defiled.'

Then she began to chase him. He ran again. He hadn't had to run like this for fifty years. His dhoti came undone and started to fall off but there was no time to tie it up again. The poor fellow was veritably flying on the wings of religion. At some moment or other his moneybag slipped from the knot at his waist. When he stopped after another ten yards to pull up his dhoti he no longer had the purse. He turned back and looked. The ekka man's wife showed him the purse in her hand and beckoned to him to come back. But religion meant even more than money to Sethji. He went another few steps, but then he stopped again.

Suddenly his piety asserted itself. Could he throw religion over for a few rupees? He'd get plenty more rupees but where would he get another soul?

With these thoughts he took his way like a dog mauled in a dog-fight, his tail drooping, and every so often he stopped to turn back and see whether those devils were coming after him.

NOTE

Original title, '*Tagādā*', 'Dunning', A story from the early thirties.

A Car-Splashing

Well, it's like this: early in the morning I finish off my bath and my prayers, paint a vermillion circle on my forehead, get into my yellow robe and wooden sandals, tuck my astrological charts under my arm, grab hold of my stick—a regular skull-cracker —and start out for a client's house. I was supposed to settle the right day for a wedding; it was going to earn me at least a rupee. Over and above the breakfast. And my breakfast is no ordinary breakfast. Common clerks don't have the courage to invite me to a meal. A whole month of breakfasts for them is just one day's meals for me. In this connection I fully appreciate rich gentlemen and wine-merchants—how they feed you, how they feed you! So generously that you feel happy all over! After I get an idea of the generosity of the client I accept his invitation. If somebody puts on a long face when it's time to feed me I lose my appetite. How can anybody feed you if he's weeping? I can't digest a meal like that at all. I like a client who hails me with, 'Hey, Shastriji, have some sweets!' whom I can answer, 'No, friend—not yet.'

It had rained a lot during the night. There were puddles everywhere on the road. I was walking along all wrapped up in my thoughts when a car came along splashing through the pud- dles. My face got spattered. And then what do I see but my dhoti looking as though somebody mixed up a mess of mud and flung it all over it. My clothes were ruined; apart from that, I was filthy, to say nothing of the money lost. If I'd caught those people in the car I'd have done a job on them they wouldn't forget. I stood there, helpless. I couldn't go to a client's house in this state and my own house was at least a full mile away. The people in the street were all clapping to ridicule me. I never was in such a mess. Well, old heart, what are you going to do now? If you go home what will the wife say?

I decided in a trice what my duty was. I got together about a dozen stones from all around and waited for the next car. I'd show them a Brahman's power!

It wasn't even ten minutes before a car came into sight. Oh no! It was the same car. He'd probably gone to get the master from the station and was returning home. As soon as it got close I let fly a rock, I shot it out with all my strength. The gentleman's cap went flying and landed on the side of the road. The car slowed down. I fired again. The window-pane smashed to pieces and one piece even landed on the fine gentleman's cheek drawing blood. The car stopped and the gentleman got out and came toward me, gave me a punch and said, 'You swine, I'll take you to the police!' I'd scarcely heard him when, throwing my books down on the ground, I grabbed him by the waist, tripped him and he fell with a smack in the mud. I jumped on top of him at once and gave him a good twenty punches one after the other until he got dizzy. In the meantime his wife got out. High-heeled shoes, silk sari, powdered cheeks, lipstick, mascara. She began to poke at me with her umbrella. I left the husband and wielding my stick said, 'Lady, don't meddle in men's business or you may get a whack and a bruise and I'd be very sorry about that.'

The gentleman found the occasion to pick himself up and give me a kick with his booted feet. I got a real knock in the knee. Losing patience, I struck out with my stick, getting him in the legs. He fell like a tree when you chop it down. Memsahib came running brandishing her umbrella. I took it away from her without any trouble and threw it away. The driver had been sitting in the car all this time. Now he got out too and came rushing at me with a cane. I brought my stick down on him too and he fell flat. A whole mob had gathered to see the fun. Still lying on the ground the sahib said, 'You rogue, we'll hand you over to the police!'

I wielded my stick again and wanted to thump him on the skull but he folded his hands and said, 'No, no, baba, we won't go to the police. Forgive me.'

I said, 'All right, leave the police out of it or I'll crack you over the skull. I'd get six months at the most for it but I'd break you of the habit. You drive along and splash up mud and you're blind with conceit. You don't give a damn who's in front of you or along side of you.'

One of the onlookers said, '*Arrey,* Maharaj! These drivers know perfectly well they're splashing and when some man gets

drenched they think it's great fun and laugh at him. You did well
to give one of them a lesson.'

'You hear what the people are saying?' I shouted at the sahib.
He gave a dirty look toward the man who'd spoken and said to
him, 'You're lying, it's a complete lie.'

'You're still just as rude, are you! Shall I have another go at
you with the stick?'

'No, baba,' he said humbly. 'It's true, it's true. Now are you
satisfied?'

Another by-stander said, 'He'll tell you what you want to hear
now but as soon as he's back in his automobile he'll start the same
old business all over again. Just put 'em in their cars and they
all think they're related to the maharaja.'

'Tell him to admit he's wrong,' said another.

'No, no, make him hold on to his ears and do kneebends.'

'And what about the driver? They're all rogues. If a rich man's
puffed up, that's one thing, but what are you drivers so conceited
about? They take hold of the wheel and they can't see straight
any more.'

I accepted the suggestion that master and driver hold on to
their ears and do kneebends, the way you punish little children,
while Memsahib counted. 'Listen, Memsahib,' I said, 'you've got
to count a whole hundred bends, not one less but as many over as
you like.'

Two men drew the master up by his hands, two others that
gentleman-driver. The poor driver's leg was bruised but he began
to do the knee-bends. The master was still pretty cocky; he lay
down and began to spew out gibberish. I was furious and swore
in my heart that I wouldn't let him go without doing a hundred
knee-bends. I ordered four men to shove the car off the edge of
the road.

They set to work at once. Instead of four fifty men crowded
around and began to shove the car. The road was built up very
high with the land below it on either side. If the car had slid
down it would have smashed to pieces. The car had already
reached the edge of the road when the sahib let out a groan and
stood up and said, 'Baba, don't wreck my car, we'll do the knee-
bends.'

I ordered the men to stand off. But they were all enjoying themselves and nobody paid any attention to me. But when I lifted up the stick and ran for them they all abandoned the car and the sahib, shutting his eyes, began to do the knee-bends.

After ten of them I said to the Memsahib, 'How many has he done?'

Very snooty, she said, 'I wasn't counting.'

'Then sahib's going to be groaning and moaning all day long, I won't let him go. If you want to take him home in good health count the knee-bends, then I'll let him go.'

The sahib saw that without his punishment he wouldn't get away with his life, so he began the knee-bends again. One, two, three, four, five. . . .

Suddenly another car came into view. Sahib saw it and said very humbly, 'Panditji, take pity on me, you are my father. Take pity on me and I won't sit in a car again.'

I felt merciful and said, 'No, I don't forbid you to sit in your car, I just want you to treat men like men when you're in it.'

The second car was speeding along. I gave a signal. All the men picked up rocks. The owner of this car was doing the driving himself. Slowing down he tried to creep through us gradually when I advanced and caught him by the ears, shook him violently and after giving him a slap on both cheeks, said, 'Don't splash with the car, understand? Move along politely.' But he began to gabble until he saw a hundred men carrying rocks, then without any more fuss he went on his way.

A minute after he left another car came along. I ordered fifty men to bar the road; the car stopped. I gave him a few slaps too but the poor fellow was a gentleman. He took them as though he enjoyed them and continued his journey.

Suddenly a man said, 'The police are coming.'

And everybody took to his heels. I too came down off the road and sidling into a little lane I disappeared.

NOTE

Original title, '*Motor ke Chhinte*', 'Splashing from a Car', A late story. Though Indian commentators have paid little attention to this story, it is interesting for a number of reasons: the title is not an abstraction (such are comparatively rare), the villain is allowed to talk for himself—unlike the other heavy-eating Pandits of the stories—and it pictures sudden, irrational violence erupting, in this case provoked by a hostility to the Westernized rich.

A Moral Victory

His Excellency the Viceroy was coming to Banaras. Government officials both high and low prepared to welcome him. In the meantime, the members of the Congress Party had given notice that they would call a general strike. This produced great consternation among the officials. On the one hand they had set flags along the streets, cleaned everything up and raised a reception dais, on the other, police and soldiers with drawn bayonettes were drilling in every street and alley. The officials were desperately trying to ensure that the strike would not occur, while the Congress was determined that it would. The officials might be able to count on brute strength but the Congress had the assurance of moral power. This time let there be a test to see which one would control the field.

From morning to night the magistrate rode out to threaten the shopkeepers that he'd put them in jail, that he'd have their shops looted, that he'd do this and do that. Folding their hands the shopkeepers would say, 'Your Lordship is a king, you can do whatever you want. But what are we to do? Those Congress people won't leave us alive. They'll have a sit-down strike on our doorsteps, they'll jump into wells, they'll fast—who knows, if a few of them give up their lives we'll be disgraced forever. If your Lordship can explain it to these Congress people we'll be very much obliged. It won't be any loss to us if we don't have to close our shops. The most important men in the country will be coming and if our shops are open we'll sell the most expensive merchandize and get double the price. But what can we do? We have no control over those devils.'

Even more disturbed than the officials were Raj Haranandan Sahib, Raja Lalchand and Khan Bahadur Maulvi Mahmud Ali. They did their utmost along with the magistrate and on their own as well. They summoned the shopkeepers to their homes, cajoled and threatened them, bullied the cart and buggy drivers, flattered the labourers. But they were so scared by that handful of Congress workers that not one of them paid any attention to these gentle-

100

men, and it reached the point where a neighbourhood green-grocer's wife boldly said, 'Your Lordships, you can have us all killed but we won't open the shops! We don't intend to get ourselves dishonoured.'

The biggest worry was that the workmen making the dais—carpenters, smiths and the like—might work. If they did it would be a calamity. Rai Sahib said:

'Gentlemen, let's invite merchants from other cities to open a separate market here.'

Khan Sahib said, 'There's not enough time left to arrange for another market. Let's arrest the Congress agitators and confiscate their property—then see whether or not we control them!'

'If we start making arrests,' Raja Lalchand said, 'the townspeople will be even more aroused. If your Lordship tells Congress that if they call off the strike they'll all get government jobs, why —since most of them are unemployed—as soon as they hear your offer they'll be wild with joy.'

But the magistrate accepted none of these proposals. And so it went on until there were only three days left before the Viceroy's visit.

2

Finally Raja Lalchand had an inspiration: why shouldn't they too resort to moral pressure? After all, Congress had made a great show in the name of religion and morality. The government ought to imitate them, beat the tiger at its own tricks. They would have to find a man who would go on a hunger strike, even fasting unto death, until the shops opened. Such a man would have to be a Brahman and someone the citizens respected and would pay attention to. Raja Sahib's colleagues thought it was a fine idea, they jumped with enthusiasm. Rai Sahib said, 'That's it, we've cracked their front! Fine, now which Brahman shall it be— Pandit Gadadhar Sharma?'

'Certainly not,' said Raja Lalchand. 'Who pays any attention to him? He only writes for the newspapers. What do the people of Banaras know about him?'

'Then would Damri Ojha be our man?' Rai Sahib suggested.

'Not at all,' Raja Sahib said. 'Who knows him except for the College students?'

'How about Pandit Moteram Shastri?'

'That's it, that's it!' Raja Sahib said. 'You've hit it on the head, he's certainly the man for us! We must send for him. He's learned, he's pious and—he's shrewd. If he's willing to help then we've won our game.'

Raja Sahib immediately despatched a message to Pandit Moteram. At that moment Shastriji was at his prayers. He no sooner heard this providential summons than he cut short his morning ritual and prepared to go. If Raja Sahib had summoned him, then what a windfall it might be! To his good wife he said, 'Today the moon's auspicious! Bring my clothes and I'll find out why they've sent for me.'

'Your food's ready,' his wife said. 'Go and eat—you don't know when you'll get back.'

But Shastriji did not think it proper to keep a man waiting so long. He put on his long green broadcloth jacket with the red fringe, wound a gold-embroidered scarf around his neck, then set a Banaras gold silk turban on his head. He put on a silk dhoti with a wide red border and stepped into his pattens. His Brahmanic glory radiated from his countenance. From a long way off it was plain that some great holy personage was approaching. People who met him on the road bowed their heads and many shopkeepers stood up to greeet him. Today the very name of Banaras, it seemed, was illustrious only because of him, there was nobody else at all worth taking note of. And what a gentle soul, pausing to say a few words to the children! It was in this style that Panditji made his way to Raja Sahib's house. The three friends rose and greeted him. Khan Sahib said:

'Tell us, Panditji, how have you been feeling? By God, you're worthy of being put on display! You must weigh a good ten maunds.'

Raja Sahib said, 'For one maund of learning you need ten maunds of intellect. According to this rule, for every maund of intellect you need ten of flesh, otherwise who could lift up the burden?'

'You people don't understand,' Raja Sahib said, 'wisdom is

like a cold : if it doesn't affect the head, it goes down into the body.'

Khan Sahib said, 'But I've heard the great ones say that a fat man's the enemy of wisdom.'

'Your reckoning was wrong,' Raja Sahib said, 'otherwise you would surely have understood that if the ratio of mind to body is one to ten then the fatter the man the bigger the intellect.'

'From which it is proven,' Raja Sahib said, 'that the fatter the man the fatter the head.'

Pandit Moteram said, 'If I've been summoned to your noble presence because of my fat head, then why should I bother to bring my sharp wits too?'

After this exchange of pleasantries, Raja Sahib explained the present problem to Panditji as well as the plan for solving it which he had conceived. He said, 'So there it is. Just understand that this time your future prosperity is in your own hands. Probably nobody has ever had so magnificent an opportunity to decide his fortune. If there's no general strike, for the rest of your life you won't have to ask for anything from anybody. So you must resolve on such a fast that the whole town is shaken. Congress has gained its power by hiding behind a screen of religious piety —so you must manage to shock the religious sensibilities of the people.'

Gravely Moteram replied, 'This is not such a difficult job. I can perform ceremonies that bring the rain down from the skies, I can calm the small pox fever, I can raise or lower the price of grain. So it's no great matter to take care of those Congress people. Great British dignitaries who can read and write think no one can do the work I do. But they have no knowledge of the occult sciences.'

'Well then, sir,' said Khan Sahib, 'one must declare you a second God! Had we known the powers you have we wouldn't have worried for such a long time.'

'Sir,' Moteram said, 'I can locate hidden treasures, summon the dead—all I need is customers to appreciate my powers. It's not virtues that are lacking in the world but connoisseurs—that is to say, virtuous people—to appreciate them. As the Bhojpuri proverb has it, "Good things galore but a dearth of good folk." '

'Fine,' Raja Lalchand said. 'Now how much will you want for this ceremony?'

'Whatever your respect for me suggests.'

'Well, can you tell us just what sort of a ceremony you're going to perform?'

'It will be a total fast, during which I'll recite spells and prayers. If I don't cause a sensation in the city my name isn't Moteram.'

'And when will you start?'

'I can start right away. But first you might give me just a few rupees to offer in my invocations to the gods. . . .'

And to be sure there was no shortage of rupees. Panditji took his money and set out for home in high spirits. But when he told the news to his wife, she looked worried and said, 'It was silly to get yourself into this mess! Since when can you tolerate being hungry? You'll be the laughing stock of the whole town, they'll die laughing. Better give them back their rupees.'

Moteram reassured her. 'Who says I can't stand being hungry? I'm not such a fool as to do this on an empty stomach. First of all, prepare a meal for me. Go out and get some pastry and fudge and ras-goolas. I'll simply stuff myself. Then I'll eat a pound of cream with almonds. Whatever room is left I'll fill with butter curds. Then we'll see how hungry I get! For three days I won't be able to draw a breath so who's going to be hungry? Our luck is on the upswing, we'd regret it if we hesitated now. If the market doesn't close, think of how rich I'll be. If it does, well, it's no money out of my pocket. I've already got my hands on a hundred rupees.'

While she set about preparing his meal Pandit Moteram sent out the town crier with the news that that evening Moteram Shastri was going to discuss the country's political problems in the square before the Town Hall. People surely would come. Panditji had always stayed out of political matters; if he was to speak about them today everyone would be extremely curious to hear him for he had a great repuation in the city. At the appointed time a crowd of several thousand gathered. After all the proper preparations Panditji arrived from home. His belly was so stuffed that he could scarcely walk. As soon as he reached the square the audience stood up and bowed right to the ground in greeting.

Moteram said, 'Citizens, merchants, bankers and money-lenders! I've heard that after listening to the Congress people you have decided to close your shops on the occasion of the auspicious visit of the British Viceroy. What sort of ingratitude is this? Why, if he wanted to the Viceroy could have you all shot out of cannons this very minute and the whole city plowed under as well. It's no joke, this man is a king! He overlooks your mistakes and takes pity on your poverty and you're ready to go out like sheep to the slaughter. If the Viceroy wishes he can close down the railway and the post offices and shut off all your supplies. Tell me, what would you do then? If he wanted, he could put everybody in Banaras in jail—tell me, what would you do then? Can you run away from him? Is there any place where you could find shelter? Therefore, if you have to remain in this country as his subjects why do you contrive all this mischief? Remember, your lives are in his power. If you let the rabble take over the town, then the whole city will be laid low with grief. Do you think you can stop a hurricane with a broom? Beware, anybody who closes up his shop! If anybody does, I tell you, I'll fast on this very spot until I die.'

One skeptic shouted, 'Sir, it will take you at least a full month of fasting to die—what can happen in three days?

Moteram roared back, 'The breath of life doesn't reside in the body but in the head. If I want, I can escape this life this very minute by my yogic powers. I have warned you, now you know and your way is plain. Heed my words and you will prosper. Heed them not and you will be destroyed, you'll never be able to show your faces anywhere in the world. Enough! Understand this, here I take my seat.'

3

When they heard the news the townspeople were stunned. This latest trick of the officials left them bewildered. The Congress leaders at once pronounced it hypocritical. The Government supporters had given the Pandit some money and got up the whole fraud. When every other means—army, police and courts—had failed, they had devised this new trick. It was nothing else than political bankruptcy. Since when had Moteram Shastri been such a patriot that, concerned about the condition of the country, he would take a fast upon himself for it? Let him die of hunger indeed—in two days he'd give up. This new stratagem had to be nipped in the bud lest it actually succeed—imagine what it would be like if the government got its hands on a new weapon like this and used it all the time. The ordinary people were not so sophisticated that they would understand these mysteries, they would let themselves be bullied.

But the city merchants and money-lenders were most of them so under the thumb of their religion that these remonstrations had not the slightest effect on them. They said, 'Gentlemen, because of you people the Government has turned against us, they're ready to take action, put us out of business. How many will go bankrupt and not even be able to show their faces to the officials? When we used to go to them before the officials would say, "Come in, Sethji", and treat us with respect, but now they shove us around in the railway carriages and no one pays any attention. Whether you have an income or not, they glance at our account books and raise the taxes. We have borne all this and will go on bearing it, but we cannot accept leadership in religious matters from you people. When a noble, learned and pious Brahman renounces food and water because of us, then how can we eat and sleep with a quiet conscience? If he should die, what answer would we have ready for the Lord?'

The upshot of the matter was that not one of them heeded the Congress. At nine o'clock a deputation of merchants set out to attend on Panditji.

Now, today Panditji had eaten as much as he could, but eating as much as he could was no uncommon occurrence for him. About twenty days of every month he managed to get himself invited out to dine, and over-eating is natural when you're invited out. Seeing one's fellow-diners one is inclined to rivalry and to demonstrating one's appreciation to the host, and above all because of the excellence of the food itself one consumes more than an ordinary amount. Panditji's appetite had never failed to meet these challenges successfully. So at this moment, at the arrival of the dinner hour, his resolution somewhat wavered. Not that he was actually beset by hunger, but at meal times if his stomach was not absolutely crammed then in his imagination he begin to suffer the pangs of appetite. Such was the condition of Shastriji at this moment. He was tempted to call some street vendor and help himself to a few sweets, but the officials had posted several soldiers around for his protection. They would not hear of withdrawing. Panditji's vast wisdom was now busy with the problem of how to get rid of those kill-joys. What reason was there to post those louts there? Was he a prisoner, were they afraid he'd run away?

It was possible the authorities had put him in this situation because they feared the Congress people might try to use force to remove him. Nobody knew the tricks they might try, and of course it was the duty of the authorities to protect Punditji from any such disgraceful underhanded conduct.

Panditji was sunk in these reflections when the merchants' deputation arrive. He was reclining comfortably, propped up on his elbows. The leaders touched his feet in greeting and said, 'Maharaj, why have you brought this wrath down upon us? We shall respectfully do whatever you command. Rise up and take food and drink. We didn't know you really were going to take this vow or we would have begged you not to before you did. Be gracious to us. It's long past dinner time now. We will never disregard what you tell us.'

'These Congress people will ruin you,' Panditji said. 'They're already sinking and they'll take you with them. If the market's closed, it will be your loss alone. What does the Government care? You'll starve to death if you go on strike. Does the Government care? You'll go to jail and hard labour. The Government doesn't care! I don't know what crazy idea's got into your skulls to cut off your own noses to spite others. Don't listen to those rogues. Why do you want to shut up the shops?'

'Maharaj,' a merchant answered, 'so long as the whole city's agreed on it how can we oppose them? If the Congress gives the order to have us looted, who'll help us? Rise up and take food! Tomorrow we'll hold a meeting and let you know whatever happens.'

'So go and have your meeting and then come back,' Moteram said.

As the disappointed deputation was about to leave, Panditji said, 'Would any of you happen to have a pinch of snuff?'

One gentleman took out his snuff box and gave it to him.

When they were gone Moteram said to the policemen, 'What are you standing around here for?'

'It's the magistrate's order,' one of them answered. 'What can we do?'

'Get moving,' Panditji said.

'Can we go on your say-so? If we do we'll be dismissed tomorrow—will you feed us?'

'I'm telling you to go away. If you don't, then I will myself. Am I some kind of prisoner to have you surrounding me?'

'Just go then,' the policemen said. 'If you think you can.'

'Why shouldn't I be able to? Have I committed any crime?'

'So go,' the policeman said, 'and then we'll see what happens.'

Panditji leapt up in all his Brahmanical splendour and slapped the policeman so hard that he fell back several steps. The others lost their nerve—they'd all assumed he was a flabby weakling, but when they saw how fierce he was they silently slipped away.

Moteram now sat gazing here and there to see if some food vendor were in sight so that he could get something from him. But then he reflected that if such a person said a word to anyone people would begin to clap their hands in derision. Decidedly, he would have to operate so deftly that not a soul would suspect a thing. These were predicaments that tested one's wits. He went on struggling for a moment with this thorny problem.

By chance at that instant a peddler appeared. Eleven o'clock had just struck, there was complete stillness on all sides. 'Peddler!' Panditji called out, 'Oh, peddler!'

The peddler said, 'Tell me—what shall I give you? You're hungry, aren't you? Giving up food and water is work for holy men, not for the likes of you and me.'

'What the devil are you talking about?' said Panditji. 'Am I less than any holy man? If I want, why I can go for months without feeling hungry or thirsty. I called you only because I want you to give me your oil lamp. I just wanted to see what was crawling around—I was afraid it was a snake.'

The peddler handed his oil lamp to Panditji, who had begun to scan the ground about him. Suddenly the lamp fell from his grasp and went out. The oil overflowed and he gave it another knock so that whatever oil was left spilled out too.

Shaking the lamp the peddler said, 'Maharaj, there's no oil left in it at all. I'd have sold another four pice worth of goods tonight if you hadn't put me out of business.'

'Brother, it's only the hand—because I dropped the lamp do you want me to cut off my hand? Take these pice and go somewhere and fill your lamp with oil.'

The peddler took the coins. 'After I've got it filled why should I come back here?'

'Just set your basket down and go and get your oil quickly. Otherwise, a snake might bite me and then my death will be on your head. There's some animal around for sure. See, it's crawling! Now it's disappeared. Run, lad, and come back with the oil, I'll look after your basket. If you're afraid, take your money with you.'

The vendor fell into a quandary. If he took his money from the basket then he feared lest Panditji think ill of him, believing that he considered the Brahman dishonourable. But if he left it who could say what Panditji intended? Nobody's intentions remained honourable all the time. Finally he decided that he would leave the basket there and let fate take its course. He set out in the direction of the market, leaving Panditji staring at the basket and feeling rather desperate. There were very few sweets left. There were some five or six bags but from each he could extract no more than two pieces. He was afraid his secret would become known. He thought, 'But what if I ate them? My hunger would only get worse, I'd be like a tiger smelling blood. There wouldn't be much fun in a sin like that.' He sat back in his place. But after a moment his hunger grew stronger. 'Still, it would be nice,' he thought. 'No matter how insignificant the amount of food, it's still food.' He got up, took out the sweets. But just as he was about to stick the very first piece of fudge into his mouth he saw the peddler hastening toward him with his lamp lit. He had to finish off the sweets before he arrived. He put two pieces together into his mouth and was still chewing them when that devil of a peddler had come another ten steps. Panditji stuffed four pieces into his mouth and swallowed them half-chewed. There were still six pieces left and by now the peddler had gotten as far as the gate. Panditji thrust all that was left into his mouth. Now he could neither chew it nor spit it out. That demon was charging him like an automobile with his lamp blazing away. When he was right in front of him Panditji swiftly swallowed all the sweets. But after all he was a man and not a crocodile: his eyes filled with water, he choked, he shuddered, coughed violently. Holding out his lamp the vendor said, 'Take this and look around, though if you're ready to fast to death why are you afraid of dying from snakebite? Why worry? If you die the Government will look after your kids, won't it?'

Panditji was so angry that he determined to scold this vulgar troublemaker, but he was unable to produce a sound. He silently took the lamp and after pretending to look around handed it back.

The peddler said, 'What ever possessed you to take the side of the Government anyway? If they're going to meet all day tomorrow they'll hardly make a decision until nightfall. By that time you'll be feeling pretty dizzy.'

With this he went away and Panditji, after coughing a little while, fell asleep.

4

The next day as soon as it was light the merchants began to discuss the problem, and there was a regular commotion among the Congress Party leaders as well. The Vigilance Committee officials also pricked up their ears. They'd devised a splendid plan to intimidate those simple-minded bunyas. The Association of Brahmans held a separate meeting and decided that Pandit Moteram had no right at all to meddle in political affairs. What did Brahmans have to do with politics? In short, the whole day was passed in debating the pros and cons, and nobody paid any attention to Panditji. People said openly that he'd been given a thousand rupees by the Government for taking this fast on himself. Poor Panditji had passed the night tossing about and when he rose his body felt stiff as a corpse's. When he stood up he saw stars before his eyes, his head began to spin. His stomach felt as though someone were scraping it. He kept his eyes glued on the road to see if anybody would come to conciliate him or not. He was still full of this expectation when the time of evening prayer went by. At this hour it had always been his custom to eat a snack after the ritual. Today he had not even had a sip of water. Who could say when the happy moment might arrive? Then he began to feel a great anger against his wife. She must have slept the whole night with her belly full. At this moment she would have just finished a good meal but hadn't even come here to have a look to see whether he was alive or dead. Couldn't she, under some pretext or other, bring him just a little bit of fruit pastry? But why should she care about that? She'd taken the rupees and kept them and whatever else he got she would keep as well and make a regular jackass out of him.

At any rate, Panditji waited the whole day through and no conciliator appeared. They were reluctant to come because of the suspicion in their hearts that Panditji, overcome by his own selfishness, had become involved in some fraudulent bargain and was only putting on a show.

5

At nine o'clock that evening Seth Bhondumal, the leader of the merchants' association, said decisively, 'I suppose Panditji is going through this performance only for his own profit, but since he's only a mere mortal it's none the less painful for him to go without food and water. It's against religion for a Brahman to renounce food and water while we sleep peacefully with full stomachs. If he has conducted himself against religion then he will have to suffer for it. But why do we turn away from our duty?'

The Congress Secretary was not enthusiastic. 'I've said what I had to say. You people are the leaders of society. Whatever you decide we will accept, act and we'll move with you. I also have my share of religious feeling. But listen to one request: will you people let me got there before you? I want to talk with him alone for ten minutes. You can be waiting at the gate. When I return, then you can go to him. What objection can anybody have to this?' They granted his request.

The Secretary had spent a considerable time in the police department and knew something of the weaknesses of human character. He went straight to the market and bought four rupees worth of sweets, taking care to select a large quantity of the most fragrant. He had them wrapped in tinfoil and went off to make his offering to the sulky Brahman. He also took a jug of cold scented water. Waves of fragrance emanated from both the bag and the jug. The power of scent is such that it can make a man hungry even when he's not hungry—and how much more a really hungry man?

At this time Panditji was lying on the ground dozing. He'd eaten nothing during the night—for of what account were a half dozen or so pigmy-sized sweets? And he'd had nothing at noon. Now once again meal time had slipped by. He no longer felt the restlessness of the expectation of food but the very chill of desperation. All his limbs were slack, he could not even open his eyes. He tried several times but they closed automatically. His lips were dry. If he gave any sign of life it was only a very slow moaning. He had never before been in such a fix. A couple of times a month he suffered from indigestion, which he would assuage with myrobalans and other medicines. But he'd never suffered indigestion so acutely that he'd given up eating. He whole-heartedly cursed the inhabitants of the city, the Vigilance Committee, the Government, God, the Congress Party and his own true wife. There was nothing to be hoped for from any of them. Now he was no longer strong enough even to stand up and go to the market. He was convinced that by tonight his spirit would have taken flight. For he knew that the thread of life is not some string that won't break no matter how much it's pulled.

'Shastriji!' the Secretary called.

Still lying down Moteram opened his eyes. They were as full of self-pity as those of a child whose candy's been snatched from his hand by a crow.

The Secretary set the bag of sweets down before him and the pot of water with a cup on it. Then he said casually, 'How long are you going to go on lying here?'

The aroma put Panditji's faculties back into operation. He sat up and said, 'Until an agreement has been reached.'

'But there's not going to be any agreement. The Council met all day without settling it. Anyway, tomorrow evening the Viceroy will be here. Do you have any idea of what kind of shape you'll be in by then? Your face has already turned pale!'

'If I'm fated to die here, who can avert fate? Are those ras-goolas in that bag?'

'Yes, all kinds of sweets. They were made specially to be sent to one of my relatives for a ceremony.'

'That's why they smell so good. Open up the bag a little, will you?'

Smiling, the secretary opened the bag and Panditji began to devour the sweets with his eyes. A blind man whose sight has been restored would not gaze upon the world with greedier eyes. Moteram's mouth watered. The Secretary said, 'If you hadn't taken a vow, I'd give you a taste of them. They cost two and a half rupees a pound.'

'They must be magnificent! I haven't had any ras-goolas for several days.'

'And you've gotten yourself into a pickle for nothing! If you don't survive, of what use is the money?'

'What can I do? I'm trapped!' Panditji said. 'I might have made a meal of this many sweets.' He delicately touched them. 'They must be from Bhola's shop.'

'Just try a couple of them.'

'How can I? I'd be breaking a sacred oath.'

'Come on, taste them! The pleasure they'll give you right now couldn't be bought for thousands of rupees. Who's going to know about it anyway?'

'Who am I afraid of?' Moteram said. 'Here I am dying of thirst and hunger and nobody cares in the least. So why be afraid? Bring it here, hand me the bag. Go on, tell everybody, Shastriji's broken his vow. To hell with business and the market! I don't care about anybody. When there's no religion left in the world, why should I bother to take it on myself alone?'

With this Panditji drew the bag toward himself and steadily applied his hand with the result that in a flash the bag was half empty. By this time the merchants had reached the gate and were standing there. Going to them, the Secretary said, 'Come a little closer and see the fun. You people won't have to open your bazaar; nor will you have to toady to anybody. I've solved the whole problem. This is the Congress spirit!'

Moonlight filled the square. They came closer and saw Panditji

113

engaged in doing away with the sweets with the profound absorption of a holy man in a trance.

Bhondumal said, 'I touch Panditji's feet in reverence. We were all coming, why didn't you wait? We had devised a plan so that you would have accomplished your purpose without breaking your vow.'

But Moteram said, 'I *have* accomplished my purpose. This is a divine joy that can't be obtained for any amount of money. If you have any respect for me, then order some more sweets exactly like this from the same shop.'

NOTE

Original title, '*Satyāgrah*', the Gandhian term for an act of civil disobedience, literally, 'grasping the truth'. First published in 1923.

This is one of the more elaborate episodes in the cycle of Moteram Shastri stories. Premchand obviously enjoyed the fat rogue's shrewdness, cheek, garbled eloquence and unabashed wickedness, and most of the stories about him share a vitality of narration that is not matched by structure and direction.

Man's Highest Duty

One Holi morning Pandit Moteram Shastri—that devotee of pastries and lover of sweets—sat on a broken cot in his yard, his head hanging low, on his face an expression of care and melancholy. His faithful spouse sat nearby watching him anxiously and trying in her gentle voice to wheedle him out of his depression.

After he had remained plunged in gloomy reflections for some time Panditji said sadly, 'My good luck has gone the devil knows where. Even on Holi it deserts me.'

'Evil days have come upon us,' his wife said. 'Ever since you told me to, I pray the Sun God twice a day, morning and evening, to get an invitation sent to you from somewhere. I've lit hundreds of lamps to Mother Tulsi, but the fact is, they've all deserted you. Not one of them will come to help you through these hard times.'

'The Gods and Goddesses have nothing to do with it,' said Moteram. 'When they come and help us through our difficulties then we can start talking about Gods and Goddesses. But there are an awful lot of people sitting around gobbling up pancakes and halva without paying for them.'

'But isn't there one single gentleman left in this whole town? Have they all died?'

'They've all died—or rather, they've all gone rotten. There may be five or ten of them but in a whole year only a couple of them show their generosity even once. And when they do, they give you only five or six pounds of sweets to eat. If I had my way, I'd send the whole lot of them off to hard labour. It's all the work of those Arya Samaj religious reformers.'

'But you just sit around the house! Even these days there must be some generous person who'd invite you out. Some time or other you ought to go out and offer sermons and blessings.'

'How do you know I haven't? If any such gentleman existed in this town, I wouldn't give him a blessing when I went to see him. But who the devil is around to listen to me? Everybody's wrapped up in his own business.'

In the meantime Pandit Chintamani had put in an appearance. This was Moteram's best friend. To be sure, he was a little younger than Moteram and accordingly his paunch had not attained the splendid proportions of the latter's.

'Tell me, friend,' Moteram said, 'what news? Do you know of any good opportunities?'

'No opportunities,' Chintamani said, 'just my own luck and now even that's run out.'

'Then you must have just come from home?'

'Brother, let's become wandering sadhus. When there's not the slightest pleasure left in life, what's a man to do? Now tell me, if you don't get something decent to eat even on a day like this, how's a body to keep going?'

'Yes, brother, what you say is true.'

'Then you can't think of anything to do now either? Say it straight out and then we'll renounce the world.'

'No, friend, don't despair. Don't you know, without dying you can't get into heaven? For obtaining dainty morsels you have to undergo strict austerities. My opinion is that we should act, go right away to the banks of the Ganges and give a talk. Who knows, we may stir the heart of some gentle soul.'

'A fine idea,' said Chintamani. 'Let's get going.'

The two gentlemen got up and made their way toward holy Ganges. It was still early morning. Hundreds of people were bathing there or reading scriptures aloud or thronging the steps and applying the auspicious vermillion to their foreheads. Some were already setting out for home, their dhotis still wet from the river.

As soon as the two pious gentlemen appeared they were greeted on all sides with cries of 'Reverence! Blessings!' After replying to these salutations the two friends went to the edge of the river and busied themselves in the ritual of bathing. After this they climbed up the steps and began to sing a hymn. This was so remarkable an occurrence that hundreds of curious people gathered around. When the audience was several hundreds strong Pandit Moteram said with great dignity:

'Good people, you know that when Brahma created this unprofitable world he made the Brahmans from his mouth. Is there anyone who doubts this?'

'No, maharaj,' they said, 'What you say is true—who can deny it?'

'So the Brahman emerged from the mouth of the god Brahma, this is certain. Therefore, the mouth is the most sublime part of the human body. Thus the highest duty of any living creature is to afford delight to the mouth. Is this true or isn't it? Does any one deny it? Let him come forward! We can prove our theory by the scriptures.'

'Maharaj, you are a learned man—who would dare refute you?'

'Very well, then, now that it's been determined that to delight the mouth is man's highest duty, is it difficult to see that people who do not contribute to the mouth are creatures of sorrow—will any one deny this?'

'Maharaj, you are blessed, a teacher of the true scriptures.'

'Now the question arises, how shall we delight the mouth? We say: according to your faith and according to your capacity. There are different ways. To sing the glories of the Gods, to offer prayers to the Lord, to converse with holy men and avoid wicked speech. From all these things the mouth will derive pleasure. But the highest, the most sublime and effective way is something different: Can any of you say what it is? Let him speak.'

'Maharaj,' they said, 'who can open his mouth in your presence? Please tell us.'

'Very well, I'll shout it out and sing it to the skies. Its greatness is as the full moon's light compared to all the other lunar phases.'

'Do not delay, tell us the way you mean.'

'Listen, then, pay attention: the way is this—to feast the mouth with the finest foods, to feed it the very best dishes. Does anyone deny this? Let him speak and we shall call scripture to witness.'

There was a sceptic among the crowd. 'I can't understand how the mouth can obtain greater pleasure in eating fine foods than in speaking truth.'

Several others agreed with him. 'We doubt it too. Maharaj, remove our doubt.'

'Does anyone else disbelieve? I shall be delighted to refute you. Good people, you ask how there can be greater pleasure in eating than in speaking truth. My answer is that the first way is visible and substantial, while the second is invisible. To illustrate, just imagine that I have committed a crime. If the judge summoned me and explained gently that what I had done was bad, unbefitting for me, such treatment would not succeed in setting me on the right path. Gentlemen, I'm not a saint. I'm a poor mortal caught in the toils of worldliness and delusion. Such a punishment would not have any effect on me. As soon as I'd left the judge's presence I'd begin again on the evil path. Have you understood me? Does anyone deny it?'

'Maharaj! You are an ocean of knowledge, a pearl among the Pandits—may you prosper!'

'Now let's turn back to the illustration I gave. If the judge had summoned me, promptly thrown me in jail and there subjected me to various hardships, then when I left prison I would remember those sufferings for years, and of course I would renounce the path of evil. You will ask why this is so—since both are forms of punishment why should one have an effect and the other none? The reason is that the form of one is visible and the other's hidden. Do you understand this?'

'May you prosper for your kindness! God has bestowed great sense and wisdom on you!'

'Very well, now your question will naturally be what kind of food is best. I will explain. Just as God created different kinds of colours for the gratification of the eyes, so he created diverse flavours for the mouth. But of all these flavours which is finest? This is according to each one's taste, but according to the Vedas and Shastras the taste of sweetness is the most esteemed. The gods become intoxicated with sweetness to the point where even the omnipotent, all-encompassing supreme deity himself prefers sweet foods above all. Can anyone name a god who takes salty good? Can anybody name even one such deity? There's not one. None of the gods therefore hanker after foods that are sour, tart, acid or pungent.'

'Maharaj, your wisdom has no limits!'

'Thus I have proven that of all foods, sweet foods are the best. Now again you will ask a question: will all sweet foods afford the mouth equal pleasure? If I said yes, you would all set up a cry that Panditji has gone mad. Therefore, I will say no and say it over and over again. Not all sweets have equal savour. There's a lot of difference between refined sugar and the cane. So our first duty is to see that we eat and serve only the best of sweets. In my opinion, for a feast fit for God, you should fill a plate with

Jaunpur "nectars", Agra "pearl-drops", Mathura creams, ras-
goolas from Lucknow, rose-apple candy from Ayodhya and Delhi
halva. The gods would go wild over such a dish. And the enterprising and noble soul who gets together such a tasty dish for
the Brahmans—he will find an abode in heaven in his own corp-
oreal form! If you have faith, then we urge you emphatically to
fulfill your religious obligations—for otherwise you cannot consider yourselves men.'

Pandit Moteram's speech was over. People applauded. Some
gentlemen, overwhelmed by the sermon and display of knowledge,
showered flowers upon him. Then Pandit Chintamani began his
own flowery discourse:

'Good people, you have heard the powerful utterance of my
best friend Pandit Moteram and there was no need for me to
be standing by. However, although I am in agreement with him
on almost every question, I hold a different doctrine on one
point. In my opinion if he put only Jaunpur nectars on the plate,
it would be far tastier, far more delicious than five different kinds
of sweets. And I can prove my point by reference to the scriptures.'

Flaring up, Moteram said, 'Your idea is utterly wrong. Jaunpur nectars are not fit to be compared with pearl-drops from
Agra and Delhi halva.'

'Prove it!' Chintamani shouted.

'Visibly and substantially?'

'That shows how stupid you are!'

'All your life you've been gobbling down everything in sight,'
Moteram said, 'but you don't know a thing about food.'

In reply Chintamani flung his prayer-mat at Pandit Moteram,
who dodged the blow and charged Chintamani like a wild
elephant. But at this moment the people gathered around separ-
ated the two mahatmas.

NOTE

Original title, '*Manushya kā Param Dharm*', 'Man's Supreme Religious Obligation. First published in 1920. In the opening paragraphs some of the humour comes from the fact that while the

Pandit speaks fairly highflown and not always correct Hindi, his wife speaks in her own sensible and plain Bhojpuri, a phase of Eastern Hindi that is more than a dialect and has a rich folk literature. For the names of Pandit Moteram's favourite sweets I have invented equivalents suggested by the original names. For rasgoola, see the glossary.

A Lesson in the Holy Life

Domestic squabbles and a dearth of invitations led Pandit Chintamani to consider renouncing the world and when he vowed to become a wandering ascetic his best friend, Pandit Moteram Shastri, gave him this advice.

'Friend, I've been intimately acquainted with a good many first-class mahatmas. Now when they arrive at some well-to-do citizen's door they don't fall in a heap and hold out their hands and call down hypocritical blessings such as "God keep you in body and soul, may you always be happy". Such is the way of beggars. As soon as a holy man reaches the door he lets out his war-cry in a regular yell so that everybody inside the house is astonished and comes running to see what's happened. I know two or three of these slogans—you can use any you like. Gudri Baba used to say, "If anybody dies five will die!" When they heard this battle-cry people would fall right at his feet. Siddh Bhagat had a fine slogan: "Eat, drink and be merry but watch out for the holy man's stick." Nanga Baba would say, "Give to me, feed me, let me drink, let me sleep". Just remember, your prestige depends a good deal on your slogan. What else can I tell you? Don't forget, you and I have been friends for a long time, we've enjoyed the same free dinners hundreds of times. Whenever we were at the same banquet we used to compete to eat up one dish more than the other. I'm going to miss you! May God give you a happy life.'

Chintamani wasn't pleased with any of the slogans. He said, 'Think up some special cry for me.'

'All right—how's this one; "If you don't give to me I'll run you into the ground".'

'Yes, I like that one, but if you'll allow me, I'll shorten it.'

'Go right ahead.'

'Then how about this: "Give or I'll run you into the ground".'

Moteram leaped up. 'By the Lord above, that's absolutely unique! Devotion has illuminated you. Splendid! Now try it out just once and we'll see how you do it.'

Chintamani stuck his fingers in his ears and yelled with all his might. " 'Give or I'll run you into the ground!" ' The noise was so thunderous that even Moteram was startled. The bats flew out of the trees in dismay and dogs began to bark.

Moteram said, 'Friend, hearing your cry I was stirred to the depths of my heart. Such a cry has never been heard before, it was like the roar of a lion. Now your slogan has been decided, I have a few other things to tell you, so pay attention. The language of holy men is quite distinct from our ordinary way of speaking. We say "Sir", for example, to some people, and just "you" to others. But the holy man says "thou" to everybody, important or insignificant, rich or poor, old or young; however, go on treating old people with respect. Also remember never to talk plain Hindi. Otherwise the secret will be out that you're an ordinary Brahman and not a real holy man. Make your language fancy. To say, for example, "My good woman, give me something to eat", is not the style of the holy man. A genuine mahatma will say it like this: "Woman, spread a feast before me, and you will be walking in the paths of righteousness." '

'Friend,' Chintamani said, 'how can I praise you enough? You've helped me beyond measure.'

Having given this advice, Moteram took his leave. Chintamani set out and what should he see right away but a crowd of holy men sitting in front of a *bhang* and hashish shop smoking hashish. When they saw Chintamani one of the holy men pronounced his slogan:

> 'Move along, move along,
> Otherwise I'll prove you wrong'.

Another holy man proclaimed,

> 'Fee fi fo fum
> The holy men have finally come,
> From now on only fun'.

While these syllables were still echoing in the skies a third mahatma roared out,

> Here and there
>   down and up
> Hurry up and fill my cup'.

Chintamani could not restrain himself. He burst out with 'Give or I'll run you into the ground!'

As soon as they heard this the holy men greeted him. The bowl of the hooka was refilled at once and the task of lighting it was assigned to Pandit Chintamani. He thought, if I don't accept the pipe my secret will be out. Nervously he took it. Now anyone who has never smoked hashish can try and try without being able to make the pipe draw. Closing his eyes Chintamani inhaled with all his might. The pipe fell from his hands, his eyes popped, he foamed at the mouth but not the least bit of smoke came from his lips nor was there any sign that the pipe was kindled. This lack of know-how was quite enough to ruin his standing in the society of holy men. A couple of them advanced angrily and roughly catching him by the hands, pulled him up.

'A curse on you,' one said, and another, 'Aren't you ashamed of pretending to be a mahatma?'

Humiliated, Panditji went and sat down near a sweets shop and the holy men, striking tambourines, began to sing this hymn:

> 'Illusion is the world, beloved, the world is all illusion.
> Both sin and holiness are lies—there's the philosophical solution.
> The world is all illusion.
> A curse on those who forbid us *bhang* and hashish,
> Krishna, lover, all the world's illusion.'

NOTE

Original title, *'Guru-Mantra'*, 'The Precepts of the Teacher'. Written in the twenties. In this sketch, which is a part of the satirical saga of Moteram Shastri, the slogans are half nonsensical and the concluding hymn highly ironical. The hashish is *ganja,* commonly smoked by sadhus, particularly in Banaras.

A Little Trick

Whenever Seth Chandumal took a look at his shop and warehouse crammed full with goods he would heave up a long sigh. How could he sell it? The bank interest was going up, the shop rent was climbing, the clerks' wages had to come out of whatever was left. He had to provide all this money out of his own pocket. If this situation lasted a few more days there would be no alternative to bankruptcy. And still those Congress boycotters kept after him like devils.

Seth Chandumal's shop was in Chandni Chowk in Delhi and he also had some shops out in the provinces. When the city Congress Committee tried to get him to sign the pledge not to deal in English cloth he didn't so much as consider the possibility. Then several wholesale dealers in the market, following his example, refused to put their signatures to the pledge letter. Chandumal, who had never attained any eminence as a leader, won it now without even trying. He was sympathetic to the Government. At various times he would offer a little contribution to the official bigshots. He was also chummy with the police and he belonged to the municipal council as well. As an opponent of the Congress programme for action he had become the treasurer of the Peace Council, which supported cooperation with the British—this was the reward for his colllaboration. The officials had purchased 24,000 rupeees worth of cloth for the welcome prepared for the Prince of Wales. Why should so powerful a man fear the Congress? What was their importance anyway? The police encouraged him too: 'Never sign their pledge. Just see what those people are doing. You can blame us if we don't put every one of them in jail.' So Sethji's courage grew and he determined to do battle with the Congress. The result of this was that for three months Congress volunteers blockaded his shop from nine in the morning until dark. The police squad fired at them several times and several times beat them up, while Sethji himself often showered volleys of abuse on them. But the boycotters could not be budged; on the contrary, because of these outbreaks of violence

Chandumal's business fell off still more. From the provinces his storekeepers kept on sending even more desperate news. It was a complicated problem, he saw no way out of the impasse. He had observed that the people who'd signed the pledge went right on selling foreign cloth on the sly—there were no boycott demonstrators in front of *their* shops. He was forced to bear the full brunt of the disaster alone.

He reflected, 'What advantage has my friendship with the police and judges brought me? *They* can't get rid of these demonstrators! Customers won't come at the command of soldiers. If only the boycott can be sopped somehow or other the business might still be saved.'

Meantime his chief accountant said, 'Lalaji, just look, a few traders were coming over our way. Those boycotters told them some kind of nonsense and now they've all gone away.'

'I'd be perfectly satisfied if those sinners were all shot,' Chandumal said. 'They won't give up until they destroy me.'

'If you signed the pledge—it would be a disgrace, of course—but then they'd lift the boycott and somehow or other we'd sell off everything.'

'I've considered that too,' Chandumal said. 'But think how great the loss of face would be. After putting up such a front I can't give in, I'd lose all my prestige with the judges and they'd taunt me for backing down. "Just an idiot fighting the Congress!" After a defeat like that my pride would be crushed. How would I look asking for help from the people I struck and had beaten and insulted and ridiculed? But there might be a way out. If a little trick could work then we'd be out of the soup. The thing is to kill the snake without breaking the stick! If I can just lift the boycott without toadying up to anybody. . . .'

2

At nine in the morning Chandumal had come back from a ritual dip in the Jumna and reclining, propped up by his bolster, he began to read through some letters. The managers of his other shops all related the same tale of woe. With each letter he read

Sethji's anger mounted. In the meantime two volunteers came with banners to stand guard outside his shop.

Sethji shouted, 'Get away from my shop, you!'

'Maharaj,' one of the volunteers answered, 'we're on the road —do you want us to stay out of the road too?'

'I don't want to have to look at your faces,' Sethji said.

'Then be good enough to write to the Congress Committee. We got our orders from them to come and stand guard here.'

A constable came along and said, 'What's the matter, Sethji, is this fellow talking back to you?'

Chandumal said, 'I told him to get away from in front of my shop but he says he won't leave. Just look at the way they persecute me!'

The constable said to the volunteers, 'Both of you get moving or I'll come and pin back your ears.'

'We're on the road,' the volunteer said, 'not in his shop.'

The constable was eager to show his efficiency. He also hoped for some little compensation if he did Sethji a favour. He yelled at the volunteers and when they paid no attention he struck one of them such a blow that the poor fellow fell flat on the ground. Several demonstrators came clustering from here and there, and a number of policeman gathered too. Idle onlookers enjoy nothing more than an incident like this and they flocked around as wel. Someone shouted, 'Long live Mahatma Gandhi!' and everyone chimed in, and in a twinkling there was a regular mob.

One onlooker said, 'What's up, Chandumal? Can you have these poor people treated so barbarously in front of your shop without being ashamed? Have you no fear of God?'

Sethji said, 'I give you my oath I never said a word to any policeman. These people came out of nowhere after the poor fellows. You're slandering me without any cause.'

'But Lalaji,' the constable protested, 'you yourself said these two volunteers were scaring off your customers. Are you trying to slip out of that now?'

'A lie, a complete lie, a hundred-per-cent lie!' Sethji said. 'You people started a fight with them just to show how good you are at your work. These poor fellows were standing way off from my shop, they weren't talking to anybody or causing any trouble.

Then you started after them. Is my business selling or fighting with people?'

'Lalaji,' said another constable, 'be sensible now. You got us worked up and then you kept out of it. If you hadn't told us to, why would we have hit these people? And the Inspector ordered us to pay special attention to Seth Chandumal's shop. "Don't let any volunteers gather there!" he said. So we come to protect your shop. If you hadn't made the request why should the Inspector have given us this assignment?'

'The Inspector must have wanted to show how efficient he is, I suppose,' Chandumal said. 'Why should I ask him for anything? Everybody's against Congress anyway, but the police go all to pieces just to hear them mentioned. Do you mean you do your duty only if I make a complaint?'

In the meantime somebody had informed the police station that violence had broken out between police and volunteers in front of Lala Chandumal's shop. The news got to the Congress office too. In a little while the captain of the armed police and the Inspector arrived, and a whole force of Congress officials came on the run. The crowd was enormous. Shouts of victory rang out occasionally. The police and congress leaders began to argue. The result of it all was that the police arrested the two volunteers and marched them off toward the police station.

After the police officials had gone Sethji said to the Congress president, 'I've learned today how brutally those people treat the volunteers.'

'Then those two volunteers weren't arrested in vain,' the president said. 'You don't have any doubts about this matter now, do you? Have you really learned how violent and destructive they are?'

'Yes indeed, I really have learned.'

'But the police will surely ask you to testify.'

'Let them ask,' Chandumal said. 'I'll just tell the truth straight out, whether it ruins me or not. From now on there's not going to be any police brutality in front of my door. I hadn't understood at all.'

'The police will put a lot of pressure on you,' the Congress secretary said.

'Let them do their utmost, I'll never lie. The Government's

127

not going to get off in the *real* courthouse,' and Chandumal looked heavenward for an instant.

'Now our honour is in your hands,' the secretary said.

'You won't find me an enemy of my country,' Chandumal said.

Afterwards when the president and other officials were about to leave the secretary said, 'The man appears truthful.'

Dubiously the president observed, 'By tomorrow we'll have the proof of it.'

3

In the evening the police inspector called Lala Chandumal to the station and said, 'You'll have to testify and we're counting on your collaboration.'

'I'm ready,' said Chandumal.

'Did the volunteers insult the constables?'

'I didn't hear any insults.'

'Whether you heard any or not, that's not the point. You'll have to say that they kept customers away by hitting them, that there were scuffles, that they threatened to kill—you'll have to say all this.' To the sub-inspector he said, 'Copy this description which I've taken down at Sethji's dictation.'

'You won't hear *me* lying in a packed courtroom,' Seth Chandumal said. 'There'll be thousands in court who know me. How could I show my face to anybody, where could I go?'

'These are all personal matters,' the Inspector said. 'In politics nobody worries about truth and falsehood or honour and shame.'

'But I'd be dishonoured,' Sethji said.

'In the eyes of the Government your prestige would be four times as great.'

Chandumal reflected. 'No,' he said, 'I can't testify. Get some other witness.'

'You'd better think about it, now! This could ruin you completely.'

'If it does, then so be it.'

'Your rank as treasurer of the Peace Council will be taken away from you.'

'Well,' Chandumal said, 'that's not what pays my bills.'

'You'll forfeit your license to carry a gun.'

'So I'll forfeit it—who cares?'

'And then there'll be an income tax investigation.'

'Investigate by all means—it will be to my advantage, the way business is.'

'You won't have a chair left to sit in!'

'I'm going bankrupt anyway—what good is a chair?'

'All right then. You may go now. But one of these days we'll take care of you!'

4

At this time the next day in the Congress office a programme was decided on for the morrow. The president said, 'Send a couple of volunteers to blockade Chandumal's shop.'

'In my opinion,' said the secretary, 'there's no need to now.'

'Why? He still hasn't signed the pledge letter, has he?'

'He didn't sign but he's certainly on our side now. He's made this plain by refusing to testify on behalf of the police. You can imagine how the officials will be after him for that. Moral courage like this can't come without a transformation of his ideas as well.'

'Yes, certainly there's been some change in his ideas.'

'No sir, it's a total revolution,' the secretary said. 'You know what it means to scorn the authorities in such matters—it's like a declaration of treason. It means just as much as a vow of renunciation for an ascetic. Now every judge in the district will be positively thirsting for his blood. It wouldn't be surprising if the governor himself was informed about this.'

'Then there's nothing else but for him to sign the pledge if only as a matter of form. Somehow or other get him over here and let's settle the matter.'

'He's very proud, he'll never come. On the contrary, if he sees that we don't trust him he's liable to try to go back over to the other side.'

'Very well then, if we're to trust him let's take the volunteers away from his shop. But still I say that you'll have to keep an eye on him by finding some pretext for going to see him.'

'You really don't have to be so suspicious,' said the secretary.

When Sethji came to his shop at nine o'clock he didn't see a single volunteer. He broke into a grin. 'We won the toss,' he said to the accountant.

'So it seems—not one of those gentlemen's put in an appearance.'

'And they're not going to. The game is in our hands now. We gambled and we got everything. Aren't you convinced? How quickly I made them my friends. Just ask me to and I'll send for 'em and make 'em lick my boots! They're not anybody's friends and nobody's enemies, they're just slaves of money. Tell the truth now, what did you think of my little trick?'

'I could go right down on my knees to you for it! The snake is dead and the stick didn't break. But those Congress fellows will be keeping an eye on you.'

'I'm ready for 'em, I can match wits with them and give them tit for tat. There are people coming, so get out a bale of the English cloth and start giving it to the traders. In a week we'll be out of the woods!'

NOTE

Original title, '*Chakmā*', 'A Trick'. First published in 1922. This is one of about a dozen stories by Premchand that deal with the boycott of British cloth as a part of the Congress drive for independence.

Penalty

Scarcely a month ever went by without Alarakkhi having some fine deducted from her pay. Once in a while she would actually get five of her six rupees; but though she put up with just about anything she had managed not to let Khan Sahib put his hands on her. Munshi Khairat Ali Khan was the Inspector of Sanitation and hundreds of sweeper women depended on him. He was good-hearted and well thought of—not the sort who cut their pay, scolded them or fined them. But he went on regularly rebuking and punishing Alarakkhi. She was not a shirker, not saucy or slovenly, nor was she at all bad-looking. During these chilly days she would be out with her broom before it was light and go on assiduously sweeping the road until nine. But all the same, she would be penalized. Huseni, her husband, would help her with the work too when he found the chance, but it was in Alarakkhi's fate that she was going to be fined. For others pay-day was an occasion to celebrate, for Alarakkhi it was a time to weep. On that day it was as though her heart had broken. Who could tell how much would be deducted? Like students awaiting the results of their examinations, over and over again she would speculate on the amount of the deduction.

Whenever she got so tired that she'd sit down a moment to catch her breath, precisely then the Inspector would arrive riding in his ekka. No matter how much she'd say, 'Please, Excellency, I'll go back to work again,' he would jot her name down in his book without listening. A few days later the very same thing would happen again. If she bought a few cents worth of candy from the sweets-vendor and started to eat it, just at that moment the Inspector would drop on her from the devil knew where and once more write her name down in his book. Where could he have been hiding? The minute she began to rest the least bit he was upon her like an evil spirit. If he wrote her name down on only two days, how much would the penalty be then? God knew. More than eight annas? If only it weren't a whole rupee! With her head bowed she'd go to collect her pay and find even more deducted

131

than she'd estimated. Taking her money with trembling hands she'd go home, her eyes full of tears. There was no one to turn to, no one who'd listen, where the Inspector was concerned.

Today was pay-day again. The past month her unweaned daughter had suffered from coughing and fever. The weather had been exceptionally cold. Partly because of the cold, partly because of the little girl's crying she was kept awake the whole night. Several times she'd come to work late. Khan Sahib had noted down her name, and this time she would be fined a half rupee. But if it were only a half rupee it would be a blessing. It was impossible to say how much might be deducted. Early in the morning she picked up the baby, took her broom and went to the street. But the naughty creature wouldn't let itself be put down. Time after time Alarakkhi would threaten her with the arrival of the Inspector. 'He's on his way and he'll beat me and as for you, he'll cut off your nose and ears!' The child was willing to sacrifice her nose and ears but not to be put down. At last, when Alarakkhi had failed to get rid of her with threats and coaxing alike, she set her down and left her crying and wailing while she started to sweep. But the little wretch wouldn't sit in one place to cry her heart out; she crawled after her mother time and time again, caught her sari, clung to her legs, then wallowed around on the ground and a moment later sat up to start crying again.

'Shut up!' Alarakkhi said, brandishing the broom. 'If you don't, I'll hit you with the broom and that'll be the end of you. That bastard of an Inspector's going to show up at any moment.'

She had hardly gotten the words out of her mouth when Inspector Khairat Ali Khan dismounted from his bicycle directly in front of her. She turned pale, her heart began to thump. 'Oh God, may my head fall off if he heard me! Right in front of me and I didn't see him. Who could tell he'd come on his bicycle today? He's always come in his ekka.' The blood froze in her veins, she stood holding the broom as though paralyzed.

Angrily the Inspector said, 'Why do you drag the kid after you to work? Why didn't you leave it at home?'

'She's sick, Excellency,' Alarakkhi said timidly. 'Who's at home to leave her with?'

'What's the matter with her?'

'She has a fever, Huzoor.'

'And you make her cry by leaving her? Don't you care if she lives or dies?'

'How can I do my work if I carry her?'

'Why don't you ask for leave?'

'If my pay is cut, Huzoor, what will we have to live on?'

'Pick her up and take her home. When Huseni comes back send him here to finish the sweeping.'

She picked up the baby and was about to go when he asked, 'Why were you abusing me?'

Alarakkhi felt all her breath knocked out of her. If you'd cut her there wouldn't have been any blood. Trembling she said, 'No, Huzoor, may my head fall off if I was abusing you.'

And she burst into tears.

2

In the evening Huseni and Alarakkhi went to collect her pay. She was very downcast.

'Why so sad?' Huseni tried to console her. 'The pay's going to be cut, so let them cut it. I swear on your life from now on I won't touch another drop of booze or toddy.'

'I'm afraid I'm fired. Damn my tongue! How could I. . . .'

'If you're fired, then you're fired, but let Allah be merciful to *him*. Why go on crying about it?'

'You've made me come for nothing. Everyone of those women will laugh at me.'

'If he's fired you, won't we ask on what grounds? And who heard you abuse him? Can there be so much injustice that he can fire anyone he pleases? If I'm not heard I'll complain to the panchayat, I'll beat my head on the headman's gate—'

'If our people stuck together like that would Khan Sahib ever dare fine us so much?'

'No matter how serious the sickness there's a medicine for it, silly.'

But Alarakkhi was not set at rest. Dejection covered her face like a cloud. When the Inspector heard her abuse him why didn't he even scold her? Why didn't he fire her on the spot? She wasn't able to work it out, he actually seemed kind. She couldn't manage to understand this mystery and not understanding it she was afraid. If he meant only to fine her he would have written her name in his book. He had decided to fire her—that must have been why he was so nice. She'd heard that a man about to be hanged is given a fine last meal, they have to give him anything he wants—so surely the Inspector was going to dismiss her.

They reached the municipal office building. Thousands of sweeper women were gathered there, all made up and wearing their brightest clothes and jewelry. The *pan* and cigarette vendors had also come, along with the sweets peddlers. A swarm of Pathan money-lenders were on hand to collect money from those who owed them. Huseni and Alarakkhi went and stood with the others.

They began to distribute the pay. The sweeper women were first. Whoever's name was called would go running and taking her money call down undeserved blessings on the Inspector and go away. Alarakkhi's name was always called after Champa's. Today she was passed over. After Champa, Jahuran's name was called, and she always followed Alarakkhi.

In despair she looked at Huseni. The women were watching her and beginning to whisper. She longed just to be able to go home, she couldn't bear this derision. She wished the earth would open and swallow her up.

One after another the names were called and Alarakkhi went on looking at the trees across the way. Now she no longer cared whose name was called and who went and who stared at her and who was laughing at her.

Suddenly startled she heard her name. Slowly she stood up and walked ahead with the slow tread of a new bride. The paymaster put the full amount of six rupees in her hand.

She was stupefied. Surely the paymaster was mistaken! In these three years she had never once gotten her full pay. And now to get even half would have been a windfall. She stood there for a second in case the paymaster should ask for the money back. When he asked her, 'Why are you standing here now, why don't you move along?' she said softly, 'But it's the full amount.'

Puzzled the paymaster looked at her and said, 'What else do you want—do you want to get less?'

'There's no penalty deducted?'

Penalty

'No, today there aren't any deductions.'

She came away but in her heart she was not content. She was full of remorse for having abused the Inspector.

NOTE

Original title, '*Jurmānā*', 'Penalty'. A late story. The story hinges on a point that may be obscure—the fact that the Inspector is persecuting Alarakkhi because she has rejected his advances. The Inspector's return to decency is a favourite theme of Premchand's and, in view of what we know of the character, not so surprising as it may at first appear. His one conversation with Alarakkhi is a kind of précis of the dialectics of poverty, developed in similar though much longer dialogues in the novels and other stories. Premchand's affinity with the Russian novelists is clear here in the affecting way he brings out the simplicity and humility of the poor.

A Coward

The boy's name was Keshav, the girl's Prema. They went to the same college and they were in the same class. Keshav believed in new ways and was opposed to the old caste customs. Prema adhered to the old order and fully accepted the traditions. But all the same there was a strong attachment between them and the whole college was aware of it. Although he was a Brahman Keshav regarded marriage with this Banya girl as the culmination of his life. He didn't care a straw about his father and mother. Caste traditions he considerel a fraud. If anything embodied the truth for him it was Prema. But for Prema it was impossible to take one step in opposition to the dictates of caste and family.

One evening the two of them met in a secluded corner of Victoria Park and sat down on the grass facing one another. The strollers had gone off one by one but these two lingered on. They had got into a discussion it was impossible to end.

Keshav said angrily, 'All it means is that you don't care about me.'

Prema tried to calm him down. 'You're being unjust to me, Keshav. It's only that I don't know how I can bring it up at home without upsetting them. They're devoted to the old traditions. If they hear anything about a matter like this from me can't you imagine how distressed they'll be?'

'And aren't you a slave of those old traditions too then?' Keshav asked her sharply.

'No, I'm not,' Prema said, her eyes tender, 'but what my mother and father want is more important to me than anything.'

'And you yourself don't count at all?'

'If that's how you want to understand it.'

'I used to think those old ways were just for silly hypocrites but now it seems that educated girls like you knuckle under to them too. Since I'm ready to give up everything for you I expect the same thing from you.'

In silence Prema wondered what authority she had over her own life. She had no right to go in any way against the mother

136

and father who had created her from their own blood and reared her with love. To Keshav she said humbly, 'Can love be considered only in terms of husband and wife and not friendship? I think of love as an attachment of the soul.'

'You'll drive me crazy with your rationalizations,' Keshav said harshly. 'Just understand this—if I'm disappointed I can't go on living. I'm a materialist and it's not possible for me to be satisfied with some intangible happiness in the world of the imagination.'

He caught Prema's hand and tried to draw her toward him, but she broke away and said, 'I told you I'm not free. Don't ask me to do something I have no right to do.'

If she'd spoken harshly he would not have been so hurt. For an instant he restrained himself, then he stood up and said sadly, 'Just as you wish,' and slowly walked away. Prema, in tears, continued to sit there.

2

When after supper that night Prema lay down in her mother's room she could not sleep. Keshav had said things to her that shadowed her heart like reflections in unquiet waters, changing at every moment, and she could not calm them. How could she talk to her mother about such things? Embarrassment kept her silent. She thought, 'If I don't marry Keshav what's left for me in life?' While she thought about it over and over again her mind was made up about just one thing—if she did not marry Keshav she would marry no one.

Her mother said, 'Still not sleeping? I've told you so many times you ought to do a little work around the house. But you can never take any time off from your books. In a little while you'll be going to some strange house and who knows what sort of place it will be? If you don't get accustomed to doing housework, how are you going to manage?'

Naïvely Prema asked, 'Why will I be going to a strange house?'

Smiling, her mother said, 'For a girl it's the greatest calamity, daughter. After being sheltered at home, as soon as she's grown up off she goes to live with others. If she gets a good husband her days pass happily, otherwise she has to go through life weeping. It all depends on fate. But in our community there's no family that appeals to me. There's no proper regard for girls anywhere. But we have to stay within our caste. Who knows how long caste marriages are going to go on?'

Frightened Prema said, 'But here and there they're beginning to have marriages outside the caste.' She'd said it for the sake of talking but she trembled lest her mother might guess something.

Surprised, her mother asked, 'You don't mean among Hindus?' Then she answered herself. 'If this has happened in a few places, then what's come of it?'

Prema did not reply. She was afraid her mother had understood her meaning. She saw her future in that moment before her like a great dark tunnel opening its mouth to swallow her up. It was a long time before she could fall asleep.

3

When she got up early in the morning Prema was aware of a strange new courage. We all make important decisions on the spur of the moment as though some divine power impelled us toward them, and so it was with Prema. Until yesterday she'd considered her parents' ideas as unchallengeable, but facing the problem courage was born in her, much in the way a quiet breeze coming against a mountain sweeps over the summit in a violent gust. Prema thought, 'Agreed, this body is my mother's and father's but whatever my own self, my soul, is to get must be got in this body. To hesitate now would not only be unfitting, it would be fatal. Why sacrifice your life for false principle? If a marriage isn't founded on love then it's just a business bargain with the body. Could you give yourself without love?' And she rebelled against the idea that she could be maried off to somebody she had never seen.

After breakfast she had started to read when her father called her affectionately. 'Yesterday I went to see your principal and he had a lot of praise for you.'

'You're only saying that!'

'No, it's true.' Then he opened a drawer of his desk and took out a picture set in a velvet frame. He showed it to her and said, 'This boy came out first in the Civil Service examinations. You must have heard of him.

He had brought up the subject in such a way as not to give away his intention, but it was clear to Prema, she saw through it at once. Without looking at the picture she said, 'No, I don't know who he is.'

With feigned surprise her father said, 'What? You haven't even heard his name? His picture and an article about him are in today's paper.'

'Suppose they are?' Prema said. 'The examinations don't mean anything to me. I always assumed that people who took those exams must be terribly conceited. After all, what do they aim for except to lord it over their wretched, penniless brothers? —and pile up a fortune doing it. That's no great career to aspire to.'

The objection was spiteful, unjust. Her father had assumed that after his eulogy she would be interested. When he'd listened to her answer he said sharply, 'You talk as though money and power mean nothing to you.'

'That's right,' she said, 'they don't mean a thing to me. I look for self-sacrifice in a man. I know some boys who wouldn't accept that kind of position even if you tried to force it on them.'

'Well, I've learned something new today!' he said sarcastically. 'And still I see people swarming around trying to get the meanest little jobs—I'd just like to see the face of one of these fellows capable of such self-sacrifice. If I did I'd get down on my knees to him.'

Perhaps if she'd heard these words on another occasion Prema might have hung her head in shame. But this time, like a soldier with a dark tunnel behind him, there was no way for her to go except forward. Scarcely controlling her anger, her eyes full of indignation, she went to her room and from among several pictures of Keshav picked out the one she considered the worst and brought it back and set it down in front of her father. He wanted to give it no more than a casual glance, but at the first glimpse he was drawn to it. Keshav was tall and even though thin one recognized a strength and discipline about him; he was not particularly handsome but his face reflected such intelligence that one felt confidence in him.

While he looked at it her father said, 'Who is he?'

Prema, bowing her head, said hesitantly, 'He's in my class.'

'Is he of our community?'

Prema's face clouded over: her destiny was to be decided on the answer. She realized that it was useless to have brought out the picture. The firmness she had had for an instant weakened before this simple question. In a low voice she said, 'No, he's not, he's a Brahman.' And even while she was saying it, agitated she left the room as though the atmosphere there were suffocating her, and on the other side of the wall she began to cry.

Her father's anger was so great at first that he wanted to call her out again and tell her plainly it was impossible. He got as far as the door, but seeing Prema crying his anger softened. He was aware of what Prema felt for this boy and he believed in education for women but he intended to maintain the family traditions. He would have sacrificed all his property for a suitable bridegroom of his own caste. But outside the limits of his community he could not conceive of any bridegroom worthy or noble enough; he could not imagine any disgrace greater than going beyond them.

'From today on you'll stop going to college,' he said with a harsh tone. 'If education teaches you to disregard our traditions, then education is wicked.'

Timidly Prema said, 'But it's almost time for the examinations.'

'Forget about them.'

Then he went into his room and pondered a long time.

4

One day six months later Prema's father came home and called Vriddha, his wife, for a private talk.

'As far as I know,' he said, 'Keshav's a well-brought-up and brilliant boy. I'm afraid that Prema's grieving to the point where she might take her life. You and I have tried to explain and so have others but nobody has had the slightest effect on her. What are we going to do about it?'

Anxiously his wife said, 'Let her, but if she has her way how can you face the dishonour? How could I ever have borne a wicked girl like that!'

He frowned and said with a tone of reproach, 'I've heard that a thousand times. But just how long can we moan about this caste tradition business? You're mistaken if you think the bird's going to stay hopping at home once it's spread its wings. I've thought about the problem objectively and I've come to the conclusion that we're obliged to face the emergency. I can't watch Prema die in the name of caste rules. Let people laugh but the time is not far off when all these old restrictions will be broken. Even today there have been hundreds of marriages outside the caste limitations. If the aim of marriage is a happy life for a man and a woman together we can't oppose Prema.'

Vriddha was angry. 'If that's your intention then why ask me?' she said. 'But I say that I won't have anything to do with this marriage, and I'll never look at that girl's face again, I'll consider her as dead as our sons who died.'

'Well then, what else can you suggest?'

'What if we do let her marry this boy? He'll take his civil service examinations in two years and with what he has to offer it will be a great deal if he becomes a clerk in some office.'

'But what if Prema should kill herself?'

'Then let her—you've encouraged her, haven't you? If she doesn't care about us why should we blacken our name for her? Anyway, suicide's no game— it's only a threat. The heart's like a wild horse—until it's broken and bridled nobody can touch it. If her heart stays like that who's to say that she'll look after Keshav for a whole life-time? The way she's in love with him today, well, she can be in love with somebody else just as much tomorrow. And because of this you're ready to be disgraced?'

Her husband gave her a questioning look. 'And if tomorrow she should go and marry Keshav, then what will you do? Then how much of your honour will be left? Out of shyness or consideration for us she may not have done anything yet, but if she decides to be stubborn there's nothing you or I can do.'

It had never occurred to Vriddha that the problem could have such a dreadful ending. His meaning struck her with the violence of a bullet. She sat silent for a moment as though the shock had scattered her wits. Then, backing down, she said, 'What wild ideas you have! Until today I've never heard of a decent girl marrying according to her own wish.'

'You may not have heard of it but I have, I've seen it and it's entirely possible.'

'The day it happens will be my last!'

'But if it has to be this way isn't it preferable that we make the proper arrangements? If we're to be disgraced we may as well be efficient about it. Send for Keshav tomorrow and see what he has to say.'

5

Keshav's father lived from a government pension. By nature he was ill-tempered and miserly; he found satisfaction only in religious ostentation. He was totally without imagination and unable to respect the personal feelings of anybody else. At present he was still living in the same world in which he had passed his childhood and youth. The rising tide of progress he called runination and hoped to save at least his own family from it by any means available to him. Therefore when one day Prema's father came to him and broached the prospect of her marrying Keshav, old Panditji could not control himself. Staring through eyes dim with anger he said, 'Are you drunk? Whatever this relationship may be it's not marriage. It appears that you too have had your head turned by the new ideas.'

'I don't like this sort of connection either,' Prema's father said gently. 'My ideas about it are just the same as yours. But the thing is that, being helpless, I had to come to see you. You're aware too of how willful today's youngsters have become It's getting hard for us old-timers to defend our theories. I'm afraid that if these two become desperate they may take their lives.'

Old Panditji brought his foot down with a bang and shouted, 'What are you saying, Sir! Aren't you ashamed? We're Brahmans and even among Brahmans we're of high rank. No matter how low a Brahman may fall he can never be so degraded that he can countenance a marriage with a shop-keeping Banya's daughter. The day noble Brahmans run out of daughters we can discuss the problem. I say you have a fantastic nerve even to bring this matter up with me.'

He was every bit as furious as Prema's father was humble, and the latter, unable to bear the humiliation any longer, went off cursing his luck.

Just then Keshav returned from college. Panditji sent for him at once and said severely, 'I've heard that you're betrothed to some Banya girl. How far has this actually gone?'

Pretending ignorance, Keshav said, 'Who told you this?'

'Somebody. I'm asking you, is it true or not? If it's true and you've decided to go against your caste, then there's no more room for you in this house. You won't get one pice of my money. Whatever is in this house I've earned, and it's my right to give it to whomever I want. If you're guilty of this wicked conduct, you won't be permitted to put your foot inside my house.'

Keshav was familiar with his father's temper. He loved Prema and he intended to marry her in secret. His father wouldn't always be alive and he counted on his mother's affection; sustained by that love he felt that he was ready to suffer any hardships. But Keshav was like a faint-hearted soldier who loses his courage at the sight of a gun and turns back. Like any average young fellow he would argue his theories with a passion and demonstrate his devotion with his tongue. But to suffer for them was beyond his capacity. If he persisted and his father refused to weaken he didn't know where he would turn, his life would be ruined.

In a low voice he said, 'Whoever told you that is a complete liar and nothing else.'

Staring at him, Panditji said, 'So my information is entirely mistaken?'

'Yes, entirely mistaken.'

'Then you'll write a letter to that shopkeeper this very moment and remember that if there's any more of this gossip he can regard you as his greatest enemy. Enough, go.'

Keshav could say no more. He walked away but it seemed to him that his legs were utterly numb.

6

The next day Prema sent this letter to Keshav:

Dearest Keshav,

I was terribly upset when I heard about the rude and callous way your father treated mine. Perhaps he's threatened you too, in which case I wait anxiously to hear what your decision is. I'm ready to undergo any kind of hardship with you. I'm aware of your father's wealth but all I need is your love to content me. Come tonight and have dinner with us. My mother and father are both eager to meet you.

I'm caught up in the dream of when the two of us will be joined by that bond that cannot be broken, that remains strong no matter how great the difficulties.

Your Prema

By evening there had been no reply to this letter. Prema's mother asked over and over again, 'Isn't Keshav coming?' and her father kept his eyes glued on the door. By nine o'clock there was still no sign of Keshav nor any letter.

In Prema's mind all sorts of fears and hopes revolved. Perhaps Keshav had had no chance to write a letter, no chance to come today so that tomorrow he would surely come. She read over again the love letters he'd written her earlier. How steeped in love was every word, how much emotion, anxiety and acute desire! Then she remembered the words he'd said a hundred times and often he'd wept before her. It was impossible to despair with so many proofs, but all the same throughout the night she was tormented by anxiety.

Early in the morning Keshav's answer came. Prema took the letter with trembling hands and read it. The letter fell from her hands. It seemed to her that her blood had ceased to flow. He had written:

I'm in a terrible quandary about how to answer you. I've been desperate trying to figure out what to do and I've come to the conclusion that for the present it would be impossible for me to go against my father's orders. Don't think I'm a coward. I'm not being selfish either. But I don't have the strength to get over the obstacles facing me. Forget what I told you before. At that time I had no idea of how hard it was going to be.

Prema drew a long, painful breath, then she tore up the letter and threw it away. Her eyes filled with tears. She had never had the slightest expectation that the Keshav she had taken into her heart of hearts as her husband could be so cruel. It was as though until now she'd been watching a golden vision but on opening her eyes it had vanished completely. All her hope had disappeared and she was left in darkness.

'What did Keshav write?' her mother asked.

Prema looked at the floor and said, 'He's not feeling well.' What else was there to say? She could not have borne the shame of revealing Keshav's brutal disloyalty.

She spent the whole day working around the house, as though there were nothing wrong. She made dinner for everyone that evening and ate with them, then until quite late she played the harmonium and sang.

In the morning they found her lying dead in her room at a moment when the golden rays of dawn bestowed on her face the illusory splendour of life.

NOTE

Original title, '*Kāyar*', 'Coward' or 'Cowards'—ironic and ambiguous in either case. First published in 1933.

3 The World

A Servant of the People

The servant of the people said, 'There is only one way to redeem the nation and that is to treat the low as brothers, the outcastes as equals. In the world all are brothers: no one is high, no one is low.'

The world cheered. 'How sublime a vision, how compassionate a heart!'

His beautiful daughter Indira heard and was plunged into a sea of care.

The servant of the people embraced a young man of low caste.

The world said, 'He is an angel, an apostle, the pilot of the ship of state!'

Indira watched and her eyes began to glow.

The servant of the people brought the young man of low caste inside the temple into the presence of God and said, 'Our God is in poverty, in misfortune and in degradation.'

The world said, 'How pure in heart he is! How wise!'

Indira looked and smiled.

Indira went to the servant of the people and said, 'Respected father, I wish to marry Mohan.'

The servant of the people looked at her with loving eyes and asked, 'Who is Mohan?'

Indira said joyously, 'Mohan is the honest, brave and good young man you embraced and brought into the temple.'

The servant of the people looked at her with the eyes of doom and turned away.

The Road to Hell

I don't know when I fell asleep last night. For a long time I was reading in the 'Lives of the Holy Men'. What great souls they were, caring only for the love of God, completely intoxicated with it! Devotion like that can come only from strict spiritual discipline. Wouldn't I be capable of such discipline? What other joy is left for me in this life? There may be some who love jewels, God knows but as for me jewels are a torment to my eyes; some might give up their life for wealth but for me just to hear it mentioned starts a fever in me. Yesterday that crazy Sushila had a wonderful time helping me to make myself beautiful —no matter how much I tried to stop her, she wouldn't listen. Then what I'd most feared finally happened. For every minute I laughed with her I was to cry all the more. Is there any other woman in the world whose husband goes into a violent rage when he sees her? any other woman who hears her husband say, 'You're destroying my hopes for the other world and nothing else, the way you're made up makes that plain,' without wanting to take poison? Finally I went downstairs and began to read the 'Lives'. Now I shall worship only Lord Krishna in Brindaban, I shall show him my beauty, and when he sees it he will not grow angry for he will know what is in my heart.

2

Lord! How can I say what is in my heart? You dwell within me, you know all that is most secret in me. I wish I could tell him my desires, serve him as a wife should, move only at his bidding, I wish he might never feel the slightest pain from anything I do or anything concerning me. It's not his fault—whatever was in my stars has come to pass. But even knowing all this when I see him coming then my heart sinks, I grow deathly pale, I feel dizzy, I long not to see him, not even to have to talk to him. No one could ever feel so miserable even seeing his worst enemy. The

150

moment I see him coming my heart starts to pound. Whenever he goes away for a day or two it's as though a weight is lifted off my heart. I talk, I even laugh, a little happiness starts to come into my life, but at the first news that he's come back everything grows dark around me. I don't know why I should feel this way, but it seems to me that in an earlier birth we were enemies, and to take vengeance for this old hatred he married me—that former life is still living in our hearts. Otherwise why would he be angry whenever he sees me and why would the sight of him disgust me? No marriage is meant to be like this! How much happier I was at home. Perhaps I might have stayed there and been happy. But because of the accursed custom it's felt to be inevitable that every unfortunate girl must be tied to the neck of some man or other. They don't know how many girls weep because of that custom, how many tender hearts shaken with longings are trampled under its foot. For a girl a husband is the source of the sweetest imaginings—whatever is best in man, most sublime and beautiful, its living image rises up and appears before one as soon as the word is mentioned. But what is that word for me? A spear to stab the heart, a mote in the eye, an arrow of bitterness piercing the breast. I always see Sushila laughing. She never complains about being poor. She has no jewels, no clothes, she lives in a tiny rented house, she does all the housework with her own hands, but all the same I've never seen her cry. If I had my way, I'd exchange my wealth for whatever she has today. When she sees her husband coming home smiling, all the shabbiness of her life disappears, her heart is a yard wide with joy. In his embrace there's a happiness I'd sacrifice the wealth of the three worlds for.

3

Today I couldn't control myself and I asked him, 'Why did you marry me?' The question's been in my mind for months but I'd held it back. The cup spilled over today. When he heard the question he looked confused and irritated, shrugged and said, 'To look after the house, to take the job of managing it, not for anything else. Did you think it was to have a good time?' So without a housekeeper the place would have seemed like a deserted house to you? Servants would have wasted the household money, and if something fell on the floor it would have stayed there, no one would bother to pick it up. So it seemed that I was brought to this house to keep it in order! I was supposed to maintain it and be grateful to him that everything in it belonged to me. The money's the big thing and I'm just here to look after it. A house like this ought to be set on fire at once! Until now, without knowing it, I've been the chief housekeeper, not of course as good a one as he thought I should be but according to my own capacity surely. I swear that from today on I won't touch anything under any circumstances. I know this: no man marries to get himself a house-keeper and he said what he said out of spite. But Sushila spoke true, without a wife his house would have been as empty for him as a cage without a bird. This is the fate of us women!

4

I don't know why he's so suspicious of me. From the time fate brought me to this house I've seen him glare at me suspiciously. Why? If I just put a flower in my hair he begins to scowl. I never go anywhere, never talk to anybody, and still he's suspic-ious! It's intolerable to be treated so shabbily. As though I didn't have any pride of my own. Why does he think I'm so vile?— isn't he ashamed of being suspicious of me? If a one-eyed man sees anybody laugh he thinks people are laughing at him. May-be he's got the notion that I'm mocking him. Perhaps this is what happens to your mind when you try to do something be-yond your powers. A beggar sitting on a king's throne can't sleep in peace; one enemy after another seems to appear on every side. I think this must be the state of any old man who marries.

Today I was going out to see the temple decorations for Krishna's birthday—Sushila had told me about it. Any man of average intelligence can understand that going out dressed like some old peasant woman is a way of making a fool of yourself, but suddenly he popped up from I don't know where and frown-ing at me said, 'What are you getting dressed up for?'

I told him I was just going out for a little to see the celebrations at the temple. As soon as he heard this he frowned and said,

'There's no need for you to go. For a woman who can't serve her husband properly it's not a virtue, it's a sin to go to the temple. You want to get away from me—I know women's tricks.'

I got so angry that I couldn't say a thing. I went right away to change my clothes and swore I'd never go to the temple again. Is there no limit to his distrust? I don't know what I was thinking that held me back, I ought to have answered him that I'd leave the house that instant without being afraid of anything he might do about it.

He's surprised that I'm always sad and depressed, in his heart he feels I'm ungrateful. Maybe he thinks he conferred a great privilege on me by marrying me. I was supposed to be over-whelmed with joy at becoming the mistress of such vast property and wealth, I was expected to sing his praises on every mountain-top. But I don't do anything of the sort, instead I mope around with a long face. Still, there are times when I actually feel sorry for the poor man. He doesn't understand that there's something in a woman's life which can't be lost without heaven itself turn-ing into hell.

5

He's been sick for three days. The doctor says it's pneumonia and there's no hope of saving him. But somehow I don't feel any dis-tress. I didn't used to be so hard-hearted, I don't know where my kindness has gone. Whenever I saw a sick person my heart used to grow faint with pity; I could never bear to hear anyone cry. But now for three days I've been listening to him groaning on his bed in the next room and I haven't gone once to see him. How could I possibly even shed a tear? It seems to me as though there's no relationship between us at all. I don't care if anybody calls me a monster or a bitch, but I haven't the slightest hesitation in saying that I feel a kind of spiteful pleasure in his illness. He's kept me here in a prison—I won't give it the pure name of marriage, it's just been a prison. I'm not so big-hearted that I can revere some-one who's kept me a prisoner or that I'll kiss the feet that kicked me. It occurred to me that God is punishing him for his wicked-ness. A woman doesn't become a man's wife just by being chained to him. For a marriage to be a marriage the heart has to be stirred at least once by love.

I can hear my husband cursing me over and over again while he lies in his room, blaming me entirely for his illness, but I don't care at all. Whoever wants his property and his money can take it, it's of no use to me.

6

I've been a widow now for three months, at least that's what people say. Anyone who wants to can say it, but I consider myself the very same as before. I didn't break my wedding bangles— why should I? Even before I didn't streak the part in my hair with cinnabar like other married women and I don't do it now. The grown-up son from the first marriage saw to the old man's funeral rites, I stayed out of it. Everyone in the house has his own way of criticizing me. If anybody sees me with a flower in my hair they screw up their faces, if they see me wearing jewelry they glare, but it doesn't bother me in the least. To irk them I wear bright saris and lots of jewels and I don't feel the slightest sorrow. I've been freed from captivity. A few days ago I went to Sushila's house. It's a tiny house, there's nothing fancy and no furniture, there are not even charpoys, but how happily Sushila lives in it. When I see her joy all kinds of imaginings begin to rise in my heart—why should I call them nasty when I don't really think they are? How much pleasure there is in their lives, their eyes are always smiling, tender smiles play on their lips, a stream of love seems to flow in their words. With this happiness—no matter how momentary it may be—their lives are a success, no one can mistake it, the memory of it suffices for all time, it's a plectrum to stir the heart forever with sweet music.

One day I said to Sushila, 'If your husband went somewhere far away would you just weep and die?'

Sushila answered gravely, 'No, sister, I wouldn't die. His memory would always be fresh, even if he spent years away.'

That is the love I want, my heart goes on trembling for the awakening of that music, I also want such memories as will make

my heart vibrate always, an intoxication that will engulf me fore-
ever.

7

I sobbed all through the night. I don't know why my heart
was so full. My life seemed to lie spread before me like a desert
where there was nothing green but a few scrubby weeds. The
whole house was ready to gobble me up, I was becoming so
jumpy I couldn't keep still. These days I feel no impulse to look
at the religious books, I have no wish to go walking anywhere.
I don't know myself what I want. Yet what I don't know my body
knows, I am the living embodiment of my desires, everyone of
my limbs cries out with the anguish inside me.

The restlessness of my mind has reached that final stage where
I feel neither shame nor fear of people's contempt. For the greedy,
selfish father and mother who threw me into the pit, for the heart-
less creature who hypocritically took the marriage vows with me,
for all of them I feel an endless hatred, I want to see them shamed.
I want to disgrace them by disgracing myself. By giving up my
life I want to see them die. My womanliness has vanished. In
my heart a wild fire has begun to blaze.

Everyone in the house was sleeping. Silently I went downstairs,
opened the door and left the house, as someone overcome by the
heat might go out and run toward any open place. I'd been
suffocating in that house.

On the road the shops were closed, all was still. Suddenly an
old woman appeared, startling me as though she'd been a ghost.
She came close to me and looked me up and down and said,
'What road are you looking for?'

Bitterly I said, 'The road to death.'

The old woman said, 'In your fate it is wrtten that your life
holds many joys in store. The dark night is over, the light of dawn
is in the skies.'

Laughing, I said, 'Are your eyes so sharp that even in the dark
you can read the writing of the fates?'

'I don't read with my eyes, child,' the old woman said, 'I read
with the mind—I haven't grown old without learning something.

Your evil days are past and the good ones are coming. Don't laugh, child, I've been doing this work for a long time. Because of this old woman many a girl who was about to throw herself into the river sleeps on a bed of flowers, and some who were ready to drink a cup of poison are drinking milk. And so I come out late of nights to see if by my help some unfortunate girl may be saved. I ask nothing in return—I have everything I need from the Lord —my desire is only to do some kindness to others in so far as I can—money for those who want money, children for those who want children, what else shall I say? I can recite the spell which will fulfill anyone's desires.'

I said, 'I want neither wealth nor children. What I want is not in your power to give.'

She laughed. 'Daughter, I know what you want, you want that thing which can make a heaven of this earth and which gives greater bliss than the blessings of the gods, the flower of heaven, the new moon, the rarest thing. But in my spells is the power to provide even this destiny. You thirst for love, and I can set you on a ship to bear you over the sea of love, tossed about by the very waves of love.'

Becoming curious, I asked, 'Mother, where is your house?'

'Very close, daughter, come along and I'll bring you there— trust me.'

She seemed to me to be a goddess come down from heaven. I went along with her.

8

Alas, that old woman I took for a goddess was a witch from hell. I looked for nectar and found poison; I longed for a chaste love and I fell into a foul, poisonous ditch. I did not find what was not to be found. I desired a bliss like Sushila's, not the sensual wallowing of a whore. But once in your life a step's been taken on the wrong road it's hard to come back on the right one.

Still, the responsibility for my ruin is not on my head but on my mother and father and that old man who wanted to be my husband. I would not write these lines except with the idea that people who read this history of my soul may have their eyes opened. I say again, for your daughters do not look for wealth, property or prestige, look only for a husband. If you can't find the right one then let your daughter remain a spinster or poison her, strangle her, but don't marry her to an ugly old man. A woman can bear the most agonizing grief, the greatest afflictions, anything, but she cannot bear the trampling down of the longings of her youth.

As for me, there is no hope left in this life. I would not exchange even this vile existence for the one I've left behind.

NOTE

Original title, '*Narak kā Mārg*', 'The Path of Hell'. First published in 1925.

My Big Brother

My big brother was five years older than me but only three grades ahead. He'd begun his studies at the same age I had but he didn't like the idea of moving hastily in an important matter like education. He wanted to lay a firm foundation for that great edifice, so he took two years to do one year's work; sometimes he even took three. If the foundation weren't well-made, how could the edifice endure?

I was the younger, he the elder—I was nine, he was fourteen. He had full right by seniority to supervise and instruct me. And I was expected to accept every order of his as law.

By nature he was very studious. He was always sitting with a book open. And perhaps to rest his brain he would sometimes draw pictures of birds, dogs and cats in the margin of his notebook. Occasionally he would write a name, a word or a sentence ten or twenty times. He might copy a couplet out several times in beautiful letters or create new words which made no rhyme or reason. Once, for example, I saw the following: Special Amina brothers and brothers, in reality brother-brother, Radheshyam, Mr Radheshyam, for one hour. Following this was the sketch of a man's face. I tried very hard to make some sense out of this rigmarole but I didn't succeed and I didn't dare ask him. He was in the ninth grade, I was in the sixth. To understand his creation was beyond my powers.

I wasn't really very keen about studying. To pick up a book and sit with it for an hour was a tremendous effort. As soon as I found a chance I'd leave the hostel and go to the field and play marbles or fly paper kites or sometimes just meet a chum—what could be more fun? Sometimes we'd climb on to the courtyard walls and jump down or straddle the gate and ride it back and forth enjoying it as though it were an automobile. But as soon as I came back into the room and saw my brother's scowling face I was petrified. His first question would be, 'Where were you?' Always this question, always asked in the same tone and the only answer I had was silence. I don't know why I couldn't manage to say that I'd just been outside playing. My silence was an acknowledgement of guilt and my brother's only remedy for this was to greet me with indignant words.

'If you study English this way you'll be studying your whole life and you won't get one word right! Studying English is no laughing matter that anyone who wants to can learn. Otherwise everybody and his cousin would be regular experts in English. You've got to wear out your eyes morning and night and use every ounce of energy, then maybe you'll master the subject. And even then it's just to say you have a smattering of it. Even great scholars can't write proper English, to say nothing of being able to speak it. And I ask you, how much of a blockhead are you that you can't learn a lesson from looking at me? You've seen with your own eyes how much I grind, and if you haven't seen it, there's something wrong with your eyes and with your wits as well. No matter how many shows and carnivals there may be have you ever seen me going to watch them? Every day there are cricket and hockey matches but I don't go near them. I keep on studying all the time, and even so it takes me two years or even three for one grade. So how do you expect to pass when you waste your time playing like this? If it takes me two or even three years, you'll fritter your whole life away studying in one grade. If you waste your time like this, it would be better if you just went home and played stick-ball to your heart's content. Why waste our dad's hard-earned money?'

Hearing a dressing-down like this I'd start to cry. What could I answer? I was guilty but who could endure a scolding like that? My brother was an expert in the art of giving advice. He'd say such sarcastic words, overwhelm me with such good counsel that my spirits would collapse, my courage disappear. I couldn't find in myself the power to toil so desperately, and in despair for a little while I'd think, 'Why *don't* I run away from school and go back home? Why should I spoil my life fiddling with work that's beyond my capacity?' I was willing to remain a fool, but I just got dizzy from so much work. But after an hour or two the cloud of despair would dissipate and I'd resolve to study with all my might. I'd draw up a schedule on the spot. How could I start work without first making an outline, working out a plan? In my time-table the heading of play was entirely absent. Get up at the crack

159

of dawn, wash hands and face at six, eat a snack, sit down and study. From six to eight English, eight to nine arithmetic, nine to nine-thirty history, then mealtime and afterwards off to school. A half hour's rest at 3.30 when I got back from school, geography from four to five, grammar from five to six, then a half hour's walk in front of the hostel, 6.30 to seven English composition, then supper, translation from eight to nine, Hindi from nine to ten, from ten to eleven miscellaneous, then to bed.

But it's one thing to draw up a schedule, another to follow it. It began to be neglected from the very first day. The inviting green expanse of the playground, the balmy winds, the commotion on the football field, the exciting stratagems of prisoner's-base, the speed and flurries of volley ball would all draw me mysteriously and irresistibly. As soon as I was there I forgot everything: the life-destroying schedule, the books that strained your eyes—I couldn't remember them at all. And then my big brother would have an occasion for sermons and scoldings. I would stay well out of his way, try to keep out of his sight, come into the room on tiptoe so he wouldn't know. But if he spotted me I'd just about die. It seemed that a naked sword was always swinging over my head. But just as in the midst of death and catastrophe a man may remain caught in the snares of illusion, so I, though I suffered reproaches and threats, could not renounce fun and games.

2

The yearly exams came round: my brother failed, I passed and was first in my class. Only two years difference were left between him and me. It occurred to me to taunt him. 'What was the good of all your horrible self-punishment? Look at me, I went on playing and having a good time and I'm at the head of my class.' But he was so sad and depressed that I felt genuinely sorry for him and it seemed shameful to me to pour salt on his wounds. But now I could be a little proud of myself and indeed my ego expanded. My brother's sway over me was over. I began to take part freely in the games, my spirits were running high. If he gave me another sermon, then I'd say straight out, 'With all your grinding what kind of marks did you get? Playing and having fun I ended up first in my class.' Although I didn't have the courage to say anything so outrageous it was plain from my behaviour that my brother's power over me was gone. He guessed it—his intuition was sharp and one day when I'd spent the whole morning playing stick-ball and came back exactly at meal time, he said, with all the air of pulling out a sword to rush at me :

'I see you've passed this year and you're first in your class, and you've got stuck up about it. But my dear brother, even great men live to regret their pride, and who are you compared to them? You must have read about what happened to Ravan. Didn't you learn anything from his story or did you just read it without paying any attention? Just to pass an exam isn't anything, the real thing is to develop your mind. Understand the significance of what you read. Ravan was master of the earth. Such kings arc called 'Rulers of the World'. These days the extent of the British Empire is vast, but their kings can't be called 'Rulers of the World'—many countries in the world don't accept British rule, they're completely independent. But Ravan was a Ruler of the World, all the kings of the earth paid taxes to him. Great divinities were his slaves, even the gods of fire and water. But what happened to him in the end? Pride completely finished him off, destroying even his name. There wasn't anybody left to perform all his funeral rites properly. A man can commit any sin he wants but he'd better not be proud, nor give himself airs. When he turns proud he loses both this world and the next. You must have read about what happened to Satan too. He was so proud that he thought there was no truer devotee of God than himself. Finally it came about that he got shoved out of heaven into hell. Once the king of Turkey became very stuck-up too; he died begging for alms. You've just been promoted one grade and your head's turned by it—you've gone way up in the world! Understand this, you didn't pass through your own efforts but just stumbled on it by luck, like a blind man who catches hold of a quail. But you can catch a quail only once like that, no more. Sometimes in stick-ball too a lucky shot in the dark hits the goal, but nobody gets to be a good player from it, the kind who never misses a shot.

'Don't assume that because I failed I'm stupid and you're smart. When you reach my class you'll sweat right through your teeth when you have to bite into algebra and geometry and study English history—it's not easy to memorize these kings' names. There were eight Henrys—do you think it's easy to remember all the things that happened in each Henry's time? If you write Henry the Eighth instead of Henry the Seventh you get a zero. A complete flunk! You won't get a zero, not even zero. What kind of idea do you have about it anyway? There were dozens of Jameses, dozens of Williams and scores of Charleses! You get dizzy with them, your mind's in a whirl. Those poor fellows didn't have names enough to go around. After every name they have to put second, third, fourth and fifth. If anybody'd asked me I could have reeled off thousands of names. And as for geometry, well, God help you! If you write *a c b* instead of *a b c* your whole answer is marked wrong. Nobody ever asks those hard-hearted examiners what *is* the difference, after all, between *a b c* and *a c b* or why they waste their time torturing the students with it. Does it make any difference if you eat lentils, boiled rice and bread or boiled rice, lentils and bread? But what do those examiners care? They see only what they've written in their books. They expect us to learn it word for word. And this kind of parroting they call teaching! And in the long run what's the point of learning all this nonsense? If you bring this perpendicular line down on that line it will be twice the base line. I ask you, what's the point of that? If it isn't twice as long it's four times as long or half as long, what the devil do I care? But you've got to pass so you've got to memorize all this garbage.

'They say, "Write an essay on punctuality no less than four pages long". So now you open up your notebook in front of you, take your pen and curse the whole business. Who doesn't know that punctuality's a very good thing? Man's life is organized according to it, others love him for it and his business prospers from it. How can you write four pages on something so trifling? Do I need four pages for what I can describe in one sentence? So I consider it stupidity. It's not economizing time, it's wasting it to cram it with such nonsense. We want a man to say what he has to say quickly and then get moving. But no, you've got to drag it out to four pages, whatever you write, and they're foolscap pages too. If this isn't an outrage on the students, what is it? It's a contradiction for them to ask us to write concisely. Write a concise essay on punctuality in no less than four pages. All right! If four pages is concise then maybe otherwise they'd ask us to write one or two hundred pages. Run fast and walk slow at the same time. Is that all mixed up or isn't it? We students can understand that much but those teachers don't have the sense—and despite that they claim they're teachers. When you get into my class, old man, then you'll really take a beating, and then you'll find out what's what. Just because you got a first division this time you're all puffed up—so pay attention to what I say. What if I failed, I'm still older than you, I have more experience of the world. Take what I say to heart or you'll be sorry.'

It was almost time for school, otherwise I don't know when this medley of sermons would have ended. I didn't have much appetite that day. If I got a scolding like this when I passed, maybe if I'd failed I would have had to pay with my life. My brother's terrible description of studying in the ninth grade really scared me. I'm surprised I didn't run away from school and go home. But even a scolding like this didn't change my distaste for books one bit. I didn't miss one chance to play. I also studied, but much less. Well, anyway, just enough to complete each day's assignment and not be disgraced in class. But the confidence I'd gained in myself disappeared and then I began to lead a life like a thief's.

3

Then it was the yearly exams again and it so happened that once more I passed and my brother failed again. I hadn't done much work; but somehow or other I was in the first division. I myself was astonished. My brother had just about killed himself with work, memorizing every word in the course, studying till ten at night and starting again at four in the morning, and from six until 9.30 before going to school. He'd grown pale. But the poor fellow failed again and I felt sorry for him. When he heard the results he broke down and cried, and so did I. My pleasure in passing was cut by half. If I'd failed my brother couldn't have felt so bad. But who can escape his fate?

There was only one grade left between my brother and me. The insidious thought crossed my mind that if he failed just once more then I'd be at the same level as him and then what grounds would he have for lecturing me? But I violently rejected this unworthy idea. After all, he'd scolded me only with the intention of helping me. At the time it was really obnoxious, but maybe it was only as a result of his advice that I'd passed so easily and with such good marks.

Now my brother had become much gentler toward me. Several times when he found occasion to scold me he did it without losing his temper. Perhaps he himself was beginning to understand that he no longer had the right to tell me off or at least not so much as before. My independence grew. I began to take unfair advantage of his toleration, I half started to imagine that I'd pass next time whether I studied or not, my luck was high. As a result, the little I'd studied before because of my brother, even that ceased. I found a new pleasure in flying kites and now I spent all my time at the sport. Still, I minded my manners with my brother and concealed my kite-flying from him. In preparation for the kite tournament I was secretly busy solving such problems as how best to secure the string and how to apply the paste mixed with ground glass in it to cut the other fellows' kites off their strings. I didn't want to let my brother suspect that my respect for him had in any way diminished.

One day, far from the hostel, I was running along like mad trying to grab hold of a kite. My eyes were on the heavens and that high-flying traveller in the skies that glided smoothly down like some soul emerging from paradise free of worldly attachments to be incarnated in a new life. A whole army of boys came racing out to welcome it with long, thick bamboo rods. Nobody was aware who was in front or in back of him. It was as though every one of them was flying along with that kite in the sky where everything is level, without cars or trams or trains.

Suddenly I collided with my brother, who was probably coming back from the market. He grabbed my hand and said angrily, 'Aren't you ashamed to be running with these ragamuffins after a one-penny kite? Have you forgotten that you're not in a low grade any more? You're in the eighth now, one behind me. A man's got to have some regard for his position, after all. There was a time when by passing the eighth grade people became assistant revenue collectors. I know a whole lot of men who finished only the middle grades and today are first degree deputy magistrates or superintendents. How many eighth-grade graduates today are our leaders and newspaper editors? Great scholars work under their supervision but when you get into this same eighth grade you run around with hoodlums!

'I'm sorry to see you have so little sense. You're smart, there's no doubt of that, but what use is it if it destroys your self-respect? You must have assumed, "I'm just one grade behind my brother so now he doesn't have any right to say anything to me". But you're mistaken. I'm five years older than you and even if you come into my grade today—and the examiners being what they are there's no doubt that next year you'll be on an equal footing with me and maybe a year later you'll even get ahead of me— but that difference of five years between us not even God—to say nothing of you—can remove. I'm five years older than you and I always will be. The experience I have of life and the world you can never catch up with even if you get an M.A. and a D. Litt. and even a Ph. D. Understanding doesn't come from reading books. Our mother never passed any grade and Dad probably never went beyond the fifth, but even if we studied the wisdom of the whole world mother and father would always have the right to explain to us and to correct us. Not just because they're our parents but because they'll always have more experience of the world. Maybe they don't know what kind of government they've got in America or how many wives Henry the Eighth had or how many constellations there are in the sky, but there are a thousand things they know more about than you or me. God forbid, but if I should fall sick today then you'd be in a pickle. You wouldn't be able to think of anything except sending a telegram to Dad. But in your place *he* wouldn't send anybody a telegram or get upset or be all flustered. First of all he'd diagnose the disease himself and try the remedy; then if it didn't work he'd call some doctor. And sickness is a serious matter. But you and I don't even know how to make our allowance last through the month. We spend what father sends us and then we're penniless again. We cut our breakfast, we have to hide from the barber and washerman. But as much as you and I spend today, Dad's maintained himself honourably and in good reputation the greater part of his life and brought up a family with seven children on half of it. Just look at our headmaster. Does he have an M.A. or doesn't he? And not from here either, but from Oxford. He gets a thousand rupees, but who runs his house? His old mother. There his degrees are useless. He used to manage the house himself, but he couldn't make both ends meet, he had to borrow. But since his mother has taken over it's as though Lakshmi had come into his house. So brother, don't be so proud of having almost caught up with me and being independent now. I'll see that you don't go off the track. If you don't mind, then' (showing me his fist) 'I can use this too. I know you don't like hearing all this.'

I was thoroughly shamed by this new approach of his. I had truly come to know my own insignificance and a new respect for my brother was born in my heart. With tears in my eyes, I said, 'No, no, what you say is completely true and you have the right to say it.'

My brother embraced me and said, 'I don't forbid you to fly kites. I'd like to too. But what can I do? If I go off the track myself then how can I watch out for you? That's my responsibility.'

Just then by chance a kite that had been cut loose passed over us with its string dangling down. A crowd of boys were chasing after it. My brother is very tall and leaping up he caught hold of the string and ran at top speed towards the hostel and I ran close behind him.

NOTE

Original title, *'Bare Bāhi Sāhab'*, first published 1934. The Hindi title cannot be translated by a single phrase. 'Sahab' is approximately equivalent to 'sir', so the sense is something like 'my respected big brother'. In the story the younger brother always addresses the elder as 'Bhai Sahab' and refers to him this way. Furthermore, he uses the formal style to address him (French 'vous') while the elder always addresses the narrator with the informal second person.

Intoxication

Ishwari's father was a rich landowner, mine an impecunious clerk who had no wealth beyond his working wages. There was a continual debate between us. I was forever attacking the zamindars, calling them jungle beasts, blood-sucking leeches, the flowering parasitic growth at the top of the trees. He took the side of the zamindars but of course his position was somewhat weak because he could present no real argument in their defense. It's a weak argument to say that not all men are equal, that there'd always been rich and poor and there always would be. It was difficult to prove the justness of such a system by humanitarian or moral principles. In the heat of these discussions I would often become angry and sarcastic, but even when he was defeated Ishwari would go on smiling. I never saw him lose his temper. Perhaps it was because he understood the weakness of his position. He certainly had his share of the harshness and arrogance of the rich. He never addressed a decent word to the servants. If they were the least bit late in making the bed, if the milk was by chance too hot or too cold, if his bicycle hadn't been properly cleaned, then he was beside himself. He wouldn't tolerate the least laziness or insolence. But with his friends, and particularly with me, he was always exceptionally cordial and sympathetic. Perhaps if I'd been in his place the same harshness might have sprung up in me as well, for my love of the people was not the result of conviction but rather of my personal circumstances. But perhaps if he'd been in my shoes he would have kept up the same high style, for by nature he was fond of luxury and good things.

I had decided not to go home for the coming Dussehra holidays. I didn't have the fare nor did I want to impose the burden for it on my parents—I knew that what they were giving me already was far beyond their resources. And on top of that I was concerned about exams. I had a lot left to study and who can do any studying when he goes home? But then I didn't want to stay on alone like a ghost in the hostel either, so when Ishwari invited me home with him I accepted without any urging. I could prepare for exams

167

very well with Ishwari since he was not only rich but also bright and industrious.

When he invited me he also said, 'But pay attention to one thing, old man. If you attack the zamindars in my house there'll be a row and my folks won't like it. They rule over their tenants with the claim that God created those tenants just to serve them. And the tenants feel the same way—if they ever got it into their heads that there's no basic difference between zamindars and themselves, that would be the end of the zamindars.'

I said, 'Do you expect me to go there and not be myself?'

'Yes, that's just what I expect.'

'You'll be disappointed!'

Ishwari didn't answer. Perhaps he was leaving it to my discretion and he was right to. If he'd insisted then I might have been stubborn about it.

2

Second class? Why, I'd never even travelled inter-class before and now I had the good luck to be travelling in second. The train arrived at nine at night but in our eagerness we went to the station as soon as it was dark. After wandering around here and there for a while we went and had a meal in the refreshment room. After one look at my clothes and manners it didn't take the stewards long to figure out who was the master and who the hanger-on, but I don't know why I was annoyed by their impudence. The money came out of Ishwari's pocket—probably he gave them more in tips than my father earned in a month. When we left he alone tipped them—eight annas. Nevertheless I expected from them the same attentiveness and politeness they gave to him. Why should they all run when he gave them an order and show less alacrity when I asked for something? I didn't enjoy my supper. This discrimination completely occupied my thoughts.

The train arrived and we got in. The stewards bowed farewell to Ishwari; they didn't so much as look at me.

'How well-mannered they all are,' Ishwari said. 'Not one of our servants has such good manners.'

Sourly I observed, 'If you treated your servants to eight-anna tips like these you'd find them better-mannered.'

'Do you mean you think they're polite just because they're expecting a tip?'

'Of course not! Fine manners and etiquette are doubtless in their blood.'

The train, a mail express, started. After leaving Prayag station it stopped first at Pratapgarh. A man opened the door of our compartment. I let out a yell at once: 'This is second class!' and afterwards I shouted it in English too.

The traveller came into the compartment and looking at me with singular contempt said, 'Yes, your humble servant is perfectly aware of that,' and sat down on a lower berth. I can't describe how embarrassed I was.

By morning we reached Moradabad. At the station several people were waiting to welcome us. Two of them were gentlemen of the household, five of them servants. The latter picked up our luggage and the two gentlemen walked behind. One was a Muslim named Riyasat Ali, the other a Brahman named Ramharakh. Both of them looked at me as though I struck them as outlandish. 'You're a crow,' those looks seemed to say, 'what are you doing with the swans?'

Riyasat Ali asked Ishwari, 'Is this other young gentleman studying with you?'

'Yes,' Ishwari said, 'we study together and we live together as well. I might add that it's only because of him that I stay on in Allahabad, otherwise I would have moved on to Lucknow long ago. This time I've dragged him along with me. Several telegrams came from his home but I persuaded him to refuse them. The last telegram was marked urgent at four annas per word but I got him to turn that one down too.'

Both gentlemen stared at me in astonishment. They appeared to be trying to look impressed.

In a slightly suspicious tone Riyasat Ali said, 'But he seems to be very plainly dressed.'

Ishwari dispelled his doubts. 'He's a follower of Mahatma Gandhi, sir! He won't wear anything except the native homespun cotton. He's burned all his former clothes. Actually, he's practically a maharaja—he has an income of 250,000 a year, but to look at him you'd think he'd been picked up in some orphanage.'

Ramharakh said, 'One sees very few rich people with natures like that! No one would ever guess.'

'If you'd ever seen the Maharaja of Changli,' Riyasat Ali corroborated, 'you would have swallowed your teeth. He used to go wandering around the market dressed in a coarse cotton vest and wearing village-made shoes. They say that once he was snapped up to work in a labour gang—and he was the man who founded a college with a million rupees.'

I found all this very embarrassing, and I don't know why the whole lie didn't simply strike me as ridiculous. It was as though with each sentence I was coming closer and closer to this imaginary glory.

I'm not a particularly good horseman. To be sure, when I was a child I'd several times ridden on old cart horses. I now saw that two smartly fitted out horses were standing ready for us. I was desperate. I mounted, trembling, but I managed to hide my fear. I steered the horse in back of Ishwari. It was lucky that he didn't gallop his, otherwise I might have gone back with broken arms and legs. It's possible he knew just how much of an equestrian I was.

3

Ishwari's house was a regular castle if it was anything. A gate like a mosque's, watchmen stationed at the entrance, servants beyond the counting, and an elephant tied up in the courtyard. Ishwari introduced me to his father and uncles and all the rest of his family with the same exaggerated stories. I can't tell you what a romance he invented. Not only the servants but all the people of the family as well regarded me with respect. They were landed gentry with an income of thousands, and yet the sort of people who regarded even a police constable as an officer. Several gentlemen there even called me 'Excellency'.

When we were finally alone I said to Ishwari, 'Old man, you're being a regular devil—why are you trying to get me into a jam?'

With a forced smile Ishwari said, 'The trick was necessary in front of those idiots, otherwise they wouldn't have had a decent word for you.'

In a short while the barber came to massage our feet: the young lords had just come from the station, they must be tired. Pointing to me Ishwari said, 'First massage the prince's feet.'

I was lying down on the charpoy. It had hardly ever happened to me in my whole life before to have someone massage my feet. I'd mocked Ishwari in the past for the follies of the rich, the fatuity of the gentry and the oppression of the bigshots and I don't know what all else, and today I was caught right in the middle of it posing as a rich gentleman's offspring.

By this time it was ten o'clock. The household followed the old leisurely and courtly ways; the light of the new order had managed to reach only the highest places. The call for dinner came from the women's part of the house. We went to bathe. I had always washed out my own dhoti, but now I followed Ishwari's example and left it there. I would have been ashamed to wash my dhoti with my own hands. We went in to dine. In the hostel we sat down at the table with our shoes on but here we had to have our feet washed. A servant was standing there with water. Ishwari stretched out his foot and the servant washed it. I also stretched out my foot and the servant washed it too. I have no idea where my earlier notions had flown to.

4

I had thought that out here in the country I'd be able to concentrate on my studies in earnest. But I spent the whole day in walks and excursions. We'd drift on the river in a houseboat or fish or hunt birds or go to watch the village wrestling matches or get together for a game of chess. Ishwari would have a lot of eggs brought and make omelettes on the English stove in his room. There was always a crowd of servants gathered round. No need to stir hand or foot, you just had to stir your tongue. If you sat down to bathe they were on the spot to wash you, if you lay down there were two to keep the fan going.

Mahatma Gandhi's rich young disciple had become famous. His renown spread through the whole estate. They made sure there wasn't the slightest delay in serving his breakfast lest the 'prince' be angry, and the bed was ready right on time when he wanted to go to sleep. I was even touchier than Ishwari, or felt obliged to become so. Ishwari made his own bed but the prince, as a guest—well, how could he make his bed with his own hands? It was beneath his dignity.

One day the following incident actually took place. Ishwari was in the women's part of the house where he had probably tarried to talk with his mother. Ten o'clock struck. I was so sleepy I could hardly keep my eyes open. But how could I set out the bedding? Not a prince like me! At around 11.30 a bearer came in, a rather over-familiar fellow. In his various household chores he'd forgotten to make my bed and remembering only now he came on the run. I gave him a tongue-lashing he wasn't apt to forget.

Hearing my tirade, Ishwari came along and said, 'You've done well. All these lazy fellows deserve a scolding like that.'

It happened that one day Ishwari had gone somewhere to a party. When evening came the lamp was not lit. It was on the table and there were matches there too, but Ishwari never lit the lamp so how was the prince to light it? I was exasperated. The newspaper had been set out; I was longing to read it but the lamp wasn't lit! By chance Riyasat Ali happened to come in just then. I blew up and gave him such a scolding that the poor fellow was speechless. 'You people don't bother at all to see that the lamp is lit!' I said. 'I don't know how such lazy wretches are tolerated here. They wouldn't be kept on an hour in my house.' With trembling hands Riyasat Ali lit the lamp.

There was a Thakur who often used to come to Ishwari's house. He was a very enterprising fellow and a devoted follower of Gandhi. Believing me to be a disciple of Gandhiji he was very deferential to me. But he was hesitant about asking me for anything.

One day when he saw me alone he came to me and, folding his hands, said, 'Sir, you're a follower of Gandhi Baba, aren't you? People say that when we have Independence there won't be any more of those landowners.'

Pompously I said, 'What need will there be for the landowners? What do they do except suck the blood of the poor?'

Then the Thakur asked, 'Do you mean that the land will be taken away from all the zamindars?'

I said, 'But a lot of them will give it gladly. The ones who won't will have to have their land taken away from them. We people in my family are all set. The minute Independence comes we'll make over all our land and villages to the tenants.'

I was sprawled in a chair with my legs stuck out. The Thakur started to squeeze my feet and then he said, 'The landowners are very cruel these days, master! If your honour would give me just a tiny bit of land on your estate then I'd move there and work for you.'

'I have no authority over the land now, my friend, but as soon as I get control of it I'll send for you first thing. I'll have you taught how to drive a car and you can be my chauffeur.'

That day, I heard later, the Thakur drank a good deal of *bhang,* gave his wife a good beating and was all set to fight with the village moneylender.

5

So in this way the vacation drew to a close and we set out for Allahabad again. A lot of the people of the village came to see us off and the Thakur came with us to the station. I played my part to perfection too and stamped on every heart the image of my aristocratic refinement and magnanimity. I really longed to give each one of the servants a good tip but didn't have the wherewithal. I already had my return ticket, I had only to get into the train. But when it came it was jam-packed with people coming home from the Durga-puja holidays. In second class there wasn't room to squeeze a stick and it was even worse in the inter. But this was the last train and we absolutely had to get on it. With the greatest difficulty we found room in third class. Our splendid get-up made a great impression there. But it really vexed me to be stuck in third. We'd come lying down the whole way in comfort and we were going back all twisted up—there wasn't even room to turn from one side to the other.

There were several educated people there too. Among themselves they were praising British rule. One gentleman remarked, 'No such justice has ever been seen in another government. Great and small, all are equal. If he wrongs anybody even the king will have to account to a court for it.'

173

'*Arrey,* sahib,' another man confirmed, 'you can bring a suit against the Emperor himself, the Emperor can be sentenced in court.'

There was one man going to Calcutta who had a big bundle tied to his back. He couldn't find any place to set it down. Uncomfortable with the thing on his back he frequently stood up by the door. I was sitting right next to the door so that each time he moved the bundle rubbed against my face. I didn't like it. For one thing, there was almost no air, and then this lout was just about suffocating me by crowding it into my face. I put up with it for some time, then suddenly I got mad. I caught hold of him and gave him a shove around and hit him two good slaps.

With a threatening look he said, 'Why are you hitting me, Babuji? I also paid my fare.'

I stood up and hit him two or three more times.

There was an uproar in the compartment; everyone began yelling at me from all sides.

'If you're so delicate why didn't you sit in first class?'

'He's some bigshot in his own backyard, but he's not there now. If he hit *me* like that I'd show him.'

'What did the poor man do wrong? There's no room to breathe in here and he just wanted to get a breath of fresh air at the window and this fellow goes into a rage! When a man's got money does he completely lose his human-kindness?'

'This is British rule too—the very thing you were raving about.'

A villager said, 'He wouldn't try anything like that in front of those Englishmen—why's he acting so high and mighty here?'

In English Ishwari said, 'What an idiot you are!'

And it seemed to me that at this moment my intoxication began to clear a little.

NOTE

Original title, '*Nashā*', 'Intoxication'. First published in 1934.

The Price of Milk

In the big cities these days you can find midwives, nurses and 'lady doctors', as they call the female obstetricians. But in the villages it's still the untouchable sweeper women who preside over the delivery rooms, and there is little hope of any change in this situation in the near future.

Babu Maheshnath was the zamindar of his village, an educated man and aware of the need for reform in the way babies were delivered, but he saw no way to overcome the obstacles to such reform. No nurse would agree to go out to the villages, or if after a lot of persuasion one agreed then she'd demand such a fantastic fee that Babu Sahib could do nothing but come away with his head abjectly bowed. As for the lady doctors, he did not dare approach them; to pay one of them he might have had to sell half his property. And so when, after three daughters, his fourth child, a son, was born, once again he sent word to Gudar the sweeper and his wife. Children being apt to be born most often at night, it happened that one midnight a servant from Babu Sahib's house set up such a shout at Gudar's door that he woke up the whole neighbourhood. It was no girl this time for him to whisper the news.

For months they had been preparing in Gudar's house for this happy occasion. Their only fear was that it would once again turn out to be a girl, in which case they'd get nothing more out of it than the usual rupee and a sari. A great many times husband and wife had quarrelled and made bets about this matter. Bhungi, Gudar's wife, would say, 'If it isn't a son this time I'll hide my face in shame. That's right, I'll hide my face—but all the signs are for a son.' And Gudar would say, 'But can't you see it's going to be a girl? It's plain as day! If it's a son I'll shave off my moustache, that's right, I'll shave it off!' Gudar may have felt that if in this way he strengthened his wife's determination that it should be a son it would help to assure its actually coming about.

Bhungi said, 'You can shave it off right now, you old cheat. I said it was going to be a son but instead of listening you just

175

went on talking. I'll shave it off myself and won't leave even a bristle.'

'There's my good old woman! It'll grow again, won't it? After three days take a look, it'll be just the way it was before. And anyway, I'll claim half of whatever you get, I'm telling you now.'

Bhungi made a contemptuous gesture with her thumb. Then, handing her three-month-old son to Gudar, started out with the messenger.'

'*Ari!*' Gudar called. 'Where are you running off to? I'll have to go to play the music for the celebration. Who's going to look after the baby?'

Without coming back Bhungi said, 'Get him to sleep and put him down right there on the ground, then I'll come back and nurse him.'

2

At Maheshnath's house Bhungi was warmly welcomed now. She got fruits and vegetables in the morning, puris and halva at noon, and the same things again in the afternoon and at night. And Gudar got plenty to eat as well. Since Bhungi was not able to nurse her own baby more than once or twice each day extra milk was arranged for him. It was Babu Sahib's lucky little boy who drank Bhungi's milk. And even after the twelfth-day naming ceremony* this arrangement was not stopped. The mistress of the household was a strong, healthy woman, but this time for some reason or other she had no milk. The times she'd had the three daughters she gave so much milk that they got indigestion. This time there wasn't a drop. So Bhungi was not only the midwife but the wet-nurse as well.

The mistress would say, 'Bhungi, if you take good care of my baby you'll be able to just sit around eating as long as you live. I'll see that you're given five bighas rent-free. You'll live at ease right down to your grandchildren's time.'

And Bhungi's darling, unable to digest the alien milk, would

---

*When a child is born the mother is considered impure until the twelfth-day naming; hence there is nothing amiss in her being attended by an untouchable woman like Bhungi.

throw up frequently and went on getting skinnier day by day.

Bhungi would say, 'When your son has his tonsure ceremony, I'll take some bracelets, I'll insist on that.'

'Of course, my dear,' the mistress would answer, 'why that threatening tone? Which do you want, silver or gold?'

'Oh mistress! If I wore silver bracelets who could I show my face to—and who would they make fun of?',

'Very well, my dear, I promise you gold.'

'And when your son is married I'll take a necklace and, for my husband, silver wrist-bands.'

'You shall have them—God grant we see that day!'

In the household Bhungi reigned, second only to the mistress. The cook, the maids, all the various servants paid heed to her; it reached the point where even the mistress gave way to her. Once she even scolded Maheshnath himself, and he let it go with a laugh. There had been some talk about untouchables. 'Whatever may happen in the world,' Maheshnath had said, 'sweepers will remain nothing but sweepers. It's too hard to make civilized people out of them.'

To this Bhungi had said, 'Master, it's the sweepers who make it possible for the high-caste people to be civilized. Just let somebody do the same for us!'

In any other circumstances could Bhungi have got away with this insolence without having every hair of her head yanked out? But this time Babu Sahib chuckled and said, 'Bhungi always has something wise to say.'

The period of Bhungi's rule could not continue beyond a year. The Brahmans objected to the child's being nursed with an untouchable's milk, and Moteram Shastri even enjoined a penance. So the nursing was abandoned but the matter of a penance was laughed away. To taunt the Brahman Maheshnath said, 'A penance, Shastriji? Very sensible! Until yesterday the child was nourished by the blood of this same untouchable, so he must already be contaminated. My my, that's a great religion you've got!'

Shaking his topknot violently Shastriji said, 'In truth, the child was nourished on her blood until yesterday, and indeed on flesh as well—since she is an eater of meat. But today's business for today, let yesterday take care of itself. At the Jagannath temple

177

at Puri untouchables sit down to eat together with Brahmans—
but they can't do it here. When we're ill we sit at our meals all
dressed, we eat highly spiced stews, but Babuji, upon recovering
we must once again eat according to the rules of morality. The
regulations for emergencies are strange indeed!'

'So the meaning of this then is that morality changes—sometimes one thing, sometimes another?'

'What else! There's one morality for the king, another for the
subject, one for the poor, another for the rich. Kings and princes
can eat when they want, with whom they want, they can marry
anybody they want, there are no restrictions for them! Those
people have the power. Restrictions are for ordinary folk.'

So there was no penance, but Bhungi was obliged to step down
from her eminence. But anyway she received so much in the way of
gifts and tips that she couldn't take it away by herself, and she
got the gold bracelets as well, and instead of one, two beautiful
new saris, not just plain muslin like the ones when the daughters
were born.

4

This same year there was a severe outbreak of the plague and
Gudar was the first to fall victim. Bhungi was left alone, but she
continued to live just as before. People kept an eye out to see if
she'd go away now. There was talk with a certain sweeper, a
certain headman paid a call, but Bhungi didn't go anywhere,
she was still there five years later when her boy Mangal, despite
being skinny and nearly always sick, was starting to run around.
Next to Maheshnath's Suresh he looked like a dwarf.

One day Bhungi was cleaning a drain at Maheshnath's house.
It was clogged with several months's accumulation of sludge so
that the water had begun to form pools in the courtyard. Bhungi
thrust a long stout bamboo pole into the drain and shook it
vigorously. She had stuck her right arm inside the drain up to
the elbow when suddenly she let out a shriek and drew her arm
back out. At almost the same moment a black snake came slith-
ering out of the drain. People came running and killed it. But they
could not save Bhungi. They assumed it was a harmless water

snake, so at first they took no precautions for her. It was only when the poison had spread through her body and she was seized by convulsions that they realized it was not a water snake but a venomous corn snake.

Mangal was now an orphan. He made a habit of hanging around Maheshnath's door all through the day. There was so much leftover food in the house that they might have fed a dozen such children. There was thus no shortage of food but all the same it made him feel bad when the food was dropped down from above into his clay bowls.* Everybody ate from fine plates, and clay bowls for him!

He might not have been aware at all of this discrimination but the village boys constantly shouted abuse at him. There was no one who would ask him to play with them, and even the piece of canvas he slept on was untouchable. There was a neem tree in front of the house. Mangal made his home directly under it with his piece of torn canvas, two clay bowls and a dhoti passed on from Suresh. The spot was equally comfortable in every season, winter, summer and the rains. In the scorching June winds, the freezing cold and the drenching rains lucky little Mangal stayed alive and was actually a lot healthier than he'd been before. And there was even someone he could call his own, a village dog which, fed up with being picked on by his fellows in the pack, had taken refuge with him. They both ate the same food, slept on the same canvas and even had the same temperament and understood one another's moods. There was never once a quarrel between them.

The pious people of the village were surprised at this generosity of Babu Sahib's. For Mangal to loiter and sleep right in front of his door—it couldn't have been fifty feet—seemed to them contrary to genuine religion. Disgusting! If this sort of thing continued, you could be sure that religion was finished once and for all. God created the untouchables too, we know that, to be sure, and who isn't aware that one ought not to commit any injustice against them?—after all, God is known as the redeemer of the lowly. But the traditions of society have to be considered too! One would feel embarrassed just to approach that door. Mahesh-

---

*Dropped from above so neither spoon nor vessel would be contaminated by contact with Mangal's hands or pot.

nath might be the master of the village, one would be obliged to go there, but let it be understood that it was odious.

Mangal and Tommy, the dog, had become fast friends. Mangal would say, 'Look, Tommy, move over a little and go to sleep. Where do you expect me to lie? You're spread over the whole canvas.'

Tommy would whimper, wag his tail and instead of sliding over would crowd closer and begin to lick Mangal's face.

Every evening he would go to look at his house and cry a little while. The first year the thatched roof fell in, the second one wall collapsed and now only half the walls were standing, all jagged at the top. This was the treasure of affection he had found. The memories, the yearning and the love together drew him to this ruin, and Tommy always came with him. Mangal would sit on the jagged wall and dream of his past life and the future while Tommy time and time again would try unsuccessfully to leap up into his lap.

5

One day several boys were playing and Mangal too came along, though he stood far apart. It's not certain whether Suresh took pity on him or whether the players needed someone to pair off, but in any case he decided that today Mangal should take part in the game—who was going to come along and see them here? 'Hey Mangal,' he said, 'how about playing!'

'No, brother,' Mangal said, 'what if the master should see? I'd get my hide skinned off, but as for you, you'd get away with it.'

'Who's going to see us here, you idiot? Come on, we're playing horse-and-rider. You'll be the horse and the rest of us will climb on you and ride.'

Sceptically Mangal asked, 'Will I always be the horse or will I get to be a rider, tell me that.'

This was a complicated question. Nobody had considered it. After a moment's reflection Suresh said, 'Who'd let you get on his back? Think of that! After all, are you a sweeper or not?'

But Mangal too stood his ground. 'When did I ever say I wasn't a sweeper? But it was my own mother who brought you up and fed you with her milk. So long as I'm not going to get to be a rider I won't be the horse. You people are pretty smart! You want to enjoy being riders and I'm supposed to stay just a horse.'

'You've got to be the horse!' Suresh scolded and ran to catch him. Mangal ran off with Suresh after him. Mangal quickened his step and Suresh too put on more steam. But from being so overfed he'd turned flabby and he was already panting from running.

Finally he stopped and said, 'Come and be the horse, Mangal, otherwise whenever I do get my hands on you I'll really beat you up!'

'Then you'll have to be a horse too.'

'All right, we'll be horses too.'

'You ride afterwards. Be the horse first, then I will after I've ridden.'

Suresh, in fact, wanted to play a trick. When he heard this proposal of Mangal's he said to his companions, 'Just look at the little stinker's nerve! There's a sweeper for you.'

The three of them surrounded Mangal and forced him down on all fours. Suresh jumped on his back at once and straddled him. He made a clicking sound with his tongue and said, 'Giddy-up, horse, giddyup!'

Mangal moved along for a little while but he felt as though his back would break from the burden. Slowly he flattened his back and slipped out from under Suresh's thighs. Master Suresh fell with a thud and began to sound his horn.

His mother heard him crying somewhere. Wherever Suresh might be crying her sharp ears picked it up, and his crying was really quite peculiar, like the whistle on a narrow-gauge engine.

She said to the maid, 'Go look, Suresh is crying somewhere, find out if anybody's hit him.'

In the meantime Suresh himself came, rubbing his eyes. Whenever he found an opportunity to cry he was sure to come complaining to his mother and she would wipe his eyes and give him sweets and dried fruit. It's true, he was eight years old but he was a complete blockhead. Excessive affection had done to his wits what excessive eating had done to his body.

His mother asked, 'Why are you crying, Suresh? Did someone hit you?'

Still crying Suresh said, 'Mangal touched me.'

181

She could not believe it. Mangal was so self-effacing that she would not have credited any mischief to him. But when Suresh began to swear it was true she was obliged to believe him. She sent for Mangal and scolded him. 'What's going on, Mangal, now you're dreaming up all sorts of mischief! I told you you were never to touch Suresh. Do you remember or not? Speak up!'

In a low voice Mangal said, 'How could I forget?'

'Then why did you touch him?'

'I didn't touch him.'

'If you didn't touch him why was he crying?'

'He fell, that's why.'

'Stubborn and lying too!' Madam broke off, grinding her teeth. If she beat him she would have to take a purificatory bath that very moment. Even if she just took a cane in her hand the lightning current of contact would be conducted through the cane to course through her body. And so she heaped as much abuse on him as she could and ordered him to get out at once. If he ever appeared at their door again she'd drink his blood. Though they gave him all that free food he dreamed up nasty tricks, etc. etc.

Mangal was not likely to feel humiliation, but he could feel fear. Quietly he picked up his pots, tucked the piece of canvas under his arm, put the dhoti over his shoulder and set out weeping. He would never come back there again. The result would be that he would die of hunger. What harm in that? What benefit was there in living like this? Where was there any other shelter for him in the village? Who would take in a sweeper? He went off toward the ruins of his house where memories of the happy days might dry his tears, and cried his heart out.

At that moment Tommy came looking for him, and then the two of them forgot their grief.

6

But as daylight faded Mangal's despair also began to disappear, while the hunger that had gnawed at his childhood and consumed his body had now become all the more intense. His eyes turned constantly toward his bowls. Up at the house he would be getting Suresh's left-over sweets by now, but here—not a scrap to eat. He consulted with Tommy:

'What are you going to eat? I'm just going to go to bed hungry.'

Tommy whimpered as though to say, 'You just have to put up with this sort of insult throughout life. But if you lose heart, how can you keep going? Just consider my case now, sometimes somebody beats me with a stick and yells after me, then in a little while I go back to him with my tail wagging. That's the way you and I are made, my friend.'

Mangal said, 'Get along now, eat anything you find, don't worry about me.'

In his dog language Tommy said, 'I won't go alone, I'll take you with me.'

'But I'm not going.'

'Then I won't go either.'

'You'll die of starvation.'

'Do you think you'll stay alive then?'

'But there's nobody around to cry over me.'

'I'm in the same fix, old man—that bitch I was in love with last fall has been unfaithful, she's with Kallu now. Luckily she took her pups off with her, otherwise my existence would have been miserable. Who'd look after five puppies?'

After another moment hunger produced another plan:

'The mistress must be looking for us, don't you think so, Tommy?'

'What else? Babuji and Suresh must have finished eating by now. The servant must have taken out the leftovers, he's probably calling us.'

'A lot of ghee will be left in Babuji's and Suresh's plates and best of all, cream!

'And every bit of it's going to be thrown into the garbage.'

'Let's see if someone's looking for us.'

'Who's going to come looking for us? Do you think they're priests who'll chant our name? They'll call "Mangal, Mangal!" just once and that's it, the food will be dumped into the drain.'

'All right then, let's get going. But I'll stay hidden if anybody calls out my name, then I'll come back—understand?'

They both started out and when they got to Maheshnath's

183

door stayed crouching in the shadows. But how could Tommy be patient? Slowly he found his way into the house. He saw that Maheshnath and Suresh were seated at their dinner. Quietly he settled down on the veranda but all the time he was afraid somebody might come along and whack him with a stick.

The servants were chatting. One said, 'Nobody's seen hide nor hair of that Mangal today. The mistress bawled him out so maybe he's run away.'

Another answered, 'If they threw him out it's a good thing. Who wants to have to look a sweeper in the face every single morning?

Mangal shrank back even further into the shadows. All his hopes sank deeper than the depths of the sea.

Maheshnath stood up. A servant washed his hands. Now he would smoke his hooka and fall asleep. Suresh would sit with his mother and listen to some story or other until he fell asleep. Who was there to worry about poor Mangal? he thought. It was so late now that there was no chance anyone would call for him, even by force of habit.

He lingered on for some time, disappointed, then, sighing, he was just on the point of going when a bearer appeared carrying a plate of leftovers.

Mangal came out from the darkness into the light. How could he resist now?

The servant said, 'Where the devil were you? We thought you must have gone off somewhere. Here, eat this—I was just about to dump it out.'

Humbly Mangal said, 'But I've been waiting here a long time.'

'Then why didn't you speak out?'

'Because . . . I was afraid.'

'Well, take this and eat it.'

He lifted up the leaf dish and dropped it into Mangal's outstretched hands. The eyes which Mangal turned to him were full of humble gratitude.

Tommy came out from inside too. The two of them began to eat from the leaf right there under the neem tree.

Patting Tommy's head with one hand, Mangal said, 'Just think, we were so hungry that if we hadn't at least got this bread they've thrown away what would we have done?'

The Price of Milk

Tommy wagged his tail.

'It was my mother who nursed Suresh.'

Tommy wagged his tail again.

'They say nobody can ever really pay the price of milk, and this is the payment I'm getting.'

And once more Tommy wagged his tail.

NOTE

Original title, '*Dudh kā Dām*', 'The Price of Milk'. A late story, first published in 1934. This is representative of Premchand's best work, objective, compassionate and free of editorializing. The scene of Mangal's departure from his home under the neem tree is one of the finest in all Premchand. Lest it be considered in the least sentimental, it should be pointed out that, sentimentality being an expression of emotion in excess of what is warranted by the situation, the emotion of the story is, on the contrary, beautifully banked. Nowhere else has Premchand so well dramatized the plight of the sweeper (i.e., untouchable). In his biographical study of his father Amrit Rai justly observes that in these late stories the anger of the earlier works has given way to anguish. It seems scarcely possible to do justice to Premchand's style in translation, for obviously no exact equivalent can be found for Bhungi's earthy conversation, Moteram's inflated rhetoric (complicated humourously by provincial pronunciation) or the idiomatic ellipses of Mangal's speech. In this dark story the ironic significance of Mangal's name—'auspicious, fortunate'—should be kept in mind.

The Shroud

Father and son sat in silence at the door of their hut before a burnt-out fire and inside Budhiya, the son's young wife, lay fainting in the throes of child-birth. From time to time such an agonizing cry came out of her that their hearts skipped a beat. It was a winter night, all was silent, and the whole village was obliterated in the darkness.

Ghisu said, 'It looks as though she won't make it. You spent the whole day running around—just go in and have a look.'

Annoyed, Madhav said, 'If she's going to die why doesn't she get it over with? What can I do by looking?'

'You're pretty hard-hearted, aren't you? You live at your ease with somebody a whole year and then you don't give a damn about her.'

'But I couldn't stand looking at her writhing and thrashing.'

They were a family of untouchable leather-workers and had a bad name throughout the whole village. If Ghisu worked one day he'd take three off. Madhav was such a loafer that whenever he worked for a half hour he'd stop and smoke his pipe for an hour. So they couldn't get work anywhere. If there was even a handful of grain in the house then the two of them swore off work. After a couple of days fasting Ghisu would climb up a tree and break off branches for firewood and Madhav would bring it to the market to sell. And so long as they had any of the money they got for it they'd both wander around in idleness. There was no shortage of heavy work in the village. It was a village of farmers and there was any number of chores for a hard-working man. But whenever you called these two you had to be satisfied with paying them both for doing one man's work between them. If the two of them had been wandering ascetics there would have been absolutely no need for them to practice greater restraint or austerity to attain a saint's serenity and patience. This was their nature. A strange life theirs was! They owned nothing except for some clay pots; a few torn rags was all that covered their nakedness. They were free of worldly cares! They were loaded with debts, people abused them, beat them, but they didn't suffer. People would loan them a little something even though they were so poor there was no hope of getting it back. At the time of the potato and pea harvest they would go into other people's fields and dig up potatoes and gather peas and roast them or they'd pick sugarcane to suck at night. Ghisu had reached the age of sixty living this hand-to-mouth existence, and like a good son Madhav was following in his father's foot-steps in every way, and if anything he was adding luster to his father's fame. The two of them were sitting before the fire now roasting potatoes they'd dug up in some field. Ghisu's wife had died a long time ago. Madhav had been married last year. Since his wife had come she'd established order in the family and kept those two good-for-nothings' bellies filled. And since her arrival they'd become more sluggish than ever. In fact, they'd begun to let it go to their heads. If someone sent for them to do a job, they'd bare-facedly ask for twice the wages. This same woman was dying today in child-birth and it was as though they were only waiting for her to die so they could go to sleep in peace and quiet.

Ghisu took a potato and while he peeled it said, 'Go and look, see how she is. She must be possessed by some ghost, what else? But the village conjurer wants a rupee for a visit.'

Madhav was afraid that if he went into the hut Ghisu would do away with most of the potatoes. He said, 'I'm scared to go in there.'

'What are you afraid of? I'll be right here.'

'Then why don't you go and look?'

'When my woman died I didn't stir from her side for three days. And then she'd be ashamed if I saw her bare like that when I've never even seen her face before. Won't she be worried about her modesty? If she sees me she won't feel free to thrash around.'

'I've been thinking, if there's a baby what's going to happen? There's nothing we're supposed to have in the house—ginger, sugar, oil.'

'Everything's going to be all right, God will provide. The very people who wouldn't even give us a pice before will send for us tomorrow and give us rupees. I had nine kids and there was never a thing in the house but somehow or other the Lord got us through.'

In a society where the condition of people who toiled day and night was not much better than theirs and where, on the other hand, those who knew how to profit from the weaknesses of the peasants were infinitely richer, it's no wonder they felt like this. We could even say that Ghisu was much smarter than the peasants and instead of being one of the horde of empty-headed toilers he'd found a place for himself in the disreputable society of idle gossipers. Only he didn't have the ability to stick to the rules and code of such idlers. So while others of his crowd had made themselves chiefs and bosses of the village, the whole community pointed at him in contempt. Nevertheless, there was the consolation that although he was miserably poor at least he didn't have to do the back-breaking labour the farmers did, and other people weren't able to take unfair advantage of his simplicity and lack of ambition.

They ate the potatoes piping hot. Since yesterday they'd eaten nothing and they didn't have the patience to let them cool. Several times they burned their tongues. When they were peeled the outside of the potatoes didn't seem very hot but as soon as they bit into them the inside burned their palates, tongues and throats. Rather than keep these burning coals in their mouths it was a lot safer to drop them down into their bellies, where there was plenty of equipment to cool them. So they swallowed them quickly, even though the attempt brought tears to their eyes.

At this moment Ghisu recalled the Thakur's wedding, which he'd attended twenty years before. The way the feast had gratified him was something to remember all his life, and the memory was still vivid today. He said, 'I won't forget that feast. Since then I've never seen food like it or filled my belly so well. The bride's people crammed everybody with puris, everybody! Bigshots and nobodies all ate puris fried in real ghee. Relishes and curds with spices, three kinds of dried vegetables, a tasty curry, sweets—how can I describe how delicious that food was? There was nothing to hold you back, you just asked for anything you wanted and as much as you wanted. We ate so much that nobody had any room left for water. The people serving just kept on handing out hot, round, mouth-watering pastries on leaves. And we'd say, "Stop, you mustn't", and put our hands over the plates to stop them but they kept right on handing it out. And when everybody'd rinsed his mouth we got *pan* and cardamom too. But how could

I take any *pan*? I couldn't even stand up. I just went and lay down in my blanket right away. That's how generous that Thakur was!'

Relishing the banquet in his imagination Madhav said, 'Nobody feeds us like that now.'

'Who'd feed us like that today? That was another age. Now everybody thinks about saving his money. Don't spend for weddings, don't spend for funerals! I ask you, if they keep on hoarding the wealth they've squeezed out of the poor, where are they going to put it? But they keep on hoarding. When it comes to spending any money they say they have to economize.'

'You must have eaten a good twenty puris?'

'I ate more than twenty.'

'I would have eaten fifty!'

'I couldn't have eaten any less than fifty. I was a husky lad in those days. You're not half so big.'

After finishing the potatoes they drank some water and right there in front of the fire they wrapped themselves up in their dhotis and pulling up their knees they fell asleep—just like two enormous coiled pythons.

And Budhiya was still moaning.

2

In the morning Madhav went inside the hut and saw that his wife had turned cold. Flies were buzzing around her mouth. Her stony eyes stared upwards. Her whole body was covered with dust. The child had died in her womb.

Madhav ran to get Ghisu. Then they both began to moan wildly and beat their chests. When they heard the wailing the neighbours came running and according to the old tradition began to console the bereaved.

But there was not much time for moaning and chest-beating. There was the worry about a shroud and wood for the pyre. The money in the house had disappeared like carrion in a kite's nest.

Father and son went weeping to the village zamindar. He hated the sight of the two of them and several times he'd thrashed them with his own hands for stealing or for not coming to do the work they'd promised to do. He asked, 'What is it, little Ghisu, what are you crying about? You don't show yourself much these days. It seems as though you don't want to live in this village.'

Ghisu bowed his head all the way to the ground, his eyes full of tears, and said, 'Excellency, an awful thing's happened to me. Madhav's woman passed away last night. She was in agony the whole time. The two of us never once left her side. We did whatever we could, gave her medicine—but to make a long story short, she gave us the slip. And now there's nobody left even to give us a piece of bread, master. We're ruined! My house has been destroyed! I'm your slave—except for you now who is there to see that she's given a decent funeral? Whatever we had we spent on medicine. If your excellency is merciful, then she'll have a good funeral. Whose door can we go to except yours?'

The zamindar was soft-hearted. But to be kind to Ghisu was like trying to dye a black blanket. He was tempted to say, 'Get out and don't come back! When we send for you you don't show up but today when you're in a jam you come and flatter me. You're a sponging bastard!' But this was not the occasion for anger or scolding. Exasperated, he took out a couple of rupees and threw them on the ground. But he didn't utter a word of consolation. He didn't even look at Ghisu. It was as though he'd shoved a load off his head.

When the zamindar had given two rupees how could the shopkeepers and moneylenders of the village refuse? Ghisu knew how to trumpet the zamindar's name around. Somebody gave him a couple of annas, somebody else four. Within an hour Ghisu had harvested a tidy sum of five rupees. He got grain at one place, wood from somewhere else. And at noon Ghisu and Madhav went to the market to get a shroud. There were people already cutting the bamboo to make a litter for the corpse.

The tender-hearted women of the village came and looked at the dead woman, shed a few tears over her forlorn state and went away.

3

When they reached the market Ghisu said, 'We have enough wood to burn her up completely, haven't we, Madhav?'

'Yes, there's plenty of wood, now we need the shroud.'

'That's right, come along and we'll pick up a cheap one.'

'Of course, what else? By the time we move the corpse it will be night—who can see a shroud at night?'

'What a rotten custom it is that somebody who didn't even have rags to cover herself while she was alive has to have a new shroud when she dies!'

'The shroud just burns right up with the body.'

'And what's left? If we'd had these five rupees before then we could have got some medicine.'

Each of them guessed what was in the other's mind. They went on wandering through the market, stopping at one cloth-merchant's shop after another. They looked at different kinds of cloth, silk and cotton, but nothing met with their approval. This went on until evening. Then the two of them, by some divine inspiration or other, found themselves in front of a liquor shop, and as though according to a previous agreement they went inside. For a little while they stood there, hesitant. Then Ghisu went up to where the tavern-keeper sat and said, 'Sahuji, give us a bottle too.'

Then some snacks arrived, fried fish was brought and they sat on the veranda and tranquilly began to drink.

After drinking several cups in a row they began to feel tipsy. Ghisu said, 'What's the point of throwing a shroud over her? In the end it just burns up. She can't take anything with her.'

Madhav looked toward heaven and said, as though calling on the gods to witness his innocence, 'It's the way things are done in the world, otherwise why would people throw thousands of rupees away on Brahmans? Who can tell if anybody gets it in the next world or not?'

'The bigshots have lots of money to squander so let them squander it, but what have we got to squander?'

'But how will you explain it to people? Won't they ask, "Where's the shroud?" '

Ghisu laughed. 'So what? We'll say the money fell out of the knot in our dhotis and we looked and looked but couldn't find it. They won't believe it but they'll give the money again.'

Madhav laughed too over this unexpected stroke of luck. He

said, 'She was good to us, that poor girl—even dying she got us fine things to eat and drink.'

They'd gone through more than half a bottle. Ghisu ordered four pounds of puris. Then relish, pickle, livers. There was a shop right across from the tavern. Madhav brought everything back in a trice on a couple of leaf-platters. He'd spent one and a half rupees; only a few pice were left.

The two of them sat eating their puris in the lordly manner of tigers enjoying their kill in the jungle. They felt neither fear of being called to account nor concern for a bad reputation. They had overcome those sensibilities long before.

Ghisu said philosophically, 'If our souls are content won't it be credited to her in heaven as a good deed?'

Respectfully Madhav bowed his head and confirmed, 'Absolutely will! Lord, you know all secrets. Bring her to paradise— we bless her from our hearts . . . the way we've eaten today we've never eaten before in our whole lives.'

A moment later a doubt rose in his mind. He said, 'What about us, are we going to get there some day too?'

Ghisu gave no answer to this artless question. He didn't want to dampen his pleasure by thinking about the other world.

'But if she asks us there, "Why didn't you people give me a shroud?" what will you say?'

'That's a stupid question!'

'But surely she'll ask!'

'How do you know she won't get a shroud? Do you think I'm such a jackass? Have I been wasting my time in this world for sixty years? She'll have a shroud and a good one too.'

Madhav was not convinced. He said, 'Who'll give it? You've eaten up all the money. But she'll ask *me*. I was the one who put the cinnabar in her hair at the wedding.'

Getting angry, Ghisu said, 'I tell you she'll have a shroud, aren't you listening?'

'But why don't you tell me who's going to give it?'

'The same people who gave before will give the money again— well, not the money this time but the stuff we need.'

As the darkness spread and the stars began to glitter the gaiety of the tavern also increased steadily. People sang, bragged, embraced their companions, lifted the jug to the lips of friends. All was jollity, there was intoxication in the air. Anybody who came in got drunk in an instant from just a few drops, the very air of the place turned their heads more than the liquor. The sufferings of their lives drew them all there and after a little while they were no longer aware if they were alive or dead, not alive or not dead.

And father and son went on slopping it up with zest. Everyone was staring at them. How lucky the two of them were, they had a whole bottle between themselves.

When he was crammed full Madhav handed the left-over puris on a leaf to a beggar who was standing watching them with famished eyes. And for the first time in his life he experienced the pride, the happiness and the pleasure of giving.

Ghisu said, 'Take it, eat it and say a blessing—the one who earned it is—well, she's dead. But surely your blessing will reach her. Bless her from your heart, that food's the wages for very hard labour.'

Madhav looked heavenward again and said, 'She'll go to heaven, Dada, she'll be a queen in heaven.'

Ghisu stood up and as though bathing in waves of bliss he said, 'Yes, son, she'll go to heaven. She didn't torment anybody, she didn't oppress anybody. At the moment she died she fulfilled the deepest wish of all our lives. If she doesn't go to heaven then will those big fat people go who rob the poor with both hands and swim in the Ganges and offer holy water in the temples to wash away their sins?'

Their mood of credulity suddenly changed. Volatility is the special characteristic of drunkenness. Now was the turn for grief and despair.

'But Dada,' Madhav said, 'the poor girl suffered so much in this life! How much pain she had when she died.'

He put his hands over his eyes and began to cry, he burst into sobs.

Ghisu consoled him. 'Why weep, son? Be glad she's slipped out of this maze of illusion and left the whole mess behind her. She was very lucky to escape the bonds of the world's illusion so quickly.'

And the two of them stood up and began to sing.

> 'Deceitful world, why do you dazzle us with your eyes?
> Deceitful world!'

The eyes of all the drunkards were glued on them and the two of them became intoxicated right to their hearts. Then they started to dance, they jumped and sprang, fell back, twisted, they gesticulated, they mimed their feelings, and finally they collapsed dead drunk.

NOTE

Original title, '*Kafan*', 'The Shroud'. First published in 1936.

Deliverance

Dukhi the tanner was sweeping in front of his door while Jhuriya, his wife, plastered the floor with cow-dung. When they both found a moment to rest from their work Jhuriya said, 'Aren't you going to the Brahman to ask him to come? If you don't he's likely to go off somewhere.'

'Yes, I'm going,' Dukhi said, 'But we have to think about what he's going to sit on.'

'Can't we find a cot somewhere? You could borrow one from the village headman's wife.'

'Sometimes the things you say are really aggravating! The people in the headman's house give me a cot? They won't even let a coal out of their house to light your fire with, so are they going to give me a cot? Even when they're where I can go and talk to them if I ask for a pot of water I won't get it, so who'll give me a cot? A cot isn't like the things we've got—cow-dung fuel or chaff or wood that anybody who wants can pick up and carry off. You'd better wash our own cot and set it out—in this hot weather it ought to be dry by the time he comes.'

'He won't sit on our cot,' Jhuriya said. 'You know what a stickler he is about religion and doing things according to the rule.'

A little worried, Dukhi said, 'Yes, that's true. I'll break off some *mohwa* leaves and make a mat for him, that will be the thing. Great gentlemen eat off *mohwa* leaves, they're holy. Hand me my stick and I'll break some off.'

'I'll make the mat, you go to him. But we'll have to offer him some food he can take home and cook, won't we? I'll put it in my dish—'

'Don't commit any such sacrilege!' Dukhi said. 'If you do, the offering will be wasted and the dish broken. Baba will just pick up the dish and dump it. He flies off the handle very fast, and when he's in a rage he doesn't even spare his wife, and he beat his son so badly that even now the boy goes around with a broken hand. So we'll put the offering on a leaf too. Just don't touch it.

195

Take Jhuri the Gond's daughter to the village merchant and bring back all the things we need. Let it be a complete offering— a full two pounds of flour, a half of rice, a quarter of gram, an eighth of ghee, salt, turmeric, and four annas at the edge of the leaf. If you don't find the Gond girl then get the woman who runs the parching oven, beg her to go if you have to. Just don't touch anything because that will be a great wrong.'

After these instructions Dukhi picked up his stick, took a big bundle of grass and went to make his request to the Pandit. He couldn't go empty-handed to ask a favour of the Pandit; he had nothing except the grass for a present. If Panditji ever saw him coming without an offering, he'd shout abuse at him from far away.

2

Pandit Ghasiram was completely devoted to God. As soon as he awoke he would busy himself with his rituals. After washing his hands and feet at 8 o'clock he would begin the real ceremony of worship, the first part of which consisted of the preparation of *bhang.* After that he would grind sandalwood paste for half an hour, then with a straw he would apply it to his forehead before the mirror. Between two lines of sandalwood paste he would draw a red circle. Then on his chest and arms he would draw designs of perfect circles. After this he would take out the image of the Lord, bathe it, apply the sandalwood to it, deck it with flowers, perform the ceremony of lighting the lamp before it and ringing a little bell. At ten o'clock he'd rise from his devotions and after a drink of the *bhang* go outside where a few clients would have gathered : such was the reward for his piety; this was his crop to harvest.

Today when he came from the shrine in his house he saw Dukhi the untouchable tanner sitting there with a bundle of grass. As soon as he caught sight of him Dukhi stood up, prostrated himself on the ground, stood up again and folded his hands. Seeing the Pandit's glorious figure his heart was filled with reverence. How godly a sight!—a rather short, roly-poly fellow with a bald, shiny skull, chubby cheeks and eyes aglow with brahmanical energy.

The sandalwood markings bestowed on him the aspect of the gods. At the sight of Dukhi he intoned, 'What brings you here today, little Dukhi?'

Bowing his head, Dukhi said, 'I'm arranging Bitiya's betrothal. Will your worship help us to fix an auspicious date? When can you find the time?'

'I have no time today,' Panditji said. 'But still, I'll manage to come toward evening.'

'No, maharaj, please come soon. I've arranged everything for you. Where shall I set this grass down?'

'Put it down in front of the cow and if you'll just pick up that broom sweep it clean in front of the door,' Panditji said. 'Then the floor of the sitting room hasn't been plastered for several days so plaster it with cowdung. While you're doing that I'll be having my lunch, then I'll rest a bit and after that I'll come. Oh yes, you can split that wood too, and in the storeroom there's a little pile of hay—just take it out and put it into the fodder bin.'

Dukhi began at once to carry out the orders. He swept the doorstep, he plastered the floor. This took until noon. Panditji went off to have his lunch. Dukhi, who had eaten nothing since morning, was terribly hungry. But there was no way he could eat here. His house was a mile away—if he went to eat there Panditiji would be angry. The poor fellow suppressed his hunger and began to split the wood. It was a fairly thick tree trunk on which a great many devotees had previously tried their strength and it was ready to match iron with iron in any fight. Dukhi, who was used to cutting grass and bringing it to the market, had no experience with cutting wood. The grass would bow its head before his sickle but now even when he brought the axe down with all his strength it didn't make a mark on the trunk. The axe just glanced off. He was drenched in sweat, panting, he sat down exhausted and got up again. He could scarcely lift his hands, his legs were unsteady, he couldn't straighten out his back. Then his vision blurred, he saw spots, he felt dizzy, but still he went on trying. He thought that if he could get a pipeful of tobacco to smoke then perhaps he might feel refreshed. This was a Brahman village, and Brahmans didn't smoke tobacco at all like the low castes and untouchables. Suddenly he remembered that there was a Gond living in the village too, surely he would have a pipeful. He set

197

off at a run for the man's house at once, and he was in luck. The Gond gave him both pipe and tobacco, but he had no fire to light it with. Dukhi said, 'Don't worry about the fire, brother, I'll go to Panditji's house and ask him for a light, they're still cooking there.'

With this he took the pipe and came back and stood on the veranda of the Brahman's house, and he said, 'Master, if I could get just a little bit of light I'll smoke this pipeful.'

Panditji was eating and his wife said, 'Who's that man asking for a light?'

'It's only that damned little Dukhi the tanner. I told him to cut some wood. The fire's lit, so go give him his light.'

Frowning, the Panditayin said, 'You've become so wrapped up in your books and astrological charts that you've forgotten all about caste rules. If there's a tanner or a washerman or a bird-shooter, why he can just come walking right into the house as though he owned it. You'd think it was an inn and not a decent Hindu's house. Tell that good-for-nothing to get out or I'll scorch his face with a firebrand.'

Trying to calm her down, Panditji said, 'He's come inside—so what? Nothing that belongs to you has been stolen. The floor is clean, it hasn't been desecrated. Why not just let him have his light—he's doing our work, isn't he? You'd have to pay at least four annas if you hired some labourer to split it.'

Losing her temper, the Panditayin said, 'What does he mean coming into this house!'

'It was the son of a bitch's bad luck, what else?' the Pandit said.

'It's all right,' she said, 'this time I'll give him his fire but if he ever comes into the house again like that I'll give him the coals in his face.'

Fragments of this conversation reached Dukhi's ears. He repented: it was a mistake to come. She was speaking the truth—how could a tanner ever come into a Brahman's house? These people were clean and holy, that was why the whole world worshipped them and respected them. A mere tanner was absolutely nothing. He had lived all his life in the village without understanding this before.

Therefore when the Pandit's wife came out bringing coals it was like a miracle from heaven. Folding his hands and touching his forehead to the ground he said, 'Panditayin, Mother, it was very wrong of me to come inside your house. Tanners don't have much sense—if we weren't such fools why would we get kicked so much?'

The Panditayin had brought the coals in a pair of tongs. From a few feet away, with her veil drawn over her face, she flung the coals toward Dukhi. Big sparks fell on his head and drawing back hastily he shook them out of his hair. To himself he said, 'This is what comes of dirtying a clean Brahman's house. How quickly God pays you back for it! That's why everybody's afraid of Pandits. Everybody else gives up his money and never gets it back but who ever got any money out of a Brahman? Anybody who tried would have his whole family destroyed and his legs would turn leprous.'

He went outside and smoked his pipe, then took up the axe and started to work again.

Because the sparks had fallen on him the Pandit's wife felt some pity for him. When the Pandit got up from his meal she said to him, 'Give this tanner something to eat, the poor fellow's been working for a long time, he must be hungry.'

Panditji considered this proposal entirely outside of the behaviour expected of him. He asked, 'Is there any bread?'

'There are a couple of pieces left over.'

'What's the good of two or three pieces for a tanner? Those people need at least a good two pounds.'

His wife put her hands over her ears. 'My, my, a good two pounds! Then let's forget about it.'

Majestically Panditji said, 'If there's some bran and husks mix them in flour and make a couple of pancakes. That'll fill the bastard's belly up. You can never fill up these low-caste people with good bread. Plain millet's what they need.'

'Let's forget the whole thing,' the Panditayin said, 'I'm not going to kill myself cooking in weather like this.'

3

When he took up the axe again after smoking his pipe, Dukhi found that with his rest the strength had to some extent come back into his arms. He swung the axe for about half an hour, then out of breath he sat down right there with his head in his hands.

In the meantime the Gond came. He said, 'Why are you wearing yourself out, old friend? You can whack it all you like but you won't split this trunk. You're killing yourself for nothing.'

Wiping the sweat from his forehead Dukhi said, 'I've still got to cart off a while wagon-load of hay, brother.'

'Have you had anything to eat? Or are they just making you work without feeding you? Why don't you ask them for something?'

'How can you expect me to swallow a Brahman's food, Chikhuri?'

'Swallowing it's no problem, you have to get it first. He sits in there and eats like a king and then has a nice little nap after he tells you you have to split his wood. The government officials may force you to work for them but they pay you something for it, no matter how little. This fellow's gone one better, calling himself a holy man.'

'Speak softly, brother, if they hear you we'll be in trouble.'

With that Dukhi went back to work and began to swing the axe. Chikhuri felt so sorry for him that he came and took the axe out of Dukhi's hands and worked with it for a good half hour. But there was not even a crack in the wood. Then he threw the axe down and said, 'Whack it all you like but you won't split it, you're just killing yourself,' and he went away.

Dukhi began to think, 'Where did the Baba get hold of this trunk that can't be split? There's not even a crack in it so far. How long can I keep smashing into it? I've got a hundred things to do at home by now. In a house like mine there's no end to the work, something's always left over. But he doesn't worry about that. I'll just bring him his hay and tell him, "Baba, the wood didn't split. I'll come and finish it tomorrow."'

He lifted up the basket and began to bring the hay. From the storeroom to the fodder bin was no less than a quarter of a mile. If he'd really filled up the basket the work would have been quickly finished, but then who could have hoisted up the basket on his head? He couldn't raise a fully loaded basket, so he took just a little each time. It was four o'clock by the time he'd finished with the hay. At this time Pandit Ghasiram woke up, washed his hands and face, took some *pan* and came outside. He saw Dukhi asleep with the basket still on his head. He shouted, 'Arrey, Dukhiya, sleeping? The wood's lying there just the way it was. What's taken you so long? You've used up the whole day just to bring in a little fistful of hay and then gone and fallen asleep! Pick up the axe and split that wood. You haven't even made a dent in it. So if you don't find an auspicious day for your daughter's marriage, don't blame me. This is why they say that as soon as an untouchable get's a little food in his house he can't be bothered with you any more.'

Dukhi picked up the axe again. He completely forgot what he'd been thinking about before. His stomach was pasted against his backbone—he hadn't so much as eaten breakfast that morning, there wasn't any time. Just to stand up seemed an impossible task. His spirit flagged, but only for a moment. This was the Pandit, if he didn't fix an auspicious day the marriage would be a total failure. And that was why everybody respected the Pandits —everything depended on getting the right day set. He could ruin anybody he wanted to. Panditji came close to the log and standing there began to goad him. 'That's right, give it a real hard stroke, a real hard one. Come on now, really hit it! Don't you have any strength in your arm? Smash it, what's the point of standing there thinking about it? That's it, it's going to split, there's a crack in it.'

Dukhi was in a delirium; some kind of hidden power seemed to have come into his hands. It was as though fatigue, hunger, weakness, all had left him. He was astonished at his own strength. The axe-strokes descended one after another like lightning. He went on driving the axe in this state of intoxication until finally the log split down the middle. And Dukhi's hands let the axe drop. At the same moment, overcome with dizziness, he fell, the hungry, thirsty, exhausted body gave up.

Panditji called, 'Get up, just two or three more strokes. I want it in small bits.' Dukhi did not get up. It didn't seem proper to Pandit Ghasiram to insist now. He went inside, drank some *bhang*, emptied his bowels, bathed and came forth attired in full Pandit regalia. Dukhi was still lying on the ground. Panditji shouted, 'Well, Dukhi, are you going to just stay lying here? Let's go, I'm on my way to your house! Everything's set, isn't it?' But still Dukhi did not get up.

A little alarmed, Panditji drew closer and saw that Dukhi was absolutely stiff. Startled half out of his wits he ran into the house and said to his wife, 'Little Dukhi looks as though he's dead.'

Thrown into confusion Panditayin said, 'But hasn't he just been chopping wood?'

'He died right while he was splitting it. What's going to happen?'

Calmer, the Panditayin said, 'What do you mean what's going to happen? Send word to the tanners' settlement so they can come and take the corpse away.'

In a moment the whole village knew about it. It happened that except for the Gond house everyone who lived there was a Brahman. People stayed off the road that went there. The only road to the well passed that way—how were they to get water? Who would come to draw water with a tanner's corpse nearby? One old woman said to Panditji, 'Why don't you get this body thrown away? Is anybody in the village going to be able to drink water or not?'

The Gond went from the village to the tanners' settlement and told everyone the story. 'Careful now!' he said. 'Don't go to get the body. There'll be a police investigation yet. It's no joke that somebody killed this poor fellow. The somebody may be a pandit, but just in his own house. If you move the body you'll get arrested too.'

Right after this Panditji arrived. But there was nobody in the settlement ready to carry the corpse away. To be sure, Dukhi's wife and daughter both went moaning to Panditji's door and tore their hair and wept. About a dozen other women went with them, and they wept too and they consoled them, but there was no man with them to bear up the body. Panditji threatened the tanners, he tried to wheedle them, but they were very mindful of the police and not one of them stirred. Finally Panditji went home disappointed.

4

At midnight the weeping and lamentation were still going on. It was hard for the Brahmans to fall asleep. But no tanner came to get the corpse, and how could a Brahman lift up an untouchable's body? It was expressly forbidden in the scriptures and no one could deny it.

Angrily the Panditayin said, 'Those witches are driving me out of my mind. And they're not even hoarse yet!'

'Let the hags cry as long as they want. When he was alive nobody cared a straw about him. Now that he's dead everybody in the village is making a fuss about him.'

'The wailing of tanners is bad luck,' the Panditayin said.

'Yes, very bad luck.'

'And it's beginning to stink already.'

'Wasn't the bastard a tanner? Those people eat anything, clean or not, without worrying about it.'

'No sort of food disgusts them.'

'They're all polluted!'

Somehow or other they got through the night. But even in the morning no tanner came. They could still hear the wailing of the women. The stench was beginning to spread quite a bit.

Panditji got out a rope. He made a noose and managed to get it over the dead man's feet and drew it tight. Morning mist still clouded the air. Panditji grabbed the rope and began to drag it, and he dragged it until it was out of the village. When he got back home he bathed immediately, read out prayers to Durga for purification, and sprinkled Ganges water around the house.

Out there in the field the jackals and kites, dogs and crows were picking at Dukhi's body. This was the reward of a whole life of devotion, service and faith.

NOTE

Original title, '*Sadgati*', 'Deliverance', implying a death in a state of bliss or grace. First published 1931.

Dukhi is a *chamar*, an untouchable who works with skins and hides and hence particularly objectionable to a Brahman. 'Dukhi' means 'sorrowful'— such names are common in villages and are usually bestowed to discourage or avert the envy of the gods; in this case, of course, it is ironic. The Gonds are a community of low standing but considerably above the Chamars. Cf. 'A Catastrophe'.

Two Autobiographical Sketches

My life is a level plain. There are pits here and there but no cliffs, mountains, jungles, deep ravines or desert wastes. Those good people who have a taste for mountaineering will be disappointed here.

I was born in 1880. My father was a postal employee, my mother an ailing woman. I also had an older sister. At the time of my birth my father was earning about twenty rupees a month; by the time he died his salary was forty. He had been a very thoughtful man, moving through life with his eyes wide open but in his last days he had stumbled and even fallen and brought me down with him: when I was fifteen he had me married. And scarcely a year after the marriage he died. At that time I was studying in the ninth grade. In the house were my wife, my step-mother, her two children and myself, and there was not a pice of income. Whatever savings we'd had were used up in my father's six-month illness and funeral expenses. And my ambition was to get an M.A. and become a lawyer. In those days jobs were just as hard to get as now. With a great effort you might find some post with a salary of ten or twelve rupees a month. But I insisted on going on with my studies. The chains on my ankles were not just iron but of all the metals together and I wanted to walk on the mountain tops!

I had no shoes and no decent clothes, and there were the high prices—barley was half a rupee for ten pounds. I was studying in the High School of Queens College in Banaras, where the headmaster had waived the fees. The exams were coming up soon. When I left school at half-past three I would go to the part of town known as Bamboo Gate to tutor a boy there. I'd get there at four and tutor until six, then leave for my house, which was five miles away in the country. Even walking very fast I could not get there before 8 o'clock. And I had to leave the house at eight sharp in the morning, otherwise I couldn't get to school on time. At night after supper I studied by the light of the oil lamp. I don't know when I slept. Nevertheless I was determined.

Somehow or other I passed my matriculation exams. But I made only second division and there was no hope left of being admitted to Queens College since fees could be remitted only for the first division. By chance Hindu College opened up the same year. I decided to study in this new institution. A Mr Richardson was the principal. I went to his house and found him in full Indian dress—kurta and dhoti—sitting on the floor writing something. But it had not been so easy for him to change his personality—after listening to me only long enough for me to get half my request out he said he didn't discuss college business in his house and I should go to the College. Fine, I went to the College and he saw me there but our meeting was a disappointment. He could not remit the fees. What could I do next? If I presented suitable recommendations then perhaps he might consider my request. But who in the city would know a country boy?

Every day I set out from home to try to get a recommendation from somewhere, and after an arduous twelve miles return in the evening. Who was there to ask? Nobody was concerned about me.

But after several days I found someone to recommend me, Thakur Indranarayan Singh of the board of directors of Hindu College. I had gone to him and wept, and taking pity on me he'd given me a letter of recommendation. In that instant my happiness knew no bounds. Blissful, I returned home. I intended to go see the Principal the next day, but as soon as I reached home I came down with a fever. I couldn't get rid of it for a week. I kept drinking concoctions made from neem leaves until I could barely stand it. One day I was sitting at the door when my old family priest came along. Seeing my state, he asked for details and then immediately went off into the fields. He dug up a root and when he brought it back washed it and ground it in with seven grains of black pepper and made me drink it. It had a magical effect. After no more than an hour the fever broke. It was as if the herb had taken it by the neck and throttled it. I asked Panditji many times for the name of the root but he wouldn't tell me. He said that if he did its effectiveness would vanish.

After a month I went again to see Mr Richardson and showed him the letter of recommendation. Giving me a sharp look he said, 'Where were you all this time?'

'I was ill.' 'What was wrong with you?' I wasn't ready for the question. If I told him it was a fever perhaps the Sahib would think I was lying. In my estimation a fever was a very light matter, insufficient to explain so long an absence. I felt I should name some disease which by its gravity would draw his sympathy. At the moment I could think of the name of none. When I'd gone to Thakur Singh he'd mentioned that he suffered from palpitations of the heart. And that was the word I thought of. I said in English, 'Palpitation of heart, sir.'

Astonished, the Principal looked at me and said, 'Are you completely well now?'

'Yes, sir.'

'Very well, fill out the entrance application form.'

I assumed that the worst was over. I took the form, filled it out and brought it back. At that moment the Principal was in one of his classes. At three o'clock I got the form back. Written on it was: 'Look into his ability.'

Here was a new problem. My heart sank. I could hope to pass no subject except English; I shivered at the thought of algebra and geometry. Whatever I'd learned I'd completely forgotten. But what else was there to do? Trusting to luck, I went to class and presented my application. The Professor, a Bengali, was teaching English; the subject was Washington Irving's 'Rip van Winkle.' I took a seat in the back row. In a few minutes I saw that the professor was competent in his subject. When the hour was over he questioned me about the day's lesson and then wrote on my form 'Satisfactory'.

The next hour was algebra. The teacher here was also a Bengali; I showed him the form. Most often the students who came to a new school have not been able to find admittance elsewhere, and that was the case here; the classes were full of incompetent students. Whoever came in the first rush had been enrolled —to the hungry the meanest gruel tastes good. But now the stomach was full and students were chosen only after careful selection. This professor examined me in mathematics and I failed; in the box marked 'maths' on the form he wrote. 'Unsatisfactory'.

I was so disappointed that I didn't bring the application back to the Principal. I went straight home. For me mathematics was the peak of Mount Everest, I could never reach it. In Intermediate College I'd already failed it a couple of times and, discouraged, gave up taking the exam. Ten years later when it was made optional I took another subject and passed easily. Until that time who knows how many young people's aspirations have been finished off by mathematics! Anyway, I went home disappointed, but the desire for learning was still strong. What could I do sitting at home? How to improve my maths and get enrolled in college was the problem. For this I would have to live in town.

By luck I got a post tutoring a lawyer's sons with a salary of five rupees. I decided to live on two rupees and give the other three to my family. Above the advocate's stable there was a rather small, unfinished room. I got permission to stay there. A piece of canvas was spread out for my bed, I got a very small lamp from the market and began my life in town. I also brought some pots from home. Once a day I cooked *khichri* and after washing and scouring the pots I'd set out for the library—maths was the pretext, but I would read novels and the like. In those days I read Pandit Ratannath Dar's *Fasana-e-Azad* (*The Romance of Azad*) as well as *Chandrakanta-Santati* (*The Descendants of Chandrakanta*), and I read everything of Bankim Chatterji's that I could find in Urdu translation in the library.

The brother-in-law of the advocate's sons had been a fellow student of mine for the matriculation. It was on his recommendation that I'd got this post. We were very good friends, so when I needed money I'd borrow from him and settle the account when I got my pay. Sometimes I'd have only two rupees left, sometimes three. On the day when I had two or three rupees left from my pay I'd lose all restraint—a craving for sweets would draw me towards the candy shop. I'd eat up two or three annas worth at once. On the same day I'd go home and give my family the two or two and a half rupees. The next day I'd begin to borrow again. But there were times when I was embarrassed about borrowing and day after day I'd fast.

In this way four or five months went by. Meantime I had taken two and a half rupees worth of clothes from a draper on credit. Every day I used to walk by his place—he had complete confidence in me. When after a couple of months I hadn't been able to pay him I gave up going that way and took a detour. It was three years before I could pay off this debt. In those days a labouring man who made his home in the back of the advocate's house used to come to me to learn a little Hindi. He was always saying, 'Know this, little brother!' and we had all come to call him that by way of a nickname. One day I borrowed eight annas from him too. Five years later he came to my house in the village and collected that half rupee from me.

I still longed to study, but every day I grew more and more despondent. I wanted to find a job somewhere but I had no idea of how and where to find one.

That winter I hadn't a pice left. I had spent a few days eating a pice worth of the cheapest cereal each day. Either the money-lenders had refused to loan me anything or from embarrassment I couldn't ask. One evening, just at dusk, I went to a bookseller to sell a book—'The Key to *Chakravarti's Mathematics*', which I had bought two years before. I had held on to it until now with great difficulty but today in complete despair I decided to sell it. Although it had cost me two rupees I settled for one. Taking my rupee I was just about to leave the shop when a gentleman with big moustaches who had been sitting there asked me, 'Where are you studying?' I said, 'I'm not studying anywhere but I hope to enroll somewhere.'

'Did you pass your matric exams? Then don't you want a job?'

'I can't find a job anywhere at all.'

This gentleman was the headmaster of a small school, and he needed an assistant teacher. He offered me a salary of eighteen rupees; I accepted. Eighteen rupees at that time was beyond the highest flight of my pessimistic imagination. I arranged to meet him the next day and left with my head in the clouds. I was ready to cope with any circumstances and if mathematics didn't stop me I would certainly get ahead. But the most difficult obstacle was the university's total lack of understanding, which then and for several years afterwards led it to treat everybody in the manner of that thief who made everybody, tall and short, fit one bed.

2

I began to write stories for the first time in 1907. I had read Tagore's stories in English and had Urdu translations published in the Urdu newspapers. But as early as 1901 I had begun to write novels. In 1902 one of my novels came out and a second in 1904, but until 1907 I had not written one short story. The title of my first story was 'The Most Precious Jewel in the World', published in *Zamana* in 1907. After this I wrote another four or five stories. In 1909 a collection of five stories was published with the title 'Sufferings of the Motherland'. At this time the partition of Bengal had taken place; in the Congress the radical faction had developed. In these five stories I praised devotion to the country.

At that time I was a deputy inspector in the department of education in Hamirpur district. One evening, six months after the stories had been published, while I sat in my tent I received a summons to go at once to see the District Collector, who was then on his winter tour. I harnessed the bullock-cart and travelled between thirty and forty miles through the night and reached him the next day. In front of him was placed a copy of my book. My head began to throb. At that time I was writing under the name of Navabrai. I had had some indication that the secret police were looking for the author of this book. I realized they must have traced me and that I was being called to account.

The Collector asked me, 'Did you write this book?'

I told him I had.

He asked for the theme of each one of the stories and finally losing his temper said, 'Your stories are full of sedition. It's fortunate for you that this is a British government. If it were the Mughal Empire, then both your hands would be cut off. Your stories are one-sided, you've insulted the British government.' The judgment was that I should give all copies of the book into the custody of the government and that I should not ever write anything else without the permission of the Collector. I felt I'd got off lightly. Of the thousand copies printed hardly three hundred had been sold. The remaining seven hundred I sent for from the *Zamana* office and had them delivered over to the Collector.

I assumed the danger was past. But the authorities could not be satisfied so easily. Afterwards I learned that the Collector had discussed the matter with the other officials of the district. The Superintendent of Police, two deputy collectors and the deputy inspector—whose subordinate I was—sat to consider what my fate should be. One of the deputy collectors, using quotations from the stories, asserted that in them there was nothing but sedition from beginning to end, and not just ordinary sedition but a contagious variety. The demi-god of the police said, 'So dangerous a man ought to be severely punished.' The deputy inspector was very fond of me. Afraid lest the affair be long drawn out he made the suggestion that in a friendly way he would sound out my political opinions and present a report to this committee. His idea was to explain to me and to write in his report that the writer was violent only with his pen and had nothing whatever to do with any political disturbance. The committee accepted his suggestion, although the police chief even at this moment was still blustering and threatening.

Suddenly the Collector asked the deputy inspector, 'Do you expect that he'll tell you what he really thinks?'

'Yes, I'm intimate with him.'

'By pretending to be friendly you want to find out his secret views? But that's spying! I consider it vile.'

Losing his wits the deputy inspector stammered, 'But I . . . Your Excellency's order. . . .'

'No,' the Collector interrupted, 'that's not my order. I had no intention of giving any such order. If the author's sedition can be proven from his book, then he should be put on trial in an open court, otherwise dismiss the case with a warning. I don't like the idea of a smile on the face and a knife in the hand.'

When the deputy inspector himself told me this story several days later, I asked him, 'Would you really have done this spying?'

He laughed. 'Impossible. Even if he'd given several hundred thousand rupees I wouldn't have done it. I just wanted to stop any legal proceedings, and they've been stopped. If there'd been a court case, you would definitely have been sentenced. You would have found no one to plead your cause. But the Collector is a noble gentleman.'

'Very noble indeed,' I said.

NOTE

Original title, '*Jivan-Sār*', 'The Substance of Life'. In the original there is a third sketch which deals mainly with Premchand's deteriorating health. His father's 'stumbling' and 'fall' refer apparently to the father's second marriage late in life and his early marrying of his son.

In the second sketch, the sentence Premchand would most probably have received if his case had been brought into court, was banishment to Burma. The final line is ambiguous: Indian interpreters feel that Premchand is being ironic, and irony is certainly there, but for all that he represented British oppression the Collector's sense of fairness doubtless was respected by Premchand, who makes a point of similar anomalies elsewhere in his work.

Glossary

anna—the sixteenth part of a rupee under the old reckoning, now obsolete.

arrey—Hey there! (intimate or contemptuous).

baba—father, grandfather, old man; a respectful term of address for a holy man.

babu—a title of respect, a gentleman; sometimes a clerk.

banya—a merchant, member of the third caste division and entitled, like Brahmans and Kshatryas, to wear the sacred thread.

bhang—a narcotic and intoxicant made from the hemp plant, most often drunk or chewed.

bigha—a varying land measure, usually a little over half an acre.

Brahman—a member of the first-rank caste division, including the priests, though many Brahman communities indulge in other occupations, including the professions, business and farming.

chapatti—a flat bread, something like a tortilla, made from wheat or other grains.

charpoy—a simple cot or bedstead.

cinnabar—at the time of marriage the husband streaks the part in the bride's hair with cinnabar; should she be widowed, the wife renounces it, along with jewellery and colour in her garments.

dada—father, grandfather, uncle (affectionate).

dal—any of various lentils, served dry or as a soup or sauce.

dhoti—a long cloth (six yards or more) worn by men in North India, wrapped according to various styles around the waist and thighs. The dhoti knot is where the purse and loose coins are stored.

Durga—a goddess, spouse of Shiva in her aspect of destroyer of evil.

Durga puja—an autumn festival (principally Bengali) honouring the goddess Durga, coinciding with the ten days of the Dassehra festival, which honours Rama.

ekka—a two-wheeled carriage with a sort of cupola for roof, drawn by one horse; it is found chiefly in the eastern Uttar Pradesh.

ghee—clarified butter.

halva—a kind of sweet pudding.

Holi—a spring festival characterized by boisterous celebrations, bonfires and the throwing or squirting of coloured powders and water.

huzoor—In Urdu a title of respect (literally, 'Presence').

213

inter—intermediate class on the railways, between second and third (now obsolete).

ji—an indication of respect added to a name or title.

khichri—a simple dish of rice, vegetables, etc.

Lakshmi—the goddess of prosperity.

Lala—a common term of address for banyas.

lota—a small pot, usually brass.

maharaj—a term of address for men of a great variety of groups, particularly Brahmans.

maund—a varying weight; in Banaras about eighty pounds.

Mother Tulsi—The goddess Tulsi or goddess of the sacred basil plant (tulsi), associated particularly with Rama.

munshi—a writer, scribe, secretary; a general title for a man connected with any phase of writing. In India Premchand is most commonly referred to as 'Munshi Premchand'.

neem—the margosa tree, a dense shade tree considered auspicious and healthful.

pan—betel leaf, coated with various spices and folded to be chewed as a digestive, sweet, or, occasionally, intoxicant.

panchayat—a council of five members (*panch:* five) originally but often of a much larger number that arbitrates among or represents its particular caste or village community.

pandit—a title for a Brahman, particularly in his capacity as a learned man and expounder of scriptures.

peepul—a variety of fig tree regarded as holy by Hindus.

pice—quarter of an anna; like 'brass farthing' or 'red cent' it is often used contemptuously to describe something trifling.

Puranas—any of various ancient texts chronicling the genealogy and exploits of various gods.

puri—any of various types of breads and cakes.

Ram—the Hindi vernacular form of Rama, the legendary hero who has come to be regarded as an incarnation of Vishnu; used as a greeting among Hindus.

Ramlila—a play or pageant representing the adventures of Rama, his wife, Sita, and his brother Lakshman, performed during the ten-day autumn festival of Dassehra. In some presentations, each day is devoted to a specific event—Rama going into exile, crossing the Ganges, dwelling in the forest, etc., culminating in Rama's triumph over Ravana and his return home to be crowned king.

ras-goola—a sweet, originally Bengali, consisting of balls of sugared curd etc. in syrup.

Glossary

sadhu—a wandering ascetic.

sahu—a shopkeeper or banker.

Sarasvati—the goddess of learning and the arts (including eloquence).

Satyanarayan—see note for the story 'Salvation'.

thakur—a general designation for a nobleman among Rajputs (members of the second or traditionally military and princely caste known as Kshatriyas). 'Thakur' has the same double meaning as the English 'Lord', indicating not only rank but, depending on context, the Supreme Deity.

Tulsi—See *Mother Tulsi*.

Uttar Pradesh—an Indian state, known before independence as the United Provinces. In population it is the largest of the states and includes the cities of Allahabad, Banaras, Lucknow and Agra. It is the heartland for both Hindi and Urdu as well as the older related dialects of Braj and Avadhi in which much of the great devotional poetry of the sixteenth century was written.

zamindar—a land-owner, usually owning and virtually governing large tracts, including whole villages. The system of 'zamindari' has been to a great extent weakened since Premchand's time by various 'zamindari abolition acts' to redistribute the land.